For Xander

For Xander

Breaking News is brought to you by Radio City Central: the local station you can trust.

SUNDAY 4th JUNE

BREAKING NEWS

Don't know what to do when you leave school? Be a politician. Jonathan Ludmire, current Shadow Foreign Secretary, admits in his article in *The Worm Turns* that all his colleagues couldn't get a regular job if they were turned out of the cabinet tomorrow. 'They're all jolly good chaps,' says Ludmire. 'Most of them did at least a term at Oxford, so they know how to behave and know all the right people. It's not like they expect you to know much more in this job. I'm the Shadow Foreign Secretary and I only speak English. Oh, and a bit of Pig Latin, if you count that. It's a kind of code one used to use to speak to the other boys in front of the staff. Civil Service does everything, really.' You can read further revelations on what it is like to work in politics in Ludmire's new book, *A Life of Ease*, published this Thursday.

MARTY

Marty McLaren, whose name was really Neville Martin McLaren, crouched uncomfortably in the rhododendrons.

He hadn't counted on them being wet from the morning dew. Icy drops still fell on the back of his neck and ran along his spine, making him hunch his increasingly tense shoulders. Beyond the bush he could see the garden, bathed in bright sunlight. A warm haze hung in the air, but inside his hideout he shivered. It was so frigging unfair. The second thing he hadn't counted on was that he'd be here for so long. He'd already been forced to piss out his morning coffee in the corner. The incline of the bank had ensured it hadn't all stayed in the corner and now he had to watch the way he crouched. It also smelled.

Any moment now, he told himself. Any moment now. He shifted his weight onto his other bent leg and did his best to steady the camera. It was a good camera and did its best to make up for his shoddy camera work. Marty knew he lacked certain skills, but once he got this story – once he put it up on his very own website – then the phone would start to ring. And that would be him away from his dead-end job on *The Caledonian Chronicle* and off to the lights of a big city with a proper press. Somewhere his talent would finally be appreciated.

He checked the frame of his shot once more and, to his delight, he saw the back door open.

MIKI

Miki was trying to get away from the breakfast table. She had something she needed to do upstairs. Homework. She'd already forced down two pieces of toast and jam and a cup of cold tea, but her mother had taken it upon herself to cook a Sunday brunch. Dishes of tiny roasted potatoes, fried halloumi, salad, vegan sausages and even scrambled

6

eggs lay scattered across the table. She'd managed to get the odd little electric cupboard on the wall, that had come with the house, heated up inside. The thing she normally complained looked like a hot cabinet at a cheap bakery and was, according to her, an electrical death trap, was now filled with homemade pies.

All the usual papers, catalogues and leaflets that lived on the kitchen table had been pushed to one end where they teetered in stacks. The fact her mother had actually used eggs, and this was a vegan-plus meal, meant this was a celebration of no small import. As far as her mother was concerned, this was family time. Her father hadn't been doing much talking. He seemed happy to not have cooked for himself for once and was eating his way heartily through everything on offer. Her mother had even made bread. Miki groaned internally. Her mother was a great cook, who rarely cooked. There was no easy way she was getting out of here.

'Darling, are you sure you won't come with?'

Miki tried to focus on what her mother was saying. She kept being distracted by the lilac streak in her hair. It looked suspiciously like the last of Miki's purple hair chalk. The one she'd been saving for school on Monday. They were supposed to be starting the suffragettes in history and she'd wanted to do her hair in green and purple. Mr Deacon might even notice. Not that she could say anything to her mother. For a year or so now, her mother had tried to be her friend, suggesting girls nights when they could plaster each other's faces with avocado and used coffee grain masks. She offered to share her wardrobe, with its tie-dye ensemble. Apparently she had yet to notice that Miki dressed everyday as if she was going to a funeral. Miki appreciated the effort, she really did, but she had no clue how to tell her mother that they were not peas in a pod, but rather, she was a pool of darkness in her mother's sunlit fantasy worlds and that was the way she liked it. She had about as much interest in New Age memorabilia as she did in personal mantras, possibly less.

'I mean, even if you didn't get your A levels this year…'

'I'm doing NAT 5s, Mum. I'm fifteen, remember?'

'Whatever they are, darling, you know they can always be taken again, if they matter to you so very much. But this is more than the usual fair. There are going to be some excellent speakers, who have new insights into how each of us can and must change our lives to prevent global warming. It will be very empowering. I know how your generation thinks – that my generation has ruined the planet and it's all over for you before it's started. But that isn't the case. There is strength in individuals coming together to make changes. And you'd get to know the business better. You need to meet our co-sellers. See what they're offering.'

'You mean your competition.'

'Now, darling, we're all trying to save the planet. Same side. There's a whole week of workshops and demonstrations.' She picked a leaflet out of the pile and read out, 'How to throw a pot, how to make your own sanitary pads, how to forage for nature's bounty, how to build your first soil loo, how to tie-dye – that's me. And so many more. It will be fun. You'll see.'

'It would be nice to have your company, honey,' interposed her father through a mouthful of eggs. 'What's more, the new GoPro arrived this morning.'

'Don't talk with your mouth full,' said her mother automatically.

8

'Sorry, honey,' said her father, still chewing. 'Your mother's right,' he added. 'You'd enjoy the week more than you know. Besides, it's more than time, you should see how the business you're going to inherit runs. I can't wait for the day when I retire and you take over.'

'Selling it hard there, Dad?' asked Miki. 'Anyway what's this about a new GoPro?'

'It's not new exactly,' said her father, with a nervous look at his wife, 'but it's got a lot of life left in it. As you know, your mother and I were not as successful as we had hoped with that little internet video we did. At least, not in the way we wanted.

'I don't know about that,' said her mother. 'It went viral.'

'Urgh, Mum,' said Miki. 'It was a disaster. Everyone at school kept yelling *rah,rah, go eco!* at me.'

'I did think you might be a trifle old for those pom-poms,' said her father, quietly.

'Well, this is a new idea,' said her mother. 'We will be using a trampoline.'

'Oh gods!' said Miki, 'Isn't it enough I've had to cancel all my social media accounts? I don't dare post anywhere. Now you're going to make even bigger fools of yourselves.'

'That's most unkind. But I know you'll come round,' said her father.

'Yes, dear, you are being quite tiresomely ordinary in your teenage rebellion. I had hoped for something more – more intellectual. But as your father says, you will come round. Even average teenagers eventually conform,' added her mother.

'When I'm old and grey, I'll be proud to sit back and watch you help save the world, one soil toilet at a time.'

'Yuck,' said Miki. 'We're eating!'

'Don't be so gauche, darling,' said her mother. 'The prevalence of human waste is a huge problem. Never mind those methane-bloated cows, we have to ensure a clean water supply and proper sanitation worldwide. Do you know, in some countries girls have to go into the woods to relieve themselves? Terribly risky in cultures where rape is still common. Imagine, there you are, dying for a poo...'

'M-Mum!' said Miki. 'I don't want to know!'

Her mother's face froze. 'Michelle, we have always treated you with respect. We have taught you we are all responsible for this planet and what happens here. We taught you to stand up for what is right. You are as privileged as a princess compared to some girls today. We all have to look out for each other. This uncaring, dare I say even consumerist, attitude of yours, never existed before you started at that school. I have had more than one occasion to regret ceasing to homeschool you and once more you prove my point.' She looked over at her husband. 'Father,' she said. Miki's father stopped mid-ladling. 'It's only my second portion, Meg,' he lied.

'Father, I move to have Michelle removed from our table due to her lack of respect for current world issues. Seconded?'

Miki's father looked over at her. 'Sorry, Miki,' he mouthed. 'Seconded,' he said.

Miki stood up. 'Fine, but I'm taking the dog with me. C'mon Red.'

The Irish Setter lifted his head at the sound of her voice and thumped his feathery tail on the floor. He didn't get up. 'Fine,' said Miki again and scooped up the bowl of halloumi. She stormed out. The dog got up and followed her. He loved halloumi.

10

'I hope she doesn't give him a lot,' said her father. 'It'll only make him sick.'

'He has free will, like everyone else in this house,' said her mother.

'Yes, dear,' said her father.

RORY

Rory couldn't hear them anymore. He leant against a tree. Then he bent over because it felt better. His side burned. Like he'd been struck with a lightsaber, he thought. Or shot with a laser gun. Or pierced with a hot steak knife. Or a fire poker... His imagination conjured up image after image until he was almost afraid to put his hand on his side in case it sank in through an open wound.

He coughed hard and spat up some bile. At least the blood pounding in his ears was quieting. He passed his hands gingerly over his abdomen. They came away wet with sweat, but no gore. He heaved a sigh of relief. 'I live to flee another day,' he said softly to himself. Then he noticed his Vans. His once red checkerboards were now covered in slime and mud. All the fear, all the humiliation, fled. Instead, he felt a rising fury. They were ruined. He'd had them a week and they were ruined. At that moment he wanted more than anything else to face the bullies who had been chasing him and take them on. He swore several more times. He turned to face the tree and punched it again and again, each time screaming out his rage and frustration. He didn't stop until his knuckles were raw and bloody, and his wrists ached. Then he sank down onto the ground and wept. He held his hands behind him, unable to look at the mess he had made of his knuckles.

Leon stuffed his fist in his mouth. He rocked back and
forth with laugher, feeling his sister's dresses move around
him. He peeked through the slats of the louvre doors once
more. His sister still sat on her dressing table stool, but her
boyfriend, Cliff, was perched on the edge of the bed. He
patted the space beside him. 'C'mon Alice. You can trust
me. You're so beautiful I just want to hold you in my arms.'

Leon thought any minute he was going to swallow his
whole hand. Where did this guy get his lines? Had he been
watching the Hallmark Channel? He was such a twit, with
his slicked-back hair and the tiny bits of dark fluff along
his top lip that he pretended was a moustache. Alice might
be a bit gormless, but there was no way she was going to
kiss this guy.

'Didn't you like what we did last time?' said Cliff. 'We
don't need to go further than that. Unless you want to.'

'My dad would kill me,' said Alice in what sounded to
Leon like an alarmingly wistful voice. Hiding in here was
meant to be a joke. There were some things he didn't want
to see. Surely, Alice had more sense than to do anything
with this clarty specimen of teenage boy? Leon could smell
Cliff's sweat combined with the sharp smell of the cologne
he used. He was sure he felt his nose hairs shrivelling.

'Look,' said Cliff. 'I'll take off my top first.' Leon
watched as he pulled his sweatshirt over his head. Yuk.
Cliff's skin was the same colour as toothpaste that crusted
round the top of a tube. His skin settled in a fat little roll
over his belt, but above it his ribs stood out. He was a
combination of the most unattractive features a male could
possess. Alice might be his sister, but couldn't she do better
than this?

Alice shook her head. 'It's not the same.'

'No,' said Cliff. 'You're beautiful. C'mon, Alice. You're sixteen. The other guys in our year, well, I can tell you, their girls go much further.'

'Well, you can go out with one of them then,' said Alice.

Good for you, thought Leon.

Cliff stood up and walked across to her. 'But I don't fancy any of them,' said Cliff. 'They're all skanks. You're different.' He slid his hands along her forearms, pushing her sleeves up to reveal her bare skin. 'Your skin is so soft, like feathers.'

'Feathers?' said Alice. Now she sounded confused.

'Feathers,' said Cliff. 'Soft as a bird. You're my bird, my exotic, beautiful, sweet pigeon.'

At this point Leon thought it might be possible to die of suppressed laughter.

Then he saw Cliff take the edges of his sister's top in his hands and very gently begin to lift it. He waited for Alice to object, but all she did was giggle. 'Pigeon. I don't want to be a pigeon!'

Cliff pulled the top over her head and threw it onto the ground. He stepped back to admire his handiwork. Alice stood there, smiling awkwardly. 'No, you're more like a dove. A heavenly dove.'

'I'll give you dove,' said Alice and launched herself at him. They both landed on her bed, laughing. Leon took his fist out of his mouth. Alice was only wearing her bra on top. He was pretty sure this wasn't okay. He'd seen something similar in the movies, but the people acting like what Cliff and Alice were doing had been far older, and much better looking. He could hear Cliff murmuring something and Alice giving soft giggles, but he couldn't work out what they were saying. Was he telling her jokes? Cliff had no wit at all. Leon heard the bed creak in protest, and decided he didn't want to look any closer. This mission had taken an ugly turn. He took his eye away from the slats and sat back among Alice's shoes.

Something stuck him hard in the rear and he bit his lip rather than cry out. He twisted and pulled out a black shoe with a very long and pointed heel from under his bum. He held it up for a moment. How on earth could Alice walk in that? He studied the heel. It was reminiscent of a stiletto dagger from Italy during the Middle Ages. In dire necessity perhaps it could be put to use as a weapon. He tested the heel softly against the floor, forgetting entirely for a moment the scene in the bedroom.

'What was that?' he heard Alice ask very clearly. Leon froze.

'It's nothing, don't worry about it,' said Cliff. 'Kiss me again.'

Called away from the show, Leon couldn't help himself. He put his eye to the slats once more. She wasn't really kissing him, was she?

'Are you sure?' said Alice. 'I don't want my dad to catch us.'

'No one's going to walk in on us. They think we're doing maths.' He tickled her, making her giggle. 'They think you're a good girl.'

'Don't *you* think I'm a good girl?' said Alice in a funny voice that Leon didn't understand.

'I don't know,' said Cliff, 'are you?'

'You'd better try me and find out,' said Alice.

They moved on the bed together and Leon couldn't see clearly. There was more giggling. Then Leon saw Cliff

14

twist and turn. He looked directly at the wardrobe as if he could see Leon, which Leon knew simply wasn't possible. Cliff grinned with triumph. Leon saw Cliff drop Alice's bra on the floor. The mission had gone critical. It was time to call in reinforcements. He rocketed out of the wardrobe and out the bedroom door. He heard his sister yelling behind him and a scrabble of movement, but he was fast. 'Mum! Mum!' he shouted. 'Cliff's taken off Alice's bra.'

'Leo, I'm going to kill you!'

He glanced back to see Cliff, shirtless and shoeless, at the top of the stairs, red-faced with fury. From the bottom of the stairs he heard his father roar, 'A-A-A-ALICE!' The general had arrived.

MIKI

Miki fed Red two slices of halloumi. 'No more,' she said. 'It's bad for you.'

The dog whined and pawed at her.

'Stop it,' said Miki. 'You're making me sound like Mum. You know any more will make you sick. It's fatty and salty…' Red licked her knee. 'And delicious, I know. But you can only have a little bit.' She put the bowl up on the bed and put her arms round the dog's neck. 'You love me, don't you, Red?' The dog snuffled her affectionately but kept his eyes on the bowl of cheese. 'You wouldn't make me go to some nasty fair, would you?' The dog confirmed with a lick that he loved her very much, almost as much as he loved cheese.

Miki sat up and wiped her hands roughly across her eyes. 'I won't cry,' she told the dog. 'Besides, tomorrow they will have forgotten they ever wanted me to go. If only they would forget the whole idea. They didn't even ask me what I thought before they changed everything and started this business.' She pulled the dog's ears gently. 'They say they're doing it for me. But what if I don't want it? What if I want my own life?'

Red snuffled her again and edged her towards the cheese. 'No,' said Miki. She put it higher up on her bed. Red gave a long drawn-out woolly noise that sounded like a sigh, and slumped down on the rug. When it came to cheese he had all the patience in the world.

Miki pulled a drawing pad and a box of pastels from under the bed. Within minutes, she was lost in her creation. From beneath her fingers appeared a sketch of herself as a goth clown, crying one golden tear while the rest of the world burned around her. She smeared a last shadow and held it out to look at it. 'Okay. Not bad for half an hour's effort,' she said. 'What do you think, Red?' She turned to look at her dog, and found he was right next to her. Red had his head in the cheese bowl and was oblivious to the world.

Miki sighed. 'Great critic you are. Hopefully my art teacher will prefer it to cheese. Now give that here. You'll only make yourself ill.' Red gave a low rumbling growl which wasn't in the least menacing. Miki whipped the bowl away from under his head and the growl became a howl.

JONAS

Jonas made tea and brought it through to his mother. He had a big casserole dish of food, plates and cutlery on his tray. He'd even remembered napkins. He felt pleased with himself. It was the first time he'd managed to make macaroni cheese, keep the pasta soft, not curdle the sauce and not burn any of it. And he'd daringly added some french mustard to the sauce to give it what the TV chefs kept referring to as 'kick'.

His mother was lying on the sofa in the living room with her eyes shut. Jonas hesitated with the tray in his hands. He could always heat up some for her later on. He'd just decided to go and eat his quietly in the kitchen when she stirred. 'Oh, love, is that you?' she said sitting up. She looked pale. Jonas was sure there were more lines around her eyes than yesterday.

'I made mac and cheese, Mum,' he said.

'Oh, how lovely,' said his mother. 'I was going to do that. I must have fallen asleep after being in the garden.'

Jonas set the tray down on the coffee table. 'I think it's my best yet,' he said.

'It looks wonderful,' said his mother. She reached out for a plate, but her hand spasmed sharply and she quickly drew it back.

'Does it hurt a lot?' said Jonas.

'No, dear,' said his mother. 'I just think I overdid it a bit today. After my little sleep, and some of your excellent food, I'll be right as rain.' She paused briefly. 'Perhaps you could put some on the plate for me? You know how this wretched disease goes – all swings and roundabouts, with none of the fun.' She gave him a smile. 'I read yesterday on the internet that there's a doctor in Italy who thinks he has found a cure. Something to do with having too much lead in your brain. You'd think that was the kind of thing you'd notice, wouldn't you? Still, can't believe everything you read on the web, can you?'

'No, Mum,' said Jonas quietly.

His mother pulled herself up to a sitting position,

grunting with the effort. 'Goodness, I sound like a hog in a sty! Still, darling, even our own GP thinks there's every chance that there will be a cure in my lifetime. And you do remember, don't you, that there's no way you'll develop this? It doesn't matter how bad my MS gets, it can never, ever pass to you.'

'Of course, Mum,' said Jonas. He kept his face away from her as he ladled the mac and cheese out, so she couldn't see that he was trying not to cry. He hated seeing his mum in so much pain.

RORY

Rory scrubbed desperately at his shoes in the downstairs cloakroom. He'd tried using only water and it had made the stain worse. The only good thing about the chase was they hadn't got his phone. God, that would have been a disaster. What they could find on there. His life would be over.

Now, as a last-ditch effort, he'd tried using the liquid soap his mother put out for guests – jasmine and mint. To his astonishment the stains were coming away in froths of bubbles. Forty-five minutes later his Vans, if not as good as when they were bought, were looking better than he ever thought they'd look again. He took them through to his bedroom and went to open his window, so he could put them on the sill to dry in the sunlight. But the window was already open. He always kept it shut and locked when he was out, but here it was, open.

Who could have been here? He looked around wildly. Now he took the time to check, he realised that several things had been moved. He was a particularly tidy boy, so he spotted that his chest of drawers had been opened. The

18

drawers weren't level anymore. He went over and opened one. Everything inside had been mixed up. He opened another drawer. It was the same. He threw open the door to his wardrobe and found half his clothes lying on the floor. His shoes, once neatly arranged in pairs, were now all in a tumbled mess.

His heart beat faster. Someone knew. Someone had found out. But had they found *it*? Whoever had been here wanted him not to realise something was wrong when he got home. But they hadn't had time to tidy things properly. No one looking at the room would think there had been a burglary. They'd just think he was untidy, like most boys his age. Now Rory's heart beat faster than ever. Was that why they'd chased him, so he'd be late home? So they could find…? But how could they have known.

On the verge of a full-blown panic attack, he crawled under his bed. He pulled off a small piece of the skirting board and felt behind it. The box met his hand. He pulled it out, almost sobbing with relief. Then he opened it and his world crashed.

The box was empty.

MARTY

Back home, Marty plugged in the camera and pulled up the photos on his iMac. They were even better than he could have hoped for. For once they were well-framed and in focus. It really was his lucky day. It had been worth ruining his shoes. Everything he could have wanted was right in his lap. He began to compose the story in his head. He reached for the keyboard. Then he stopped. He shouldn't rush this. It had to be pitch perfect. He'd go and have a shower. He was cold and filthy. Besides, he always thought better in the shower. It was the white noise effect of the water that blocked out everything else – especially those rude letters from his bank manager. Then he'd defrost something nice and have a glass of wine before he sat down to do the first draft. He deserved it. This was day one of the new successful Marty.

BREAKING NEWS

Argentinian archaeologists have uncovered the body of a 2000-year-old man who appears to be wearing white ear buds, similar to those of a very popular technology brand. Could this shine a new light on the fruit Eve took from Eden?

OTHER BREAKING NEWS

There are reports in Yorkshire of a pig laying six large eggs. Unfortunately, the eggs were removed before the contents could be inspected. One local farmer, who wished to remain anonymous, said he believed it was a new government-led genetic project to make British breakfasts more profitable by having eggs and bacon from the same source.

FURTHER BREAKING NEWS

Dutch authorities are holding a group of self-declared British civil servants prior to deportation. Supposedly, the government officials held a most uncivil party in a hired windmill, which included a bungee jump, a large vodka luge, several live bands and a fireworks display. Local farmers claimed the noise frightened their cows and the flower growers complained the ashes from the fireworks had damaged the tulips.

Breaking News is brought to you by Radio City Central: the local station you can trust.

MONDAY 5th JUNE

BREAKING NEWS

The Prime Minster today condemned Jonathan Ludmire's assertion that the Civil Service does everything in government. The PM said 'I want people to know that politicians work long and hard hours to serve the British people. We rely on no one but ourselves. The Civil Service is there mainly for the paperwork.' The Prime Minister was unavailable for further comment as he had fallen asleep during the session in the House of Commons this morning and no one was available to wake him up.

OTHER BREAKING NEWS

It has been confirmed today that all asteroids come from Outer Space, so the likelihood they are sent to Earth by aliens in a co-ordinated attack remains a distinct possibility. Patrick Loss of the Protect the Earth from Aliens Society (PEAS) said on last night's TV show, *The Perspective*, 'The British People deserve to know the truth. A whole region, Tunguska, was wiped out in Russia in the early years of last century. Newspapers at the time reported it was an exploding asteroid, but what are the chances? Fifty years later, NASA was founded, and they've been secretly protecting us ever since. We're lucky the aliens didn't land in the first half of the twentieth century. Unless, of course, they did.' Mr Loss' new book, *How to Befriend Alien Overlords: An Emergency Guide*, is published on Monday.

FURTHER BREAKING NEWS

In a small rural village in Italy, the local mayor has verified that a young girl has a talking pet rabbit. More on this later.

AND ABROAD

The President-Elect for the United States has said he will ban peanut allergies. His statement has caused an uproar in the medical and judicial worlds with people wondering if allergy treatments are to be outlawed, and if people suffering from severe allergies will be imprisoned immediately. The head of the US Health Board said the suggestion was 'utter tosh', but other US dignitaries have been more guarded in their comments.

9.15 AM HISTORY CLASS

Miki took a deep breath and turned the door handle. Mr Deacon, now shorter than her at five foot nothing, paused dramatically, caught in an exaggerated pose indicating at the white board. Miki waited for it.

'So nice of you join us, Ms Barton. Do have a seat. We

are discussing Western propaganda during World War I. I feel certain you will have some views.' There was never anything overtly rude about what Mr Deacon said, but somehow his words always stung her. Miki thought him a good-looking man, and when she was younger she had found him intriguing. Now she was taller than him she saw things differently. The man had so many chips on his shoulder it was a surprise he didn't topple over.

All eyes in class turned to her. Miki forced her features into her strongest *I couldn't care less* expression (practiced nightly in the bathroom mirror). Her upper lip slightly raised in the right corner, her eyebrows also raised and her eyes slightly squinted. On a good day it worked. On a bad day she looked like she was about to fart.

'I'm sorry, Mr Deacon,' said Miki, pushing her way through the rows of desks and not reacting when her book-filled satchel unintentionally connected with Mark Stuart's head. 'Bitch' hissed Stuart, but she'd moved on before he could reach out a hand to pinch her, or worse.

'I must stop you there, Ms Barton. Whatever excuse you have prepared, kindly abandon it. I have no interest in any of your tiny little lives outside of this classroom. In here, history is all, and as far as I am aware, none of you have yet done anything worthy enough to be noted in the annals of history. Or am I mistaken?' Deacon's gaze swept around the room with a haughty expression. As everyone else was sitting and he was standing, for once, he could actually look down his nose at them.

'Not yet, Mr Deacon, sir. Give me time!' said Rory. Miki smiled at him, glad someone else was taking the spotlight off her. Today, Rory's blonde hair stood on end and had pink streaks. He wore his yellow-framed specs that

24

emphasised his large brown eyes, giving him a wide-eyed, innocent look that was in complete contrast to his general demeanour.

'I think it unlikely you will achieve as much as a footnote in history, Rory,' said Deacon. 'But if you do, what an odd footnote it will be. Multi-hued and attention-seeking, one presumes.'

'Oh, you know me, sir. I love the spotlight,' said Rory.

Mr Deacon gave him a tight little smile. 'Well, unless you desire to look up at the one outside the Head's office, I suggest you kindly shut it and let me continue to install what little learning is possible into your tiny little minds. Now, what would you say, Jonas, was the dominant political party at the time?'

Jonas didn't answer. Everyone looked round to see that Jonas had his head down on his desk. He gave the tiniest snore.

'Jonas,' said Deacon sharply.

Jonas jerked awake.

'I do apologise,' said Deacon, 'Are we disturbing your nap time? Only, I was under the impression this was meant to be a history class.' A nervous whinny of laughter went round the room, as the more nervous pupils attempted to show they were on their teacher's side.

'Sorry, sir,' said Jonas. Miki could see his face was pale as milk and his eyes bleary. He was clearly not in a good way. 'I didn't sleep well last night,' he said.

Deacon moved down the row of desks, stopping to drum his fingers on the desk of the girl in front of Jonas. 'What did I just say to Ms Barton, Ms Klein?' he asked.

Susan Klein brushed her long hair unnecessarily back from her face and said in an overly sweet voice, 'That

25

outside these walls you are uninterested in our lives.'

'Tiny little lives,' corrected Deacon. 'But, yes, Ms Klein, you are essentially correct. Kindly do not wear mascara again in my class. It makes me think your eyes are being attacked by spiders, as well as being against school rules.' Susan Klein flushed red.

'Propaganda by the West during WWI? Anybody?'

'Inside the British Empire or outside it?' said Miki without raising her hand.

Deacon pretended to be deaf until she went through the actions of raising her hand and being given permission to speak, despite the fact no one else wanted to open their mouths.

'I said, inside the British Empire or outside it?'

'I was under the impression I was the one who asked the questions,' said Deacon, 'But expand.'

'The war years of 1914-1918 were the last years of the stately homes and of the overbearing social class system. Not only did so many men die during the battles, making the once great houses of the time impossible to staff, but men of all classes dying alongside each other in the trenches broke the illusion of the superiority of the so-called upper classes. Although the class system remained up to the Second World War, broken and reformed. We still have the separation between the ultra rich, with or without titles, and us mere mortals. The system of the have and the have-nots persists.

'But the old class system never recovered from the loss of personnel during the First World War. Prior to 1914 it was considered a good position to go into service as a servant. Afterwards it was seen as an anachronism and a step down. During the war years there was a great effort to secure the privilege of the upper classes. Efforts attempting to teach the lower classes that they were inferior, that officers straight out of school knew best because of their class, I would count that as propaganda. Internal propaganda, but propaganda none the less. To attempt to convince any man he is the lesser than another…'

'Yes. Yes, we all know your views on inequality,' said Deacon, cutting her off. He turned so that his back was facing her. 'Now, has anyone anything intelligent to offer?'

'Rude little man,' said Miki quietly under her breath, and had the satisfaction of seeing Deacon's shoulders stiffen. However, he didn't choose to rebuke her this time. Doubtless, he didn't want her repeating her comment any louder. Or maybe, she thought, he knew she'd follow it up, if questioned, with how people should pick on others their own size. Across the aisle came a tiny little snore. Jonas was asleep again. However, Mr Deacon was still wandering down the classroom, talking and gesticulating widely with this arms. What an arse, she thought.

The relief when the bell went was palpable throughout the class. In the corridor outside Miki caught up with Jonas. 'Hey,' she said. 'You okay? You look like the belly of a dead fish.'

'Just tired,' said Jonas. 'Excuse me. I have to get to my locker before next period.' He half walked, half jogged off. Miki watched him go. She considered calling out after him, but they weren't exactly friends. It was just that… a hand landed hard on her bottom. Miki spun around to find Mark Stuart standing there. 'That's what naughty girls like you need,' he said. Miki whirled her book bag up and round to hit him firmly in the face. Stuart went down as if she'd hit him with a concrete pillar which, considering how many books Miki carried around with her, wasn't that far off the truth. He lay stunned on the floor. Miki was secretly rather surprised. She'd forgotten how much she had in her bag. But she decided to play it cool and began to walk away when she heard a muffled shout, 'You fuck'n' bitch. You broke my fuck'n' dose,' said Mark.

Miki turned back to see Mark sitting on the floor, blood streaming from his hands as he held them against his face. 'You broke my fuck'n' dose,' he repeated. Miki, torn between laughter and horror, didn't see Deacon come up behind her and put his hand on her shoulder. 'Oh dear, Ms Barton. Have we been...?' But Miki, still filled with adrenaline and righteous anger, reacted instinctively. Drawing on the aikido classes she had done in her first year of high school, before art had begun to take up all of her free time, she trapped the hand on her shoulder, turned and threw... Deacon. She had time to note that he flew through the air quite nicely before landing on Mark in a tangle of limbs and blood. Deacon struggled to sit up, pushing Mark roughly aside. 'Ms Barton,' he said in accents like thunder. He scrambled to his feet, yanking at his trouser legs, which had risen up to show – what? Snoopy socks! Miki tried to think of something clever to say and failed. Deacon, his usually immaculate hair, flopping forward over one eye, marched up to her and took her upper arm in a vice-like grip. 'You, young lady, are coming with me!' Miki had no doubt she could forcibly detach him from her arm but going quietly to the Head's office seemed like the better option.

JONAS

Behind him Jonas could hear some kind of commotion

in the corridor. Dealing with school schisms was the last thing he needed. He ignored it and headed for his locker. He thrust his head into the space and snatched up his hidden phone, stuck to the underside of the shelf at the back. Since the new headteacher had taken office, phones weren't allowed to be used within the school building. He unlocked it and read several messages from his mother, all reassuring him she was fine. He would have been less concerned if she had sent fewer messages. However, this morning he could barely keep his eyes open. Last night he'd done his usual round of tidying the house and making soup and simple salads that she could have for lunch. But when he'd got to his room, his brain wouldn't switch off. He kept wondering how much longer he could cope. He'd deleted all his accounts online. He was too afraid that one night he'd crack and ask for help. Then his mother would be sent to some institute somewhere and he'd be sent into care. He'd never see her again. He had to hang on. He had to do it alone. The only way to stop the thoughts had been to play Grand Theft Auto. He'd lost himself so deeply in the game that it was 5 a.m. before he knew it.

He stowed the phone back in its hiding place.

'Watch out!' said Rory colliding with Jonas' shoulder as he attempted to reemerge from the locker. 'There's been enough blood spilt today to appease the gods! Fair Miki has trounced the evil Mark!'

'What are you talking about?' Jonas asked.

'Not even a sorry from the surly knave,' said Rory. 'Why, fie, he be but a mortal after all!'

'You're rehearsing for the school play?' said Jonas. '*A Midsummer Night's Dream*? I'm doing the lights.'

'I'm trying to get into character,' said Rory, taking Jonas

by the elbow. 'You're in Comp Sci with me next, aren't you?' Jonas nodded. 'Problem is, they cast everyone when I was off last week. Very little left of interest. So, I thought I'd go for a smaller part and hope one of the others gets ill on the night.'

Jonas frowned.

'I don't mean like really ill, but you know, a little tummy upset or some such thing.'

'Are you going for a part as a fairy? Is that why your hair is pink?'

'Smart boy! I thought Peaseblossom.'

Jonas shook his head. 'Isn't whoever plays Peaseblossom the understudy for the part of Helena? You can't.'

'Shakespeare's original work was played entirely by men,' said Rory.

'Yeah,' said Jonas. 'But look around. We have equality now.'

'That's fine,' said Rory. 'But why can't I play a girl?'

'Because it's not a farce,' said Jonas. 'Everyone would laugh at you.'

'But I can mope so magnificently,' said Rory. 'Besides, true equality would mean I had every right to play a girl!'

They entered the computer lab. 'Is there no end to your talents?' said Jonas. 'I mean the way you can copy code so well too. I know why you are suddenly so friendly,' said Jonas.

Rory stuck out his tongue at him. 'Oh fie, what fools these mortals be.' He then made fluttering motions with his arms and flew off to the other side of the lab.

RORY

Rory sat down and looked at the blank computer screen. It wasn't even worth his time to turn it on. He hadn't read any of the chapters of the textbook last night. He hadn't the faintest idea how to go about the current programme. Jonas was always such a lonely little geek; he'd thought he'd be glad of a friendly chat.

He studied his reflection in the blank screen, idly twitching a hair or two back into place. He had to admit he looked good today. Not that it would cut any ice with Ms Wishart. He doubted she knew much more about computing than he did, but he'd give her kudos for always staying a chapter ahead of the class. The only way he might have a chance of distracting her from his lack of knowledge was by asking her something that was beyond her. The flaw in his plan was that he couldn't think of anything to ask. He couldn't even remember what the code he was meant to be writing was supposed to do.

Karl had been useless last night. No help whatsoever. Usually he said all the right things. But not in this time of crisis. Maybe that was it. Maybe Karl was the kind of person who went to pieces in a crisis. But it wasn't his crisis! It was Rory's.

'I think it would help to turn the machine on, Rory.' Rory jumped in his seat. Ms Wishart, all woollen suit, harsh perfume and fading perm, stood over him.

'Goodness, Miss, do you have Ninja training? I never heard you at all.'

'Your computer, Rory.'

'I'm sorry, Miss. I can't get my head around it. I think I've been born into the wrong age.'

'To turn on a computer?'

'To be able to code this project,' said Rory. He tilted his head up towards her and opened his eyes wide. The harsh light of the classroom made his eyes tear up. He forced himself not to blink at once in case he was going to need to cry.

'Are you struggling, dear? You can always come and talk to me.'

Rory heaved a big sigh. 'Do you think, Miss, if you don't mind, you could go through with me again what we're meant to do. I read the chapter, but it was like it was in an alien language. I simply couldn't get it through this thick head of mine.'

Ms Wishart pulled up a chair. 'Now, you mustn't think you're stupid, Rory. You're really very bright. A bit of a class clown at times, but there's nothing you couldn't do if you set your mind to it. Now, let's take a look at the problem, shall we? Where's your book?'

Rory rummaged in his bag and pulled it out. He handed it to her with the sweetest smile. 'You are such a kind lady,' he said. 'If only all teachers were as wonderful as you, I'm sure I would do better in school.' He felt he was laying it on a bit thick, but he knew she'd just had S1.12 in and even S6 thought they were hellspawn. At least he could be the balm to someone's day. He settled back in his seat and let her words wash over him as she demonstrated what he was meant to be coding. She had such a relaxing voice.

LEON

In Maths Room 3b Leon stood under the hole in the ceiling and gathered his courage. By pulling the teacher's desk across he'd found he could scrape at the side of one of the ceiling tiles to loosen it. He'd visited the room over several days' worth of breaks, working to free it. Today, just now, it had come away in his hands. Today was the day. He double-checked the blinds were pulled down on the door. Then, carefully, he placed a chair on the desk and climbed up. He put his hands on either side of the panels, leaning on the metal lattice that held the suspended ceiling in place. Yes, he was tall enough to get the necessary leverage to pull himself up. The question was, would the metal framework hold while he did so?

Very gently he eased his weight onto the palms of his hands. The thought of landing in a heap of furniture and metal girders was not enticing. Leon didn't like pain. He didn't even like heights. He inwardly recited the motto he had created for himself. *Without daring there is no adventure.* He stood on tiptoe, ready to ascend. The frame held firm. This was going to be glorious. The whole of the lower floor of the school had a false ceiling. If he could get up there, he could get anywhere. Why, he might even be able to get above the teachers' staffroom. The things he could hear! He'd finally know if it meant something that Ms Wishart often got a lift after school with Mr Deacon. They were always the last staff to leave and seemed to go to the car only when they thought the pupils had all left. Leon found this very suspicious. For two teachers to be so friendly and for no one else to have noticed, suggested some kind of shenanigans. Were they secret agents from Ofsted? Or better yet, were they some kind of government scouting team? If so, Ms Wishart must be highly skilled. She didn't come across as very bright when she was teaching computer science. That could be an act, or she could be Deacon's liaison to their HQ. They might be in love – if teachers could fall in love. He wasn't clear on that point. That would be a truly icky solution. Besides, Ms Wishart looked older than Mr Deacon. But then Mr Deacon wasn't very tall. He needed to check out Ms Wishart's shoes. Perhaps when she took her shoes off she was the perfect height for Mr Deacon to kiss. He threw up slightly in his mouth at the thought.

He should have thought of that. He'd read that you could tell a lot about a person by looking at their watch and their shoes. He wasn't sure what the watch would mean, unless it was to tell you if they kept it to time. (And why wouldn't they? Maybe if they set it to Russian time. That would mean something, wouldn't it?) But looking at someone's footwear properly would let you work out how tall they were. Unless they had placed paper inside their shoes. Enemy spies could be tricky. That was why Leon had to get all the practice he could in now, while he was still at school. By the time he applied to MI5, or simply '5', as those in the know called it, he'd have super skills and they would welcome him with open arms. He'd be a new breed of superspy. He still held out hope he'd be taken on as a teen apprentice due to his outstanding abilities. The problem was how to get those abilities noticed.

Gingerly, Leon pushed his weight further onto to his hands. The tips of his toes separated from the seat of the chair. Very faintly, he heard a voice. At first Leon thought it came from the ceiling above, so he pushed himself up a bit higher. His waist came level with the opening and he leaned the top half of his body across in preparation for wiggling his legs in. Points of light pierced through the ceiling tiles from the room below, sending shafts of faint illumination across the space. Leon forgot about the voice. He reached his arms out and pushed himself up onto to his stomach. He kicked out with his feet. He could see the edges of a metal frame running across the bottom of the space. Brilliant! There were also struts sticking into the ceiling every now and then. He could see some of them were coming loose, but not many. With luck the frame would also be bolted into the walls. If he kept his weight spread evenly across that he would be able to move around the room. This could be a way to get between classrooms. Perhaps a duct space or something? A conduit? There were always conduits in American TV shows.

Now he had his upper body and half his legs in the ceiling space. He'd planned to kick the chair away about now. The ceiling tile he'd removed lay in front of him, waiting to be replaced. With luck no one would ever guess where he had gone. Of course, this made the idea of getting out a little problematic, but trainee spies had to get used to thinking on their feet or in this case, their stomachs.

Leon heard the voice again. Definitely an adult and coming from somewhere below. He hadn't heard the classroom door open, so it was unlikely anyone had come into the room. They must be out in the corridor. He couldn't risk kicking the chair away now. It might be heard. The best thing he could do was wait.

He inched his legs in and rolled onto his side. Slowly, and as quietly as possible, he slid the tile over the hole, taking care to leave it ever so slightly out of alignment. If someone came in, they might think it was odd that a chair was on the desk, but hopefully they wouldn't notice there was anything up with the ceiling now that the tile mostly filled the gap once more. Then, when they were gone, he could free the tile, knock down the chair, replace the tile properly and he'd be free to roam above the ground floor, listening in for critical intel from below.

At least, that was the plan.

He carefully spread his weight flat across the frame to wait for whoever it was to pass. The metal struts dug into his back uncomfortably, but it was nothing he couldn't handle. After all, spies had to be able to withstand torture. This was nothing.

Except, as he lay there, Leon noticed that grey stuff was falling down on him. He brushed it away from his face. It felt soft. He suddenly thought of asbestos and how it damaged people's lungs; they'd never leave that in a school, surely? His heart raced and sweat broke out on his forehead. But it only took him a moment to realise his foolishness. No one had been up here since the suspended ceiling had been constructed. It was dust. Lots of dust. He almost laughed in relief but managed to swallow the rising giggle when he heard footsteps approach and stop. Whoever it was must be standing outside the classroom door. Leon held his breath. Under him the ceiling frame shifted a tiny amount. He felt the give, but it was tiny. Obviously, the frame was well-bolted into the walls and ceiling.

He continued to hold his breath – he could manage two minutes. He'd timed himself in the bath. By the end of that, surely whoever it was would have either moved on or come in. He waited.

He hadn't run out of breath, but it still seemed like an age later when he heard the footsteps – he could now make out two sets – begin walking again. The door opened and then closed. A low murmur of voices. Words he couldn't make out. Whoever it was, they passed under him and

36

towards the back of the room. He let loose an exhalation of relief that, whoever they were, they hadn't realised he was up here. This loosened a large clump of dust which freed itself from the old ceiling and deposited itself on his face. Leon felt his nose twitch. He rubbed it, still listening to the departing footsteps. He rubbed it again. Every time he rubbed his nose the itch grew worse, but he couldn't help it. It was so itchy. He could feel a sneeze building. He tried holding his breath again, but it wasn't working. Perhaps they were far enough away now, because he couldn't hold out any longer. Aa-choo! He sneezed violently. The frame underneath him gave ever so slightly more. Another cloud of dust floated down from the old ceiling. Leon tried to cover his face with his hands, but it was no good. The air was thick with dust. He sneezed again. And again. And again, until he was helplessly in the throes of a sneezing fit. Every time a sneeze shook his body the frame gave way slightly more. He could no longer hear the footsteps. But they were the least of his problems. If he didn't stop sneezing, then…

The frame shook loose from whatever aged mounts it had. The whole ceiling came crashing down, and Leon with it. As he fell, he got a look at the room's occupants and saw the startled faces of his sister Alice and her boyfriend, Cliff, looking up, mid romantic clinch, as the tiles rained down on them. 'Leo! Not again!' screamed Alice.

MIKI

Outside the headteacher's office, Miki sat on a nasty, stained, blue padded seat and swung her legs. She had been waiting at least an hour and a half. Mr Deacon had informed the office secretary, in the little room off to the right, that she was there and promised her dire consequences should she move. Then he had gone off. She presumed he had gone to try and clean up. Stuart's blood had stained his jacket and his hair looked as if he had lost a battle with an angry hen.

Miki had both her own art books from home (which made the bag so heavy) and her phone in her bag, but she decided it was wiser to leave those hidden. There was no saying that Deacon might come back and confiscate anything he found her using. He'd been pretty mad. Too angry to listen to her side of the story. As far as he was concerned, she had assaulted a teacher and would, in all likelihood, be expelled from the school. She really, really didn't want that to happen. But at least if it did, she'd be going out as a legend. Maybe she could tweet something quickly about Diving Deacon before he came back. It would be good to leave him with a nickname that would haunt him for the rest of his career. He'd had no right to touch her and entirely deserved what he had got. She rolled up her blouse sleeve and looked at her upper arm. Tiny blue bruises were blossoming where his fingers had gripped her. She understood he'd been in shock, but still, he'd technically injured her. All he had suffered was disturbance to his hair. He was completely out of order.

Miki genuinely believed this. Especially as it came on the back of her being physically assaulted by Mark Stuart. However, she also knew that she had a reputation of her own, that she had spent much of the previous lesson winding up Deacon for fun, and that it was quite possible Deacon had thought he was breaking up an actual fight. She would be more than happy to shake hands with Deacon and call it quits as long as Mark Stuart got what he deserved. At the

38

very least the acknowledgement that her action in breaking his nose had been perfectly justified. Besides, she hadn't meant to do more than make him think twice about ever touching her inappropriately again. More than once she'd felt her bum being pinched when she'd passed his chair, but she'd never managed to catch him in the act. She knew it was him, but she couldn't prove it. He'd only got what he more than deserved today. Why, there were countries in the world where his hand would have been removed for touching her inappropriately. He should count himself lucky.

'Smiling to yourself over this mornings's escapades, are you, Ms Barton? I wonder if seeing your parents here will wipe that smile off your face?'

Miki looked up to see Deacon standing in front of her, arms folded and a triumphant grin on his face. Behind him she could see the approaching figures of her parents. 'Oh shit, you didn't!' she exploded.

Deacon bent down over her and said in a harsh whisper, 'Oh yes, I did. Let's see what Mummy and Daddy think of their precious daughter's actions.'

'You don't know what you've done,' said Miki. 'They'll side with me and then there will be real trouble.'

Deacon stood up, frowning. 'Side with you?'

'I've been trying to tell you, Mark Stuart assaulted me. He slapped me on the butt. I hit him with my book bag after that. My parents will see it as resisting sexual assault and ask for you to call the police in. When you put a hand on my shoulder, I thought you were one of his friends – after all, you're about the same height.' She stopped. 'Sorry, didn't mean to offend.'

Deacon was still frowning. 'You couldn't tell me this earlier?'

She showed him her rolled up sleeve. 'I know you didn't mean to,' she said, 'but you hurt me when you marched me up here. They are going to crucify you.'

'I repeat,' said Deacon, looking somewhat paler and a lot less sure of himself now, 'why didn't you tell me about this earlier?'

'I tried,' said Miki, rising to her feet. 'Oh shit. Shit. Shit. Here they come. They were meant to be at some fair today. They are going to be livid to miss it. I don't know which of us is going to come off the worst in this, Mr Deacon, but I guarantee it's not going to be pleasant for either of us.'

Deacon swallowed hard. 'I was only doing what I thought was right,' he said.

'Yeah, me too,' said Miki. 'But you're not allowed to touch a pupil, remember? Especially one of the opposite sex. Let alone leave them with bruises.'

'It was never my intention to injure you, Miss Barton,' said Deacon frowning. 'You're an annoying termagant of a girl, but I bear you no personal animosity.'

'I know,' said Miki, giving him a slight smile. 'You dislike all of us equally.'

Deacon passed his hand through his hair again, frowning harder. He seemed younger and even slightly vulnerable. Suddenly, Miki remembered why she had fancied him.

Both of them could now clearly see the disgruntled expressions on the faces of Miki's parents. 'Shit,' said Miki. 'Yes, Miss Barton' said Deacon. 'I fear we are indeed in the shit.'

Miki considered remarking he'd be up to his neck sooner than her, but decided it was too easy, and too cruel a shot.

RORY

Today, in usual terms, would have been a good day. No one harassed Rory on his way home, despite his pink hair. His red Vans returned home in pristine condition. But the moment he walked through the door of his home it was as if he became another character. The confidence, the brashness and his flamboyant air fell away like the thick skin that sloughed off the school custard. He managed to get to his room. Then he dropped his bag and coat on the floor and threw himself face forward onto the bed. He lay there for several minutes, just breathing, his arms held out stiffly at forty five degrees.

He heard a knock at his door. 'Go away, I'm dead,' said Rory.

The door opened. 'Dead people don't talk,' came his sister's voice. 'Besides, I came to do you a favour.'

Rory rolled over on the bed and propped himself up on his pillows. 'What is this favour and what will it cost me?' Susan, two years older than him, stood in the doorway, carrying an armful of clothes.

'I don't want these anymore,' she said. 'I'm going to tell Mum and Dad I've outgrown them. I thought you might like them. You could take them in for the wardrobe on that play. Put you in good favour with the casting director.'

'What's wrong with them?' asked Rory, sitting up a bit further.

'They're not black,' said Susan. 'I'm a goth now.'

'This is about your new boyfriend? Jamie, isn't it? He uses more eyeshadow than you!'

'So?'

'So, he should learn to apply it properly. He always

41

looks like he's come out of a coal mine.'

'Whatever. If you don't want them…'

'I didn't say that,' said Rory, getting up. 'Thanks, Susan. It might help. I'll take them in tomorrow.' He took the dresses off her.

'If Mum or Dad asks, tell them you've already taken them in and they've been cut up for fairy dresses, yeah?' She turned to go.

'Sure,' said Rory. He put out a hand to touch her lightly on the arm. 'Sorry, Sue. I've had a hell of a day.'

'At least it wasn't you going off in the ambulance at lunchtime,' said his sister.

'There was an ambulance?'

'Yeah, some kid got carried out on a stretcher. One of the younger ones.'

'Wow,' said Rory.

'Oh, don't worry, he didn't have the blanket over his face, so he was alive.'

'Morbid, much?' said Rory.

'Goth, much,' said Susan and went out, closing the door behind her.

Rory went over to the mirror and held up one of her dresses. Green and composed of several translucent layers of material. It would be perfect, once reworked, for Peaseblossom. Then the reality of the missing box under his bed came crashing down on him. No one had spoken to him about the contents today – but it was only a matter of time. Rory collapsed onto his knees, dropping a cascade of colour around him. He curled into a ball and cried softly so no one would hear him.

MIKI

Miki could hardly believe her own ears; she found herself arguing that school was great. Her parents were all for storming out on the spot. 'You're sixteen, darling,' said her mother. 'You don't have to stay in this institutionalised hellhole a moment longer. My God, you've been assaulted, and they tried to get you to take the blame.'

'Sexually assaulted,' said her father.

'I'm not sure we can categorise it quite like that,' said the headteacher, Mr Murray. An older man with greying hair, he had long given up hope of helping students achieve academic excellence, or even, as he had dreamt of as a young man, of having an ex-student win a Nobel prize. Now, he was merely trying to glide into retirement. It was all very well younger teachers like Robin Deacon wading in to fight the good fight, but all he wanted to do was go home. His wife, Margaret, had promised him macaroni cheese for his tea tonight. He had a mound of paperwork to do – not that he could see the point of most of it, but if he didn't get these people out of his office and settle to task then he'd not be home before six. The macaroni would all be all dried up in the oven, and Margaret's affections with it.

'And how exactly would you like to categorise it?' Miki's mother was saying, 'Boys will be boys?' Her voice had risen to an alarming pitch by the end of this sentence. 'I've a good mind to sue!' she screeched.

'Of course, what the boy did was totally unacceptable,' said Mr Murray quickly. 'He will be severely punished.'

'And how will that be done?' demanded Miki's mother.

'A one week...' he flinched under her gaze and corrected himself, 'A two-week suspension and a period of three months probation when he returns.'

'If he causes any trouble during his probation period he will be expelled?' asked Miki's father.

'Of course,' said Mr Murray, wiping his sweating palms on his trousers under his desk. 'I will telephone his parents as soon as this interview is over. As for Ms Barton, I think we can understand what she did, can't we, Mr Deacon?'

'I hardly think that violence against a teacher can go unrebuked,' said Deacon, his voice quivering with rage.

Miki revealed her arm. 'Or violence against a student?'

'Ms Barton, Mr Deacon, consider yourselves rebuked,' said Mr Murray. He held up his hand to prevent Deacon from speaking. 'I will call Mark Stuart's mother myself. I hope we will see Miki back in school tomorrow, but perhaps she should have the rest of the day off after her trauma?'

'We shall have to see,' said Miki's mother, rising. She offered her hand to Mr Murray, who took it and had to bite his lip not to yelp under her vice-like grip. 'I do believe in all humanity working together. Once the issue is satisfactorily resolved I will not bear you a personal grudge.'

'Thank you,' said Mr Murray, slightly shaken.

'However, whether my daughter returns or not remains to be seen.' She pointed an accusing finger at Deacon. 'That man injured my daughter. Don't think you've heard the last of this, Deacon!'

Miki willed for the ground to open up and swallow her. She caught Deacon's eye and they exchanged a look of mutual misery. A year ago she would have found such a moment thrilling. Now she felt only sick and embarrassed.

BREAKING NEWS

The White House has clarified that the President is to ban the sale of peanuts and not the allergy, as previously stated. See page link for our article on reactions from Furious Peanut Farmers.

More on the talking rabbit soon.

OTHER BREAKING NEWS

A secret source reports that violence against staff has broken out at an Edinburgh school. At least one teacher has been injured during a brawl that apparently started between two pupils. The cause of the argument is not known, nor is it known how many police officers are attending the incident. There have been unconfirmed rumours that two teachers are being held hostage. An ambulance was seen leaving the school. More later…

Breaking News is brought to you by Radio City Central: the local station you can trust.

TUESDAY 6th JUNE

BREAKING NEWS

Sources have clarified that the riot that broke out at an Edinburgh school yesterday, causing material damage to the building and personnel, began over a political disagreement. A local girl, whose family are known for their eco-liberal sympathies, launched an attack on a middle-class boy.

OTHER BREAKING NEWS

Follow this link to see pictures of a benefit fraudster living the high life at your expense. This story is brought to you by our correspondent, Marty Mclaren.

JONAS

Jonas had a modern studies essay due in this morning and had completely forgotten about it. He opened up the news on several websites, looking for something that he could write about. He scrolled through page after page. 'Do people really believe this stuff?' he said out loud in astonishment as he read article after article. So far, he hadn't found anything that his teacher wouldn't think he had made up. Then he saw the benefit fraud case by Marty McLaren. It sounded more real than anything else he had read, so he clicked on the link. Moments later he was staring at a picture of his mother in their own back garden.

Jonas sat perfectly still. He even forgot to blink until his eyes began to tear up. He could not believe what he was seeing. His mother was shown kneeling by a flower bed, a small garden fork in her hand. She was resting back on her heels, smiling and looking the picture of health. The photographer had taken care to include the whole back exterior of the large bungalow. His mother was wearing her favourite blue sundress, as she had been yesterday. He realised the photo must have been taken moments before she had come back in and collapsed from exhaustion. That was how Multiple Sclerosis worked. One minute she could be perfectly fine and the next she could be so exhausted she barely had the energy to sit upright. Sometimes she found it difficult to get out of bed and he had to help her. And then there were the terrible days when she couldn't walk at all. But this Marty McLaren hadn't shown any of that.

Jonas scanned down the piece. Phrases like 'living at our expense', 'falsely claiming benefits for a disability she can seemingly turn on and off at will', 'her son, being coached in the ways of deceit', 'What can the authorities do?' It finished with the line, 'It's up to us, as concerned citizens, to root out and expose these fraudsters. They are using money to support their lifestyle that could be used for more serious purposes, like equipping a children's hospital. How can people like this justify their laziness and self-centred ways when they are depriving sick children of much needed medicine?'

Jonas felt physically sick. His mother was still asleep in her bedroom. He usually made her a cup of tea immediately before he left for school. With luck, this piece would disappear down the news pages of the day. It wasn't as if the site he was looking at was particularly well known. He had to hope that no one else would pick up the story.

Rage boiled inside him. He wanted to find this Marty McLaren and ask him where he had trained as a doctor. What right he had to attempt to destroy someone else's life – and for what? A few measly lines in print and a byline that would be forgotten by lunchtime. But he had no idea who Marty McLaren was. He had to be local, but the name meant nothing to him.

Jonas clenched his hands into fists to prevent him hurling the keyboard across the room. His modern studies teacher had talked about citizen journalists and how everyone could post on the internet now. She'd said how everyone had more information at their fingertips than ever before. She'd even talked about how, when she was young, her parents had only had one encyclopaedia set in the house, and an incomplete set at that. She hadn't understood that they had stopped buying any volumes after 'M to N', and everything beyond 'O' had remained a mystery to her till she reached high school. She'd made it sound like the world had made progress.

Jonas opened a new document. He typed THE MODERN WORLD OF FAKE NEWS. Then he poured all his rage and frustration into taking apart the habit of news websites publishing unconfirmed and, sometimes, clearly false stories on their sites and presenting them all as facts.

LEON

The nice nurse brought Leon a breakfast of scrambled eggs on toast, baked beans, juice and cereal. The eggs were underdone. It took a lot of chewing to swallow the toast, it was so rubbery. The cereal arrived soggy and only got worse. However, she brought it with a smile, which was more than his father would have given him after this latest escapade. He knew he would be able to get around his mother. He was the youngest of five: three boys and two girls. This made him the baby of the family. Usually this was annoying, except for times like this. For once he didn't mind the trade-off of being thought the baby and given leeway the others didn't enjoy.

After he'd swallowed down his breakfast, the nice nurse helped him pack up. 'You're very lucky, you know, sweetheart. Only bruises.' She gave him another of her wide smiles. For an old woman in her thirties, Leon liked her a lot. She had unruly dark curly hair that she kept having to tuck away. He grinned back. 'I bounce like a rubber ball. That's what the doctor said last night.'

The nurse laughed and leaned closer so she could speak softly. 'I fell out of a tree when I was twelve and broke my arm.' She folded his pjs and put them at the bottom of the suitcase.

'Did it hurt?' asked Leon.

'Oh, it sure did. Not at first, I was too startled. By the time my mum got me to the hospital I was crying my eyes out. But that wasn't the worst bit. It was the itching.'

'The itching?'

'I had a plaster cast from here to here,' she indicated from her upper arm to her wrist. "And it itched something

49

terrible. Problem is, you can't scratch under a cast! Drove me wild.'

'Were you parents cross?'

'At first I think they were frightened,' said the nurse. 'Then they were angry.' She discreetly tucked the teddy bear his mum had included under his slippers. 'Then they were simply fed up with me moaning!' She smiled again. 'I have to say, for a quick trip up a tree, it wasn't worth months of wearing that dratted cast.'

'I'll be more careful next time,' said Leon.

'I think it might be a good idea if you stopped climbing things,' said the nurse. 'Or, there are a couple of excellent climbing centres in Edinburgh. Why don't you ask your parents to take you to one of those? Then you'd be able to climb safely, with ropes and everything.'

'It's an idea,' said Leon. He spied his father entering at the far end of the ward. 'But I think I might wait a while. Dad's already moved on to the angry stage,' he pointed discreetly at him.

The nurse, taking a peek, winked at Leon. 'You stay safe now, honey.'

'Hi, Dad,' said Leon, putting on his best aren't-I-cute face. 'Where's Mum?'

'Your mother couldn't get time off work, so I said I would come and get you. After all, what else do I have to do? Oh wait, that's right, I have a company to run.' He picked up the suitcase from the bed. 'Now that all the excitement is over, I think it's time you told me what happened. And it had better be good. The way things stand, you're grounded until you're twenty-five.' He frowned, looking down at his son. 'As for your sister, she'll never forgive you. She's grounded till she's thirty, and I've banned Cliff from the house until he buys her an engagement ring.'

'Cliff is going to be my brother-in-law?' said Leon, his eyes bulging.

'Over my dead body,' said his father as he strode out of the ward. Leon hurried after him and in doing so discovered he ached everywhere.

MIKI

Miki's parents left in a flurry of forgotten papers and agitation. Both of them had spoken to her separately, using low, serious voices. Her mother had concentrated mostly on how her school would never teach her anything she wanted to know. Her father had gone the more conventional route of asking her to report any boy who so much as looked at her the wrong way. Then he fell back into the usual diatribe about the failings of modern education and how it didn't prepare anyone for modern life. Miki had found herself standing with her hands clenched at her sides, desperately trying to remain firm but polite. At least he hadn't brought up the subject of the 'University of Life', of which he was such a big fan. Not only did the term make her want to scream, but both her parents were Oxford graduates. She knew if she announced her intention to go there and study they would be (hypocritically) over the moon. But there was no chance of that. She'd rather die. Well, maybe not die, but rather have compulsory maths lessons for the rest of her life – or something equally dire.

Finally, they left to return to the eco-fair, barely consolable that their own daughter chose to attend high school. The irony was not lost on her. She started eating her good-for-you muesli, which her mother made in batches at home, with almond milk, but she added the chocolate buttons she'd bought yesterday. Then, in a feat of defiance, she ransacked the special Christmas cupboard, where items normally off-limits were stored through the year, and added a handful of Christmas cake raisins to her bowl. Now, it tasted slightly less like the bottom of a birdcage.

She had double maths first thing and had no qualms about missing the start of that, or registration. In fact, if she was late, that would make Mr Murray worry that her parents had been serious about suing the school. As if! She remembered all too well when her father had decided they should make living wills and her mother had screamed the place down about how lawyers stole all your money and that she wouldn't go near them in a thousand years.

Miki wouldn't go as far as to say she wanted to be normal, but she did feel it was unfair that she had such outrageous parents, who had given up their regular lives to help save the planet. It wasn't as if she could actually explain it to anyone. She got only as far as her eco-warrior parents and most other adults said how brave they were and how proud she must be. Other kids just assumed she was as mad as her parents. The only things she could do that would ever make them truly angry would be something like buy factory-farmed chicken or decide she wanted to be an investment banker. However, her conscience would allow her to do neither.

She turned on the radio. Radio Four's dulcet tones wafted across the room. Miki retuned to Radio One and poured herself another bowl of muesli. This time she added both raisins and glacé cherries from the Christmas stash.

This made her suddenly aware of the lack of dog under the table begging for food. 'Red!' she called. Silence. She got up and wandered into the living room. 'Red?' Again, there was no answer. Puzzled, Miki checked upstairs, but there was no sign of the big retriever. She tried to recall if her parents had said they were taking the dog with them. Admittedly she had gone into a mode where she no longer listened and merely grunted her replies in order to make them hurry up and leave. However, she couldn't imagine them taking the dog to an eco-fair. Red tended to forget any discipline he'd been taught the moment he came across an outdoor food stand. She came downstairs calling 'Red'. Midway down the stairs she realised, despite walking past the front door several times, she'd blanked the fact that it was open. Her parents had not closed it properly. She flew down the rest of the stairs, pausing only to pick up her key, before bolting out into the front garden, calling Red's name. She stopped at the end of the path and looked up and down the street. There was no sign of the dog.

RORY

Rory was late, but he knew he'd have to take the make-up off. Sometimes he got away with wearing a little bit of mascara. He could even manage the slightest bit of shading below the eyeline without anyone noticing. He practised. He had skills. But the new coloured mascaras that were supposedly all the rage made him look like he had some kind of exotic eye disease. He'd either be sent home for wearing make-up, which would lead to another conversation with his parents he didn't want to have, or they'd cart him off to hospital to see an eye surgeon.

He stood peering into the bathroom mirror. He'd had to take his contact lenses back out too. These mascaras might be badly coloured, but sod's law dictated that it was the most covering, longest lasting one he'd ever encountered. He'd already used all his eye make-up remover and was on to his sister's. The bathroom bucket was already full of used cotton wool pads. He looked down at the pile gathering around the sink in astonishment. How could so little mascara make so much mess on his face? He peered short-sightedly into the mirror. He'd been pulling at his eyelids so much he looked like he had conjunctivitis. It would have to do. Carefully, he put his contact lenses back in, but now his eyes were sore, and the lenses felt horrible: gritty and uncomfortable. He tried washing out his eyes with saline, but they kept misting over with gunk as they attempted to rid themselves of the last bits of mascara under his lids. 'Never again,' he muttered to himself. 'From now on, it's false eyelashes all the way.' He immediately began to wonder if he could order them online. He didn't much fancy trying the local high street.

He picked up his school bag and headed to the front door. His vision still hadn't cleared. He opened the front door and stepped out. The next thing he knew, he was flat on his back as a blur of bright red raced away from him.

MIKI

Miki's heart raced and tears pricked the back of her eyes. Her parents had spent ages taking things out to the car this morning, going back and forth, arguing and removing each other's things. This was not unusual, but it had made Miki realise that the door could have been left open at any time. They'd had him since he was a tiny puppy, all big paws and floof. He might not be the brightest dog to ever steal from a biscuit tin, but he was her dog and she loved him. Miki ran up and down the streets closest to her house and there was no sign of Red. How long had he been out? How far could he have got? Miki bent double to catch her breath. Then she ran on, still calling.

LEON

In his father's car going home, Leon sat silently gazing out of the window. He saw a red blur moving across a front lawn at the end of the street. He swivelled his head as they came level. His mouth dropped open. 'Dad,' he said.

'What?' said his father in a stern voice.

The red blur disappeared through a hedge. Leon thought better of his revelation. 'Nothing,' he said and went back to being quiet. In his mind's eye he replayed what he had seen. This was an excellent spy skill, but what could it have been? An enemy drone? Or even an alien? Did you get fluffy red aliens?

JONAS

Jonas knew he would be slightly late, but he felt sure the essay would get him an A. He reckoned it was one of the best he had ever done. It would be good to spend another few minutes checking it, but he wanted it in his teacher's inbox when she arrived at school. He attached the essay to an email and pressed send. He leaned back in his chair and breathed deeply. He felt good. If the essay was as good as he thought, perhaps he could send it to some of the news sites that published rubbish. He could dare them to publish this! That would show them. If they wouldn't, he'd put it up on his blog and even pay to advertise it on other sites. He'd written with passion and a burning desire for justice.

He got up and wandered through to the kitchen to make his mother her cup of tea. In his head he continued to make what he knew were unrealistic and fantastic plans for his essay, but at least it made him feel better. When he saw something out the kitchen window, he almost dropped the mug into the sink.

Now that was odd.

He opened the fridge and took out a slice of ham. Then he opened the back door and went out.

MIKI

Miki stood in the street looking this way and that. A figure jogged down the road towards her. As he came into sight, she realised it was Rory. His usually carefully spiked hair was flattened and there was a big smear of red across his legs.

'What happened to you?' she asked. 'Have you seen my dog?'

'In reverse order, I don't know, and I was knocked over by a running thing covered in paint. Have you painted your dog recently?' Rory meant it as a joke, but he stepped back involuntarily when he saw how Miki's expression darkened.

'Mark Stuart,' said Miki through gritted teeth. 'When I get hold of him I'll turn him inside out by his testicles.'

'Oh, okay then,' said Rory, backing away. Miki grabbed him by the wrist. 'Oh no you don't,' she said. 'I need your help. We have to find Red and then you have to help me kill Stuart!'

56

JONAS

By using small pieces of ham as bait, Jonas temped the big dog into the kitchen. He even managed to get a large plastic bag on the floor before the animal sat down. So there it was, in the middle of his kitchen, eating the last of the ham from his hand. It was clearly a friendly animal, if not overly bright. It was also visibly covered in red paint from head to paws.

'How on earth did you do this to yourself?' asked Jonas.

The dog wagged his tail, leaving a trail of red across the slate floor.

'No,' wailed Jonas. 'What am I going to do with you?'

His deep brown eyes stared up into Jonas' face. As far as Red was concerned Jonas was the man with the ham. Having ham was a good thing, especially when shared with him. Red had no idea where he was, but hopefully Jonas would take him home. After all, Jonas had had ham. Maybe Jonas had more ham. More ham seemed like an excellent idea to him. Red gave a small, low woof of encouragement. Ham was usually kept behind a shiny white door that only an owner could open. He looked around the room and wagged his tail encouragingly again.

'Shh,' said Jonas. 'Don't wake my mum.'

The dog's ears pricked up. 'Woof!' he said and stood up. He went over to the back door and scratched at it with his paws. 'Woof!' he said more loudly.

'No,' said Jonas. 'I'm going to ring the Cat and Dog Home. They'll have a device to read any chip you've got. Then they'll have to see if your owners deserve you back. I'd hate to see you handed over to people who did this to you. Now, you stay here while I go and look up the number on the web.'

He went through to the hall, closing the door behind him. He hurried through to his bedroom and began to search for an animal protection charity he could ring.

'WOOF! WOOF!! WOOOFFF!!!'

'Jonas,' called his mother sleepily, 'is that a dog outside?'

'No,' called Jonas. He added under his breath. 'He's inside.' Then he called, 'I'll bring your tea in a few minutes, Mum.'

He punched the number into his phone and ran back through to the kitchen while he waited for it to ring. There he found the dog standing on his hind legs barking out the kitchen window. Outside the window he saw Rory making faces at the dog. A scratching sound came from the back door. Jonas walked quietly over to the door and flung it open. He caught Miki hunched over, a multi-tool in her hand. 'Were you trying to break into my house?' he asked angrily.

'Why have you got my dog?' demanded Miki.

'I didn't know he was yours,' said Jonas. 'He ran into the garden. It took all the ham we had to get him into the house.' Even as he said this, Red pushed his way past and ran out to play with his new friend. He leapt up at the boy making the funny faces. Rory shied backwards from the big dog's pounce, lost his balance and went down on his back. Red immediately jumped on top of him and began to thoroughly wash his face.

'Good boy,' said Rory, desperately trying to push the dog off. But Red had the upper hand. Worse still, the animal had decided his cherry hair gel tasted good. 'Get him off me,' he called to the others.

Miki turned around to see Red chewing gently on Rory's hair and failed to suppress a giggle. 'Wait till he starts on

58

your eye make-up,' she said.

'Why did you paint him red?' asked Jonas. 'It must be horrible for him.'

'I didn't,' said Miki, suddenly serious again. 'He got out when Mum and Dad were leaving this morning. I found him like this.'

'Poor chap,' said a voice from the kitchen doorway. Miki turned around and saw a middle-aged woman in a blue dressing gown, leaning heavily on a stick. 'I'm Trisha,' she said. 'Jonas' mum. I thought you said there wasn't a dog outside?'

'I'd already brought him in,' said Jonas.

Trisha stood there for a moment taking stock of the red-smeared kitchen. 'Right, you need to get the paint off him before it dries properly. We don't have any dog shampoo, but you can try washing up liquid. It should be milder than shampoo for humans. Get a good lather going, outside in the garden, and then one of you can go off to the supermarket and get the proper stuff. If you don't start the process now, he'll need his fur shaved, which would be a terrible pity. Does he belong to the boy on the ground?'

'No, Mrs – I mean Trisha,' said Miki. 'He's mine. But I didn't do that to him.'

'No,' said Trisha. 'I can see he's a friendly beast, so he must have been trained by people who loved him. What a nasty prank for someone to play. There's a large bowl under the sink and some old cloths. You can start with that. I'm only sorry I can't help. I don't think this is going to be one of my good days.' And with that she sat down on a kitchen chair.

'Are you alright?' said Miki. 'You've gone very pale.'
Trisha nodded.

'I'll make her a cup of tea,' said Jonas. 'You start on the dog. Rory might as well help you. He's already covered in red paint.'

Miki opened the cupboard to take out the bowl. 'What do you call him?' asked Jonas.

Miki looked up at him from a kneeling position. 'You're not going to believe this,' she said. 'We call him Red.'

It took a lot of effort and a great deal of mess, but eventually Red reverted to his original colour. The dog had patiently let them wash him. Now he was running around the garden barking at butterflies. The three of them knelt in a soggy patch of crimson grass that now resembled a scene from a bad horror movie. Miki started to pile all the cloths back into the bowl. 'Look at me,' said Rory. 'I am covered in paint and dog hair.' The dog broke off his game for a moment to lick Rory's face. 'I think he's saying thank you,' said Jonas, grinning. 'He does seem to like you,' said Miki. Rory pushed the dog gently away from his face. 'I'd guess he likes everyone.'

'That's a dog for you,' said Trisha, coming to the back door. 'Unconditional love and affection. They always think the best of people. Poor creatures.'

'I'm so sorry about your lawn,' said Miki.

Trisha shrugged. 'It's more important your pet is okay. Will he stay here if you come inside for a moment to clean up?'

'I think so,' said Miki. 'He likes company.'

'And ham,' muttered Jonas.

They all came inside. 'I phoned the school and said you were working on an animal emergency,' said Trisha. 'I think the receptionist thought I was a student pulling her leg at first, but I explained. She said she'll make it all right with your teachers. She sounded quite fierce. Apparently, she has a red setter too. She's going to put up a poster about people mistreating animals in the area.'

Trisha had made a large pot of tea and set mugs on the table. Neither Miki nor Rory usually drank tea, but they accepted a mug to be polite.

'Thank you,' said Miki. 'But I think I know who did this to Red.'

'Who?' said Rory.

'Mark Stuart. I broke his nose yesterday after he slapped me on the butt,' said Miki.

'I saw that,' said Rory. 'He was the red one. Blood all over him. I guess he thinks this is revenge. What a coward.'

'High school sounds much more interesting than in my day,' said Trisha. 'Still, good for you dear. Boys have to learn to treat women well, otherwise they'll end up as husbands who behave badly.'

'Bit excessive, wasn't it? Breaking his nose?' said Jonas.

'What would you have done if he'd slapped your behind?' said Rory.

Jonas looked startled. 'That's different.'

'I don't see how,' said Trisha.

Miki smiled at her. 'I didn't actually mean to break his nose. I'd forgotten I had an art book on Dali in my bag. It packs a bit of a punch.'

'Surreal!' said Rory in delight. The others groaned.

Trisha's eyelids drooped and her smile faded. The skin on her face took on a greyish aspect. 'I'm so sorry, but I think all this excitement has got to me,' she said. 'Jonas, I'm sure I can leave you to ensure our guests get everything they need. It was good to meet you, Rory and Miki. And,

61

of course, Red. Feel free to visit any time, but I'm afraid I'm away back to my bed.' Trisha pushed out her chair and stood. She levered herself up by putting a hand on the back of the chair and one on the table, but even so her whole body shook with the effort. She smiled at them again. 'Don't worry. I'll be as right as rain after a wee rest. Enjoy your afternoon at school.' She shuffled slowly out of the kitchen.

'OMG,' said Rory after she had closed the door behind her. 'It's like your mother aged a thousand years in a few minutes.'

Miki kicked him under the table.

'Ow!' said Rory. 'I was merely observing.'

'Multiple Sclerosis,' said Jonas. 'They call it a hidden disease. One minute she seems fine, the next it's like she's just run a marathon.'

'But she'll get better, right?' said Rory.

Jonas shook his head, unable to form the right words.

'My aunt has it,' said Miki. 'It's an autoimmune disease. There isn't a cure yet, but they are working on it.' She reached out and touched Jonas' hand quickly. 'It can have a range of symptoms, some of them really bad, but the common denominators are generally fatigue and pain. I'm so sorry, Jonas.'

'Harsh,' said Rory. 'Your mum is cool.'

Jonas made a decision. 'Wait here,' he said. 'I want to show you something.'

Rory pulled a face. 'Will we like it?' he said in silly coy voice. 'Ow, will you stop kicking me, Miki?'

Jonas paid him no attention. He left the room and returned moment later with two printouts of the news articles. Silently, he handed them to Miki and Rory.

A few moments later Rory said, 'What an utter scummy scrotum.'

'That's sick,' said Miki. 'Who is this guy anyway? I've never heard of him.'

'He's a nobody,' said Jonas. 'Someone who wants to get attention. Be known as a whistleblower.'

'A prick, you mean,' said Rory.

'But it's not fair,' said Miki. 'Anyone who met your mum would understand. What are you going to do?'

'Batten down the hatches and prepare to defend the castle,' said Jonas, his frown at odds with his flippant comment. He sighed. 'Seriously, what can I do?'

'It's so bloody unfair,' said Miki. 'Why should people like Stuart and this cock – Martin or whoever, get away with this? It's always the normal people, the people who haven't done anything wrong that get the shit.'

'Hey, who are you calling normal?' said Rory. The other two ignored him.

'I know,' said Jonas. 'There's always been people who were out for themselves and didn't care who they hurt in the process, but the internet has ramped everything up. It's given the trolls power.'

'Social media spun and spat out,' said Miki. 'A great way to divert and control the populous.'

'Yeah, maybe,' said Jonas. 'But I was thinking more of individuals like this so-called journalist.'

'You're both right,' said Rory. He took a big gulp of tea. 'Ugh,' he said screwing up his face. 'That is vile.'

'You're welcome,' said Jonas.

'Hey, no. I didn't mean. It was good of your mum to make it, feeling the way she did.' He took another deep breath. 'I was looking for the courage to tell you something and it clearly can't be found in tea.'

'I've got a bottle of vodka in my school bag,' said Miki.

'Really!' said Jonas, torn between awe and disapproval.

'It's alright,' said Miki. 'I don't actually drink it. I flash it around a bit. It goes with my image. And if you dare tell anyone that, I'll wallop you with my bookbag.'

'No wonder Stuart went down like he did,' said Jonas.

'Guys,' said Rory. 'I'm trying to have a moment here.' He took another deep breath.

'You're going to hyperventilate if you carry on like that,' said Miki.

'Shut the fuck up!' shouted Rory. 'I'm trying to tell you I've written a secret diary and it's been stolen and I'm bloody terrified it will end up on the internet.'

'Okay,' said Miki. 'You a serial killer or something?'

'No,' said Rory. 'It's nothing like that. It's nothing that should matter to anyone else. I just don't want anyone else to know.' He tailed off, staring into his teacup.

'Was it hidden?' asked Jonas.

Rory nodded.

'Well hidden?'

Rory nodded again. 'But I have this tiny doubt in my mind that I didn't put it away the night before. I got carried away writing in it and only stopped when my eyes were closing. I think I put it back in its right place. I mean I always do. I'd never leave it out.'

'Then someone betrayed you,' said Miki. 'If your idea of well hidden is as good as mine. No one would find my stash without trashing the whole house.'

'And you've no idea who?' said Jonas. 'That's shite. It must feel like you've got a cloud hanging over you.'

'More like a hammer,' said Rory. 'You know how I get

teased about…' he indicated his clothing and hair with an elaborate flourish. 'Looking so magnificent. Except I think I washed most of my make-up off while cleaning the dog. The bits he hadn't already licked off, that is.'

Miki rummaged in her bag and passed across some mascara and eye liner. 'Sorry, only have black.'

'Thanks,' said Rory. 'A change of look is as good as a new outfit.'

'Guys,' said Jonas. 'We need to get to school, but how about we meet up again? It seems like we've all got problems. Maybe together we can do something about them.'

'Like what?' said Miki.

'No idea, yet,' said Jonas. 'But we're all smart. Between us we should be able to come up with something.'

'I'm in,' said Rory. 'Misery loves company and all that.'

'Yeah, okay,' said Miki. 'My parents are away. You can come round to mine after school.'

LEON

Lying in bed, Leon thought he would go out of his mind with boredom. He'd had the choice of listening to his father's diatribe over what happened to people who skulked in places they had no right to be or cajoling his mum into believing he still felt battered and sore. The latter was true, but being in bed with no phone, no TV and nothing to read but old Beano annuals was dull, dull, dull. Even his father's raving would have been more interesting. He'd got to the point of saying how peeping toms like Leon ended up in jail, taking drugs, and when they got out, well, apparently even worse things happened to them. That had been the point at which he had slumped in pretend exhaustion to the floor and his mother had fussed over him. On the bedside table stood his glass of once warm milk. A thick skin had formed on the surface. However, if he didn't drink it, his mother would only bring him another, and another. They should have been having a family meeting about suing the school for having a dodgy ceiling, surely.

It wasn't as if he was really ill. The nice nurse said he hadn't even had a concussion. Apparently, he'd fainted as he landed, but then, anyone seeing his sister snogging might well faint away in disgust.

He stretched his legs experimentally. He definitely felt tender. He recalled once seeing his mother bash a chicken breast with a small wooden hammer before rolling it up full of cream cheese. He felt rather like he'd been bashed all over with that same hammer. Which reminded him, his father said he wasn't going to get any supper. What? Was that any way to treat an invalid? Confining him to bed and denying him nourishment! There were laws against that kind of thing. At least, he thought there probably were, and if there weren't, there should be. He flexed his arms. Little ripples of aches flittered along under his skin to his fingertips. It was almost like being tickled, but sore.

The next experiment was to try to sit up. Leon pushed back the blankets and decided he'd had enough. He swung himself out of bed and stood up. For a moment he wobbled like a one-legged pigeon, flapping his arms to keep his balance, and then, to his surprise, he found he could stand perfectly. Could it be he had simply been sent to bed as a punishment and he didn't need to be there at all? He began to carefully arrange the pillows and his duvet, all pain forgotten.

Fortunately, as the youngest of a large family, he'd ended up with a bedroom on the ground floor. It had once been his father's den. Something his father never failed to lament when annoyed. Filled with righteous indignation, Leon went over to his bedroom window, opened it and climbed out. Outside, the twilight cast a grey veil over the world. His family would be at dinner. No one would check on him for at least an hour. It was time for a secret mission. But what? This afternoon there had been talk about local people breeding violent animals. A recon was called for. He needed to eyeball the truth.

MIKI'S HOUSE

Jonas poured himself a glass of lemonade from the pitcher on the table. He was impressed with the way Miki had set up the meeting. Each place had a notepad and pen beside it, and there was lemonade, biscuits, crisps, and even cheese and ham sandwiches laid out. Miki saw him looking. 'Mum and Dad are directors of their own company and have these home company meetings. I have to take the minutes. Reminds me of when I played with dolls and tea sets.'

Jonas' jaw dropped slightly. 'You did?'

'Yeah, my dolls were usually planning to rob a bank or take out a bad guy. Why does everyone think dolls only discuss weather, tea and biscuits? My dolls were hardcore. Especially Barbie after I shaved her head and gave her scalp a tattoo with a felt tip.'

Jonas laughed. 'I can imagine that!'

'Do you think Rory will turn up?' said Miki.

She caught him mid-gulp, so Jonas swallowed the gassy liquid quickly and felt air lodge in his windpipe. 'I don't see why not,' he said.

'I mean you and I have – vested interests,' said Miki. 'But Rory…'

'You can't have heard half the things they say about him behind his back,' said Jonas.

'What, that he's gay?' said Miki. 'I thought people were past all that sexual discrimination bollocks.'

Jonas smothered a grin. 'You're a very straightforward sort of girl, aren't you?' he said.

'You have no idea,' said Miki. She shrugged, 'Yeah, most of the time I try to call it as it is.'

'Well, I'm not sure if Rory is gay. If he was, it would probably be easier for him. He might get teased, but lots of people, even the staff, would stick up for him. You've seen the rainbow tattooed on Mr Dunlop's wrist, haven't you?'

'So, what is he? He seemed nice enough to me. He helped with the dog, and not everyone in our year would.'

'I don't know,' said Jonas slowly. 'In fact, I wonder if Rory even knows himself. Maybe that's part of the…'

The doorbell rang. Miki threw him a look that Jonas interpreted as 'we'll talk about this later'. She went to the door. Jonas resolved not to get caught alone with her that day. She was curious, he got that. He didn't think she had any malicious intentions, but having had his family's privacy shattered today on that news site, he didn't feel like probing someone else secrets.

Rory came in. His eyes were rimmed bright red. 'What happened to you?' said Jonas.

Rory slumped down into a chair and reached for the lemonade jug. 'Blame my sister,' he said. 'Apparently she buys the cheapest false eyelashes ever. Stick on like bloody super glue.' He took a big glug of juice from a cup. 'Everyone has to start somewhere right? I mean, it's the first

68

time I've used the things, so you'd think they have a little latitude in use, right? I put them both on. I need both hands – they're tiny and fiddly. I get them in position, so I just see the ends. I'm convinced I'm looking like one of those eighties pop divas, pre-surgery, glorious and glamorous, and then I look in the mirror. What do you think I see?'

'Someone glorious and glamorous?' ventured Miki.

'Someone with two prickly sea slugs stuck to their eyelids. I mean, my God, they looked ridiculous. Zombie eyelashes – that's what they were. Although, no self-respecting zombie would ever have worn them.'

'Can you have self-respect when you're dead?' asked Jonas. Miki flapped her hand at him to be quiet. 'So, what did you do?' asked Miki.

'I pulled the bloody things off, didn't I? But that was before I read the back of the packet that said you were meant to wear them overnight, until the glue loosened. You should have seen me.' He mimed pulling at his eyelashes while pushing himself back with his other hand. Then he stage-fell onto the floor. By this time even Jonas was laughing. Rory continued miming for a bit, so that Miki was near hysterics. He sat up. 'Girl,' he said to Miki, 'you have a laugh like a goose stuck down a drain.'

Jonas tried not to laugh at this: Miki did have a honking laugh, but all that did was free the gas from the lemonade. He fought it for a moment then lost as he let loose the largest belch of his life. It was enough to ensure the three of them laughed until tears streamed down their faces.

Rory felt gratified they had enjoyed his performance, but more than that, they'd both passed his test. Neither of them had reacted to him using false eyelashes in any way. It appeared that these were two people who were prepared to accept him as he was, without asking all sorts of questions.

Leon pressed his nose against the window and watched the three teens fall about giggling. They looked like they were having fun. His intel had led him to believe that insurgents rearing wild beasts lived here, but they appeared to be harmless. Of course, any good spy knows that appearances can be deceptive. He sank down below the window before he was spotted. There was a decently large rhododendron to hide him from the street. He took out his small suction mic that he'd got last Christmas, as part of a Young Spies Kit from Santa. (A purchase his mother had come to deeply regret). He raised his hand slowly to the window – people were more likely to notice jerky, unnatural movements – and stuck it to the glass. Then he put the earphones in and listened.

A girl's voice. 'Come on, let's be serious. What are we going to do about our problems?'

First boy's voice. Slight cough. Obviously nervous. 'I've been thinking about that. It seems to me we've all got secrets, right?'

Girl's voice. 'What's my secret?'

First boy. 'Look, if I'm wrong, tell me to shut up. I'm not asking to know your secrets. Even though you and God-knows-how-many people know mine.'

Girl's voice. 'Sorry. With me it's not so much a secret as misconceptions. Misunderstandings. People not getting who I really am – or rather, gossiping about me being something I'm not. If you see what I mean.' Her voice tails off.

First boy, 'My thoughts apply even more then. Look. People, especially people reading stuff on the internet, believe anything. It doesn't matter what they actually know, they see it on a website and somehow, it legitimises the lies in their minds. The more outrageous, the more likely they seem to buy into it. Particularly if the story victimises someone.'

Girl's voice. 'That's horrible.'

Second boy's voice. 'Yeah, but it's true. That's the dystopian effect of fake news. People love it as much as they hate it.'

Girl's voice. 'I wish we could make up our own fake news and get them back.'

First boy. 'I don't want to sink to their level.'

Second boy. 'Maybe we wouldn't have to. What if we created fake news that ended up showing people how easily they accepted lies? Nothing too personal, you understand.'

First boy. 'Miki, do you usually have a sucker microphone stuck to your living room window?'

BREAKING NEWS

There are now fears that the Italian talking rabbit may have been eaten by local villagers, who believed it was possessed by the devil. Our intrepid reporter is at the scene gathering information. More soon.

OTHER BREAKING NEWS

A spokesman for the British Civil Service said 'We do much more than paperwork. Besides, most of our work is on computer now.'

FURTHER BREAKING NEWS

There are fresh concerns about the Edinburgh high school whose pupils staged a riot yesterday. Sources have confirmed at least one child was taken to hospital and kept in overnight – possibly with serious injuries requiring surgery. However, this morning, everything at the school appeared normal, begging the question, are the local authorities attempting a cover up?

Breaking News is brought to you by Radio City Central: the local station you can trust.

WEDNESDAY 7th JUNE

BREAKING NEWS

Sadly, it has been confirmed that the talking rabbit has indeed been eaten. Our man at the scene reports it was cooked in white wine, with garlic, chives, olive oil, salt, and served with homemade bread. A man at the supper, who wished to remain anonymous, said the creature tasted 'divine'. We have reached out to the Vatican to discover if these local people have accidentally eaten a miracle, and if they have, what will happen to them? Are they now blessed? Or, as some villagers are claiming, will the wrath of God descend on them?

OTHER BREAKING NEWS

Should our correspondent, Marvin McMacy, be forced to reveal the identity and location of his benefit fraudster? If he doesn't, is he complicit in her offence? 89 percent of late-night callers to the Jeremy Jives Radio Show believe that he should. We're opening up a comments section for readers to leave their thoughts online. More on this later.

LEON

Leon opened his eyes. The moon cast a sliver of light between his curtains. He could only have been asleep for a couple of hours, but he felt fully refreshed. He stared at the ceiling above his bed, reaching out a finger to trace patterns in the old stippled-effect paint. The raised platform bed he'd chosen allowed him to have an office-like space beneath it. One that he covered with a black-out curtain. The rest of his room remained much like one belonging to any child his age – a mixture of cuddly bears and video game consoles. He'd left his tree lamp on. A small cylinder with shapes of trees cut out of it, it threw ghostly projections of fine, winter branches across the room. It spooked his sister and even his mother disliked it. Leon regarded it as one of his major security protocols.

Sleep appeared to be as far away as morning, so he climbed down the ladder and slipped behind the curtain, leaving his duvet rumpled up so that any cursory inspection of the room would leave the observer thinking he was still in bed.

He turned on his laptop. The machine launched facial recognition, and logged him in. He loved this feature. It meant that whatever he wrote on here was totally secure. He began typing.

Day One of Infiltration

When my surveillance of the suspected insurgents' safe house was disturbed, I was forced to make a snap decision. I opted to go undercover, using my persona of an over-curious, but cute, schoolboy. I persuaded the group to let me in. They had been discussing the phenomenon of fake news and how to combat it with counterintelligence (of sorts). Although, of course, they didn't use that specific term. When Rory, an older boy, prone to wearing garish colours and of an exuberant manner, demanded to know what I had heard, I had to make a second snap decision. As the saying goes, the best lies are wrapped up in the truth, and so that's what I told them. I expressed empathy for their situation. Miki was all for making me a peanut butter sandwich and letting me go. At this point, the other boy, Jonas, whose mother was recently exposed on the web as a criminal mastermind, said there was no point going ahead as I knew their plan.

I confess, my natural instinct to take control took over and I explained they did not have a plan, merely an idea. This led to some squabbling, but I managed to quieten them by suggesting we set up a website and put out fake news stories to lure in the local population. At our chosen time, the truth of each story would be revealed. I admit, it's more or less what the boy, Jonas, had already suggested, but I made it sound workable. Rory was keen no one individual was targeted. Miki pointed out that none of them were web designers.

At this point, I had to reveal my status as an over-achiever for my age and explain that I could set up the website for them and oversee the dissemination of news. This caused further debate, but as Miki's parents were away at some kind of hippy fair, we have decided to regroup later and take things further.

I am, of course, interested only in exposing the safe house, and the degree to which the three teenagers are involved in subversive interests. I believe that if I help them with the basics of their plan, I will uncover their true motivations and dastardly plots. In the meantime, I've warned them not to use their mobile phones, but to rely on landlines, and direct verbal interactions, to communicate. Mobile phones are too easily found by family members and they leave trails that are hard to delete. I'd rather they did nothing other than speak face to face, and from the blank looks I got mentioning landlines, I infer this is what they will do. I don't want them texting each other and leaving me out of the loop. Having limited their communication options, I feel the situation is under control and I can move things forward.

Leon sat back and looked at his file with pride. He knew his writing style was above his age – even antiquated at times, but then that happened when you were a child protégé. This would be his masterpiece. With this he would finally be able to show the British Secret Service how useful he could be as a child recruit. He had a mild twinge of guilt about Miki. She had seemed nice. Doubtless her parents had forced her into their deviant anti-government ways. He'd have to remember to put in a good word for her when they were arrested.

He read over his file again. It seemed an excellent start, but he wasn't sure about the word 'dastardly'. It reflected what he meant, but maybe it gave the wrong feel. Leon yawned. He'd have to think about it. He shut down the computer and picked up one of his favourite books to take back up to bed with him. It was all about a spy who had worked for both the British and the German Secret

Services during World War II. The whole thing was totally true, and, in the end, it turned out the double agent was a true-blue British spy. There were some aspects of the book Leon didn't quite get, but he'd had the sense not to ask his mother, who would doubtlessly have confiscated it.

MARTY

'Marty Mclaren,' said Marty to the two policemen on his doorstep.

'Ah' said the older of the two. Grey-haired with a neatly trimmed moustache and crinkles around his eyes, and as many lines around his mouth as a laughing gnome, Marty mentally labelled him as someone marking off time until he retired. The other, a young woman, with her blonde hair tightly pulled back into a bun, and the creases in her uniform sharp enough to cut butter, was clearly gunning for promotion. Her flint-like topaz eyes bored into him, giving Marty a shiver down his back. He liked strong women, but this was hardly the time to tell her.

'Yes,' said Marty. He adopted a casual attitude, placing a hand on the door jamb and slinging one foot over the other, so his weight was entirely on one leg. 'It's an industry thing,' he said, with a slight smile. 'Time is pressing in the international media world. Names get typed in incorrectly all the time. The sentiment's there and as long as I get the paycheck,' he gave a self-assured chuckle, 'then I really don't care. I'm not in this for the fame. I'm in it to find the truth.' He gave his most serious and most charming stare to the woman PC. She met his eyes, but immediately dropped them to the notebook in her hand. *Strike one*, thought Marty. *She's impressed.* He made a mental note of the number on her shoulder. He could call the cop shop later to get her name. Wouldn't do to look too keen by asking her out on his doorstep. Besides, she was working.

'So, you got paid for this piece, Mr Mclaren?' asked the WPC.

'Not something I can talk about,' said Marty, sinking further into his pose. 'Union rules and all that. The best of us get paid more, you see.'

'Doesn't sound very fair to me,' said the PC. 'A sort of favouritism – or you could say bias, don't you think, WPC? What is the world coming to?'

'Indeed,' said the WPC. 'But in this case, it will affect the charge.'

'Charge?' said Marty, his voice sounding higher than he wanted. His throat appeared to have suddenly narrowed. His voice went up another notch. 'What charge?'

'At the moment I believe loitering with intent is being contemplated,' said the WPC. 'And all that such entails.'

'Entails?' said Marty, placing both feet on the ground and feeling like a little boy in front of a headteacher.

'Were you, or were you not, waiting with photographic equipment in the bushes of the garden of a lady, unknown to you personally?'

'Well, when you put it like that,' said Marty, 'It sounds bad. But it's all in the context. I was waiting to take a photograph of a woman who is a known benefit scrounger.'

'Really, sir? You have evidence of this?' said the PC.

'There's no law of trespass in Scotland,' said Marty.

'We are aware of that, sir. But if you could answer my colleague's question… As you are doubtless aware, being so well informed on points of law, knowing of a crime, and not reporting it, is a criminal offence in itself.'

Marty licked his lips. The words 'a journalist's source is sacred' were on the tip of his tongue, but as he considered the two grim faces in front of him, he knew that wasn't going to fly. 'It was Tracy at the job centre,' said Marty. 'She said the woman never came in because she claimed she was too ill, but then she'd seen her at the supermarket last weekend, looking as right as rain.'

'Kind of you to share your source, sir,' said the WPC. 'Tracy what?'

'Tracy Harris,' said Marty, mentally striking through the idea of asking Tracy out for a drink. 'She was clear about what she saw, but I suppose she might have been mistaken. She only had an old photo on the file to go by.'

The WPC raised an eloquent eyebrow. 'I see, sir. And to come back to our earlier question, how much were you paid?'

'I said…'

'It affects the severity of any charges, sir.'

Marty sighed. 'I did it pro bono.'

'To be clear, sir,' said the PC, 'You did all this for free? Hobby, is it? Spying on decent women in their homes?'

'Decent?' said Marty. 'There's nothing wrong with her. She's living in the lap of luxury while the rest of us are paying for her lifestyle.'

'The lady in question has MS,' said the WPC. 'Multiple Sclerosis. If you look that up on the internet, sir, you'll discover that it's a progressive neurological condition with no known cure. However, sufferers have some good days, as well as significantly bad ones.'

'Oh,' said Marty. 'I didn't know.'

The moustached PC leaned over and closed WPC Dutton's notepad with one finger. 'Seeing as how he didn't know, WPC, don't you think we can let it go with a caution this time?'

The WPC gave a deep sigh. 'If you think so.'

'I'm sure we won't have to come and see Mr McNaughty again, now will we, sir?'

Marty had the sense not to protest about his name. Instead he said, 'No, officer, you certainly won't.'

The WPC snorted and turned her back on him. As she walked away, the PC gave him a wink and then pointed from his eyes to Marty in the universal sign of 'I'll be watching you'.

Marty closed his front door, but not before he heard WPC Dutton's low chuckle. That blasted woman and her son! They'd ruined his reputation with the police – a relationship vital to any would-be investigative journalist. He'd show them. Everyone had secrets. Everyone. He recalled Tracy saying something about the husband disappearing a while back. But she didn't claim to be a widow. Had she buried him in the back garden? Or, better yet, had he run off with a co-worker? A naughty, saucy scandal was exactly what the internet loved. Why, he could even make it look as if he was on her side, pointing out how she was the poor victim, all the while destroying her privacy and spreading her secrets. Marty actually rubbed his hands together. Revenge was going to be fun.

The question remained, though, who the hell had tipped off the police to his article?

MIKI

Miki kept her head down as she walked along the school corridor. She'd delayed leaving history by spilling the contents of her pencil case on the floor. The crash and spill of the pencils drew some particularly sharp words from Deacon until he'd turned around and seen whose pencil case it was. He and Miki had looked each other in the eye, he'd restrained himself to a simple 'Hurry up, Ms Barton. History waits for no woman.' Miki had muttered, 'Herstory' under her breath as she bent to pick up her things. Glancing up through her eyelashes, she thought she saw Deacon stiffen, and when she left, his lips were pressed together so tightly they were barely more than a red slash in his face. 'Sorry, Mr Deacon. Bye, Mr Deacon,' said Miki with a smile. She got a curt nod in response. If the tussle with Mark meant Deacon would stop ragging on her, then maybe it had been worthwhile.

The corridor was empty. She had to hurry. Hopefully, Mark would be long gone. Even as she thought this, there was a light tap on her shoulder. She spun, only to see empty air. 'Over here!' called Rory from behind her. She turned and he skipped backwards so he could face her. Both his eyes were ringed with mauve and gold.

'Don't worry,' he said. 'I know better than to get in striking range.'

Miki let out a gasp of exasperation. 'What happened to your eyes.'

'It's for the play,' said Rory. 'But I can't get it off!'

'Your sister been buying the cheap stuff again?' said Miki, finally smiling.

Rory sighed. 'My own fault. She gave me a load of stuff to donate to the drama department, and I forgot all about that. So, when I see these great colours there, I go for it.'

'Not remembering they came from your sister's lame stock.'

81

'Exactly,' said Rory. 'I'm being haunted by the make-up from hell.'

'On the bright side, it does look good.'

'Just as well, if I'm wearing it for the rest of my life.'

'Are you switching to art?' asked Miki as they turned into the art class corridor.

'Nah,' said Rory. 'I thought they might have some decent paint remover.'

'You don't want to get that stuff near your eyes,' said Miki. 'They'd melt.'

Rory shrugged. 'Shit. Never mind. By the way, that little kid turned up in my computing class. Keeps being put into higher classes. When it comes to science, turns out he's a bit of genius. He wasn't lying about that. I told him about what had happened to Jonas' mother, and he anonymously sent the article, with explanation, to the local councillor. You know Peter the Cheater? The one who got caught out cheating on his wife and is always looking for good causes to champion to make himself look better? Clever kid, huh?'

'Shh,' said Miki. 'We'll find out tonight what he can do.'

'If his mum lets him out,' said Rory. Two female students walked round the corner. 'How's the dog?' said Rory, slightly too loudly.

'Nothing left but a slightly rosy blush.'

'Hey, Miki,' said one of the girls. 'Saw you got yourself on the news.' She held up her phone and read from it. 'Political punch up at local school. Extreme eco-radical, Miki Barton, daughter of Drs Barton, known eco-warriors, beat up a fellow student when he suggested she shouldn't disturb their history class with her leftist, feminist propaganda. Rumour has it, Barton was all set to be expelled, but her parents put undue pressure on the local council to let their daughter stay in school.' The girl looked up. 'The piece is called *How Eco-Terrorists are Blackmailing our Educators. The Rebel Climate Changer's Tide in our Schools.*'

'Yeah, I've heard her entire family is wacko,' said the other girl, smiling at her friend.

Rory looked at them and Miki in growing alarm. 'Did you do that to my dog?' said Miki.

'Come on. They're not worth it,' said Rory, trying to catch Miki's arm.

Miki evaded his grasp, uttered what sounded to Rory's ear like a deep growl, dropped her bag on the floor and launched herself at the two girls. Rory hesitated for a moment then waded in to try and separate the three of them.

Sitting outside the Head's office, Rory now had two black eyes and his nose was swelling fast. 'I'm really, sorry,' said Miki. 'I didn't realise it was you.'

'Don't mention it,' said Rory, as he dabbed tentatively at his nose. 'At least now there's a reason for my eyes to be black and purple.'

'There's scratches all over your face too,' said Miki. 'You look as if you've been fighting a gorse bush.'

'A gorse bush with a hefty left hook,' said Rory. He stood up and went to look at his reflection in the glass of the school's trophy case. 'Blimey, how much make-up am I going to need to regain my fairy-like complexion?'

'Huh?'

'For the play,' said Rory. 'I'll be Peaseblossom yet.'

'I'm afraid you won't,' said Mr Murray coming out of his office. 'It's been decided that Rory is to be banned from the play, and you, Miss Barton, are to be excluded for two weeks.'

'What?' said Miki, shooting to her feet. 'That's totally unfair. Rory was trying to stop the fight.'

'Then Rory should have found an adult, and not taken it upon himself to try and interrupt what Miss Archibald described as a fight between hellcats.'

'So that's the payback you get for trying to be a decent person around here,' spat Miki. 'I suppose the fact that those two hellcats covered my dog with red paint doesn't come into your equation?' Miki took a step closer to the headteacher. 'What they did is a criminal offence! You can be prosecuted for cruelty to animals!'

Mr Murray took a half step back. 'Control yourself, Miss Barton. I have asked Miss Wishart to come to the office and escort you off the school grounds. Don't make things worse for yourself. And as for you, Rory, be grateful I haven't excluded you as well.' Then he retreated rapidly into his office. If Miki hadn't been so angry, she might have found his scurrying away funny. She turned to apologise to Rory again, only to see him wiping his eye shadow off on his handkerchief. 'Turns out tears are the best make-up remover. Who knew?' he said.

'Oh, Rory,' said Miki, coming over to put an arm round his shoulder. 'I'll get my parents to speak to Murray.'

Rory pulled away from her. 'I think you've done enough,' he said.

JONAS

'Hello,' said Jonas breathlessly. He'd been coming up the path when he heard the landline ring.

'Can I speak to Mrs Wilson, please,' said an unfamiliar female voice.

'I'm sorry, she's resting. This is her son, Jonas.'

'Well, Jonas, I need you to go and wake your mother up.'

'Is it important?' said Jonas. 'Only she always rests at this time of day. Who is this?'

'This is the Department for Work and Pensions. We have received some information that your mother may not be on the right benefit.'

'What's your number?' said Jonas. 'I'll get her to call you back.'

The woman at the other end of the phone recited a number. 'Have you got that?'

'Yes,' said Jonas, who hadn't reached for the notepad by the phone. 'I've got it.' He hung up and went through to the kitchen.

'Jonas?' called his mother, sounding sleepy. 'Is that you? I thought I heard the phone ring.'

Jonas opened the door to his mother's room. She'd drawn the curtains to shut out the light, but he could make out her form lying on the bed. 'It's nothing, Mum,' he said. 'Just someone trying to sell us double glazing. I told them we lived in an underground bunker and didn't have any windows.'

Trisha laughed. 'What did they say?'

'Nothing,' said Jonas. 'They just hung up. You go back to sleep. I'll wake you at teatime. I thought perhaps pizza tonight? There's one in the freezer.'

'You're a good boy,' said Trisha, and Jonas could tell from her voice she was already halfway back to sleep again. He went through to the kitchen and made himself a cup of tea. Then he sat down at the kitchen table. He stirred two teaspoons of sugar into his mug, and continued stirring without drinking, while he thought furiously about what he would do next.

'I suppose we should have known he wouldn't show. He's just a kid. We can manage…' Miki looked over as her laptop chimed. 'Sorry, I should have turned the notifications off before we started,' she said to Jonas and Rory.

Rory shrugged. His face had turned seven distinct different colours, but his nose had gone back to normal size. Miki had been surprised he'd turned up at all and he hadn't said anything apart from to grunt when she offered him a drink. Jonas scowled furiously. 'Little punk,' he said. 'Doesn't he know how serious this is?'

The laptop chimed again. Miki went over to silence it. Then she paused. 'I think this might be him,' she said. They clustered around the screen.

Hi Guys

I'm grounded. Dad says until I'm forty, but Mum says she'll let me off at twenty-one. Of course, I was grounded when I came out to see you last night, but now I'm double grounded. My sister, Alice, had strung thread across my window, so was able to prove to my parents, beyond reasonable doubt, that I'd been out last night. Actually, I'm almost impressed. I must be rubbing off on her. Most of the time she's a real pain in the arse. All she can talk about is that Cliff character. He's tried to grow a moustache. Looks like he'd been eating caterpillars.

Anyway, they said I could let you know about the school project site I set up. Fleab.com/3bR6p7

See you there. Have a great time with testing the cookies. Save some for me.

'What the hell is he on?' said Rory. 'He's loco!'

'Why would he think we'd interested in knowing about his sister?' said Rory, frowning. 'What am I missing?'

'Oh, you guys,' said Miki. 'Do you really not get it?'

The two boys shook their heads. Miki gave a deep sigh. 'He's sending us a message, but he thinks he's being watched. Maybe he is being watched, and his parents are looking over his shoulder.'

'Why?' said Rory blankly.

Miki cocked her head on one side considering him. 'Did you ever have an Xbox ban when you were younger?'

'Of course. Hasn't everyone?'

'Well, you said this kid is a little Steve Jobs…'

'Hey, I…'

'Co-founder of Apple?' said Miki. 'You need to switch from comp sci to something else, Rory. You're a Luddite.'

'A what?'

Miki raised her hands to her head and made a 'pow' noise. 'Mind blown! Outside of drama and make-up, do you know anything?'

'I like to think I have a keen satirical sense,' said Rory.

'A what now?' said Jonas

'Guys,' snapped Miki. 'Look!' She pointed at the screen. On it was a webpage entitled 'Lunchtime News Bytes. Keeping you in the Know while you Nosh.' A logon box blinked at her.

'Oh right,' said Jonas. 'He made us a webpage.' He hunkered down beside Miki and inspected it. 'Not bad. What's the login?'

'I have no idea,' said Miki. 'I got us this far. Time for one of you to indulge your brains a little to figure out how we log on.'

'Alice and Cliff,' said Rory.

'What now?'

'Alice for the login name and Cliff for the password.'

'Okay,' said Miki and tried. 'Nope, that's not it.'

'Damn,' said Rory. 'I thought it would be something from the email.'

'Depends how paranoid he is,' said Jonas.

'Yeah,' said Miki. 'He's been cleverer than that.'

'You're not going to tell me we can't outthink someone like him?' said Rory.

Miki got up and fetched a pad and pencil from the table. 'You write down suggestions. I'll try them.'

Half an hour later the floor was strewn with crumpled up pieces of paper, Miki's hair was tangled from where she'd kept running her fingers through it and Rory was sitting on the floor miming bumping his head off the ground. Jonas had gone to make tea.

'The little shit,' said Rory. 'He did this just to torment us.'

'A fake login?' said Miki. 'I didn't think he was that kind of a kid.'

'Either that or we are as thick as proverbial planks,' said Rory.

Red came up to Miki and pushed his long head under her left arm. He craned his nose up and tried to lick her face. Miki evaded his pink tongue with the ease of long practice. The dog gave a small whine. 'Okay, boy, I'll get your dinner,' said Miki.

Rory watched the dog's wagging tail. 'Hungry boy, huh?' Then he sat bolt upright. 'That's it,' he said. 'Type Miki and then Red.' We've been too clever about this. Remember this kid thinks we're the dumb ones!

Miki did. 'Nothing.'

'Try substituting 1s for Is and 3s for Es.'

Jonas walked back in carrying a tray. 'I found these teabags in a canister. They smell a bit funny…'

'The sneaky little…' said Miki. 'We're in!'

BREAKING NEWS

Traffic in the south-east corner of Italy has ground to a standstill. Our local reporter says the blockage has been formed by a hoard of fearful villagers attempting to leave what has become known as The Village of the Blessed Rabbit before, as one woman put it, 'the wrath of God strikes us down for blasphemy'. At the same time, a great many people have taken to the roads to travel to the village hopping to see the bones of the Blessed Rabbit.

OTHER BREAKING NEWS

We would like to apologise for any offence caused by our previous bulletin. It was entirely unintentional that 'hoping' was replaced by 'hopping'. No slur on the claims of the Believers of the Blessed Rabbit was intended.

THURSDAY 8th JUNE

BREAKING NEWS

Another fight broke out yesterday at the same Edinburgh high school. Our inside contact reports that both pupils and teachers are dividing into factions. We hear they're only a hairs breadth away from a Lord of the Flies situation.

MIKI'S HOUSE, BREAKFAST

Jonas arrived at Miki's house the next morning before school with a big grin and a roll of paper in his hand. He made straight for the laptop Miki had set up. Rory arrived only minutes later, but once he saw Jonas typing, he took more interest in helping Miki put breakfast together. With his help, dishes of scrambled egg, grilled tomatoes, oven baked sausages, bacon, homemade hash browns and sautéed mushrooms were set out on the table instead of the cereal and milk Miki had originally planned. Rory looked down on his work with pride. 'All we need now is toast.' He caught Miki staring at the table.

'I don't remember the last time I saw a breakfast like this,' she said.

'Have I made too much? There's quite a few mouths to feed at home.'

'Are you sure you want to be an actor?' said Miki. 'You could be a chef.'

Rory shook his head. 'Nah, I took up cooking 'cos I liked it best among the chores Mum and Dad allocated. I mean, who wants to clean up after their stinky siblings, or worse still, do the laundry. The things you might see doesn't bear thinking about.' He shuddered dramatically.

Miki laughed and started to load a plate with food. 'As far as I'm concerned, you can come round and cook every morning.'

Rory gave an embarrassed shrug. He served himself and then wandered over, fork in hand, to see what Jonas was typing.

Lunchtime News Bytes While You Nosh

Solar Energy – solar darkness.

A group of scientists, who claim their research has been repressed for years, have today come forward with a warning about the devastating effect solar power will have.

Dr Simon Decker, ex-senior researcher with NASA, put it succinctly. 'People have been putting up solar panels without thinking about where the power comes from. All they know is that getting energy from the sun is free, but we have to remember that the sun has a limited amount of gases with which it makes that energy.

Meteorologist Sandi Mitchel confirmed. 'It's not

something we like to talk about, but every unit of heat we take from the sun and use down here, is one less unit of energy the sun has to burn.

So, have we gone too far? Is the sun about to burn out and leave us in darkness? Don't worry. Dr Decker has a solution. His suggestion is that we paint more walls and pavements white. 'White paint helps reflect the heat back up to the sun. In layman's terms, it replenishes it.'

However, it's bad news for Goths, Emos and Satanists, who traditionally wear black. Dr Decker says if they really want to help then they should consider wearing lighter-hued clothes. Every bit of reflected energy helps. But don't try and use mirrors. Decker warns, 'Mirrors might seem like a cunning idea, but in reality, they don't have the ability to reflect light back into space like white does. Instead, mirrors are more likely to trigger local fires than return the energy to the sun.'

Do you hear that? No setting up giant mirrors. Can't say I follow everything the good Dr says, but then I'm not a boffin. So, guys, pay attention, this is something the rest of the scientific community wants to hide from us. They don't believe we can all work together to save the sun and will just descend into panic instead. Why not do your bit today and wear a white shirt to work, school or wherever you're going? Let's show this group of stuck-up experts that we care about this planet and its sun.

'What do you think?' said Jonas. 'Is it too much?'

Rory read over his shoulder. 'I like the idea, but isn't it a bit too out there?'

'It's way out there,' said Miki, 'But you'd be surprised what so-called intelligent people are prepared to believe. One of my dad's friends, who works in some hush-hush department for the government, believes aliens have already landed in the US, and made contact with a secret group over there.'

'I hope he doesn't have his finger on a trigger or a button,' said Rory swallowing. 'He sounds nutso.'

'You think?' said Miki. 'Of course he is, but he has the sense to keep his personal beliefs away from his employers. Supposedly he's trying to work his way up the career ladder, so eventually he'll reach a level where someone will tell him the truth.' Miki gestured to indicate the last word was in quotes.

'Do you think Mr Deacon believes anything daft?' said Rory.

'Only that Liverpool might win the cup,' said Jonas.

Rory shook his head. 'That's all sports balls to me.' Miki stifled a giggle.

Jonas cleared his screen and closed the lid of the laptop. 'Rory and I need to move if we're going to get to school by the bell.'

'Sure, off you go and enjoy yourselves at school,' said Miki. Jonas muttered something unintelligible as he got up. 'Thanks for breakfast,' said Rory sheepishly.

'You made it,' said Miki. She grinned. 'Guys, I was kidding. I don't have to go to school today. That's great. I'm going to spend all day drawing. Red is more than enough company.'

'Okay,' said Jonas. 'You can keep an eye on the site and see how many hits it gets, and when. That would be useful to know.'

'I wouldn't be surprised if little Leo is already on to that,' said Miki. 'Probably set up some kind of tracking programme.'

The two boys headed over to the door. Just before he opened it Jonas turned and said, 'I'd look through the peephole before you let anyone in. Seeing as how you're here on your own.'

Miki, who was already lost in thought of what she might create today, didn't take offence as he thought she might. She poked out her tongue and then said, 'Yes, Dad!'

RORY & JONAS, OUTSIDE

As they walked down the path Rory said, 'Why did you say that to her? Of all of us I'd rate her as having the best chance to survive a zombie apocalypse.'

'Hmm,' said Jonas.

'Spill.'

'Just being chivalrous.'

'Yeah, right. Nowadays that's called being sexist.'

'I am not,' said Jonas hotly.

'Nah, didn't think so. So, what do you know?'

'Nothing. Really.'

Rory stopped. 'I am not moving until you tell all. And that means my fans at school will be deprived of my glorious presence until you relent.' He gestured up and down his body. 'Look at this. A kaleidoscope of teals and greens with just a muted touch of duck egg blue. I bring light into their dull little lives. Do you want to be responsible for their misery and disappointment?'

Jonas stopped. 'What I don't care for is how loud you're getting.'

Rory pirouetted on the spot. 'Loud is nothing,' he said. 'I can do outrageous. Do you want to see my outrageous?'

'Fine. Okay. I give. But you mustn't tell Miki.'

'Cross my spandex and hope to die.'

'Oh, shut it,' said Jonas. 'I got to thinking about the paint and the dog. How come someone had the paint ready when Red got out? I got the impression from Miki that usually he's kept on a tight leash.'

'They were painting a shed?' said Rory. 'I'm disappointed. That's lame.'

'You're not thinking,' said Jonas. 'It means they already had the paint ready and not on the off chance the dog would get out.'

'Oh, shit,' said Rory. 'You mean Miki was their intended target, not the dog?'

Jonas nodded.

'That's messed up,' said Rory. 'If I were a man of action I'd go after that Mark Stuart. After all, I'm sure he was the one who did it, not those girls Miki got into a fight with.' He sighed. 'Sadly, I'm not a man of action. More of a lover than a fighter. You?'

'Er, neither. More a writer.'

'Should we warn her?' said Rory. 'I'm still pissed at her over the play, but I wouldn't want her to get hurt.'

'Can we predict how she will react?' said Jonas. 'I don't know Miki that well, but I think she's equally likely to either ignore our warning or go off after Mark Stuart with a baseball bat.'

'Does she play baseball?'

'It's an expression. I meant…'

Rory put up his hand. 'I get it. Miki can be her own worst enemy. Besides we can't prove anything. I say we encourage her to be cautious and we keep an eye out for her.'

'You'd do that? Even after losing Peaseblossom?'

'Firstly, I'm not an ass, and secondly, whatever my predilection for sparkly eyeshadow, I look out for my friends. Haven't you heard of girl power?' He did an old-fashioned Wonder Woman twirl and pose.

Jonas felt the blood steal into his cheeks. 'I didn't mean...'

'Whatever,' said Rory, shrugging. 'You can strategise and I'll provide the glamour. Now we need to move, or we'll miss the bell.'

He half-trotted, half-skipped off. Jonas stared after him. He managed to keep his jaw from dropping by sheer force of will. He counted to twenty, shook his head, then walked on.

LEON

Day One of Active Project 'Black Book'

The subjects showed average intelligence in managing to work out the password clue I had sent them. However, it took them several attempts. Now the project is up and running, the first article has been about the evils of solar power. They are attempting to show how people believe fake news. The opening salvo is a half-hearted display. They obviously do not believe that there are people who would buy into this. Accordingly, I have cross-posted their piece to various Flat Earther, anti-science and extreme conspiracy groups. So far, said groups have demonstrated only a desire to further seed this disinformation. I am aware some of these may be on a watchlist, but I scrupulously avoided cross contamination with any society or group that advocates violence. Although, it should be noted, that the girl, and one of the boys, have both recently been involved in physical altercations at school. The girl perpetrated an assault by breaking the nose of Mark Stuart, but knowing Mark Stuart, I can believe he deserved it. In the interests of research and further obfuscation of my own plans, I will add my own piece to the website.

Leon sat back and regarded the screen with approval. He was particularly proud of his vocabulary. 'Obfuscation' and 'scrupulously' had taken a few attempts, and the help of the spell checker, to get right. Overall, he thought the tone professional. He knew that sometimes spies needed to seed disinformation to confuse the enemy, so he was both practising that skill as well as observing potential enemies of the state. And he'd found so many places to cross-post he was certain the website would get more and more hits, if only they could keep the interest going. He took a long gulp of milk, did his best to crack his knuckles and settled down to write the next piece of miscommunication for News Bytes While you Nosh (NBWN?) He shook his head. It was too early to use the initials only, but in the near future NBWN was going to be everyone's lips.

MARTY

As he took in the text, Marty could feel the hairs on the back of his neck rising. This was the stuff. This was the stuff he should be writing. Edgy, scary and challenging, it was exactly the kind of website he would like to work for.

What Unwanted Extras Are You Getting in Your Takeaway?

The Cold War might be over, but a new era of espionage couldn't be more active, or more dangerous. We can now confirm that the Chinese government, the Chinese having some of the best hackers in the world, have moved into a new era. Certain Chinese takeaways are serving up something extra in the hoisin sauce. A side helping of nanites. These tiny, programmable robots, invisible to the naked eye, are easily swallowed in the sauce. Once inside the host's body, they make their way to the back of the cornea and record everything the host sees. The host might be no one more important than a lollipop lady, but, just suppose, every day they see where the child of a key diplomat or minster goes to school? Something that, in the normal way of things, would be top secret. But worse, imagine if the chief engineer at the local nuclear power plant grabs a takeaway on the way home on Friday night as a treat for his family? First thing, bright and early on Monday morning, when he logs in at work, he sends all his top-secret codes and passwords direct to China's Cybernetic Espionage Centre. In a few moments he becomes a traitor to his own country and is completely oblivious to it! Just think, so much information hitchhiking its way back to China through our people's eyes. The nerve of it. The nanites don't stay in place forever. If they did, our boffins would doubtless come up with a way of scanning for them. No, typically they last for four days

– cunningly ensuring that any weekend indulgences lead to nanites being up and ready to start work on Monday morning. They leave the host's body in the usual waste cycle and go directly into our sewerage system. Whether they stay in the system as the water is cleansed or they make their way out and into other hosts has yet to be ascertained. What we do know is Chinese nanites are everywhere!

Marty saved the website address. What he needed was to find a story just as good and send it to News Bytes While you Nosh. He rubbed his hands with glee. This time next week he was determined to be their star reporter. It wouldn't be easy finding a story as outstanding as this one, but he was determined.

RORY

Karl> Have you found it yet?
Rory> I'm not stupid. I didn't just misplace it somewhere. I didn't suddenly think, you know, I think I'll leave my deepest darkest secrets on the kitchen table.
Karl> So it was in the usual place?
Rory> Yes!
Karl> Behind the skirting board under your bed?
Rory> Yes!
Karl> And you haven't told anyone?
Rory> No.
Karl> Did any of your siblings share your room, or have it before you? Any way they might know the hiding place?

Rory> No, I don't think so. I mean maybe before I was born, but they'd have been babies.

Karl> I mean, it's a good hiding place, but there are a lot of movies where people hide something behind skirting boards or under floorboards. If someone knew you had something to hide, they might have found it when searching. You are often out at school or doing other things.

Rory> Other things?

Karl> This new secret group. The website you're doing. What was that about again?

Rory> I'm not telling. I shouldn't even have mentioned it was a website.

Karl> Ah, come on. You tell me everything.

Rory> Everything about me.

Karl> Well, you're involved.

Rory> And so are others. You know as well as I do that if people found out about us, we'd be in real trouble. I don't think I could live through that.

Karl> ☹ No. I get that. You're a good friend, R.

Rory> You too K

BREAKING NEWS

A puma has been sighted on the outskirts of Edinburgh. Mrs Anne Lipscomb of Joppa said, 'I looked out my window and there it was in the middle of my washing. It'd brought down the line – a great big black cat. Bigger than a pony, it was. My Jamie isn't half going to be mad he hasn't got a clean shirt for tomorrow.'

OTHER BREAKING NEWS

Seasickness, or the lack of it, has a genetic link. A recent study showed those with a Scandic heritage are far less likely to suffer from seasickness. Researchers ascribe this to Viking ancestry.

FURTHER BREAKING NEWS

Do you know who's listening in on you? Smart technology is more hackable than ever, says *Home Smart Computing Magazine*. Your smart devices listen constantly for your demands, but that software is hackable. What's worse, that camera on your laptop? We can only suggest that you cover the camera with tape. Especially if you work from home and don't bother to get dressed properly!

FRIDAY 9th JUNE

BREAKING NEWS

More sightings of the puma! Mrs Lipscomb's neighbour, Senga Williams, claims to have seen the animal too. 'I've nae doubt it was drawn to Anne's garden by the smell. She never does a proper boil wash and her laundry is minging!' Arthur Gilbert, on his way home from a work's night out in Portobello, claims to have seen two pumas running along the shore as he walked back to his home in Pittville Street. 'Running in and out of the waves, they were,' he said. 'Playing like a couple of oversized kittens. I was in the Scouts, so I knew to keep downwind of them. I called it in, but by the time the police arrived they had vanished.' Have you seen any big cats? Call us.

OTHER BREAKING NEWS

McCleod Ferries report an increased sale of Viking helmets at unprecedented levels. They request tourists to have patience as more are on express order from their supplier.

FURTHER BREAKING NEWS

The government says it is losing massive amounts of money to fraudulent claimants. In a new and shocking move, they have now issued a statement saying that a reward will be paid to people who report false claimants who are then successfully prosecuted. We wonder what George Orwell would make of this.

RORY'S DOOR

Jonas knocked loudly on Rory's door for the third time. He could hear sounds of life within, but he was yet to hear footsteps making their way to the door. He opened up the letter box to call inside and was met with the sight of denimed legs. He leapt back startled as Rory opened the door. He stood there hands on his hips, framing a sheriff belt buckle. 'I know it's shiny,' he said, 'But you only had to ask to see it.' Jonas swallowed and reddened. 'I do seem to keep distressing you,' said Rory tossing his hair. 'Is there something you want to tell moi?'

'Stop it! I came to get you to come to Miki's for breakfast. It's the last morning before her parents come back. We need to move the base.'

Rory goggled at him for a moment. 'Oh right. We don't actually have to move anything, do we? Just meet elsewhere? Only I've just got my nails into a reasonable state.'

'I suppose not. As long as there is a computer.'

'Hang on.' Rory darted back inside the house. 'Mum,' he yelled, 'Can I have a group of friends over? We're working on a project together.' There was a muffled response. 'Yes,

Mum, boys and girls.' A pause. 'No, we don't need fizzy drinks and biscuits. Pizza would be nice.' A lengthier pause. 'Right, 7 p.m. tonight.'

Rory returned with a rucksack half slung over his shoulder. 'There, all settled.'

Jonas started at him. 'You're going to school in jeans, a denim shirt, cowboy boots and purple eyeshadow?'

'It's more of a maroon actually,' said Rory. 'Besides, what are they going to do to me? Throw me out of the play?'

'Suspend you?'

Rory closed the door behind him. 'You think I care?'

'But your education! The exams…'

Rory placed a hand on Jonas' shoulder. 'Look, mate, I'm not an academic. I'm not stupid, but exams aren't my thing. I want to go to drama school and if the school won't let me do drama, I don't see the point of my being there at all.'

BREAKFAST AT MIKI'S

Miki opened her front door and waved Rory and Jonas inside. 'Great! I thought I was going to have to do the cooking myself. I've got a ton of stuff in and it has to be gone before my parents get back. They don't approve of excess.'

Wordlessly, Rory headed off to the kitchen. Jonas followed Miki to the table where her laptop stood open. 'Are your parents political activists?' he asked. He took a step back when he saw the ferocious frown on Miki's face. He held up his hands. 'Hey, steady! I don't care if they're Russian agents. It's no skin off my nose.'

'They're Mippies. Middle-aged hippies. They call themselves eco-warriors. They gave up their jobs, sold off a ton of stuff and started a company called Worried Warriors,' said Miki, spitting each word out with loathing. 'They're above any petty political divisions. Instead they sell soil toilets, recycled yoga mats, tie-dye clothes made from junk shop finds, and a whole load of other crap. They donate twenty percent of the profits, when there are any, to various charities like Water Aid.' She scraped the chair back and slumped down in it. 'Actually, that's the only good bit about it.'

Jonas approached the chair opposite as if an angry bear sat facing him. He sat down. 'I didn't mean to offend.'

'Well, you got your answer,' snarled Miki.

'Can't say I understood it,' said Jonas, flinching. 'I mean…'

'Oh, for heaven's sake,' said Miki slamming her palms down on the table. Rory dropped the egg he was holding into the frying pan, cursed and began to pick out the shell. 'They're idiots,' said Miki. 'They really think their little effort is going to stop the world burning. What's more, they expect me to take over the business when I leave school. They keep saying nothing else matters but saving the planet.'

'Sounds like an admirable goal,' said Jonas.

Behind Miki, Rory mimed cutting his own throat. He mouthed, 'You're dead' at Jonas.

But Miki sighed. 'Would you think that if you were asked to give up acting and sell earth potties instead?'

'Easy enough. I'd put on a play to sell them. You have to think outside the box,' said Rory, pulling out the last piece of shell.

'Exactly,' said Miki, turning to face him. 'It's easy to tear things down. What we need to know is how to fix things. How to save the climate. How to eradicate poverty. How to redistribute the world's wealth so that 99% doesn't belong to just one 1%.'

'Is that right?' said Rory, '1% of humanity has all the cash? No wonder I've never had an Xbox.'

But Miki wasn't listening, 'We need to ensure that clean water and sanitation is not only a human right, but that everyone, everywhere, has them. None of this is rocket science. We need new ways of thinking. New ways of acting. We can't just go on adding to old foundations that are built on sand, or we'll end up like Venice, and they're going to sink.'

'I thought Venice was built on water?' said Rory.

'On poles that go down through the water to a sandy bed,' said Jonas. He turned his attention to Miki. 'You're really passionate about this, aren't you? Why didn't you go with your parents to their rally?'

'Yes, of course I am,' said Miki. 'But like Rory says, I think you can combine your dreams with this goal. I don't think selling a whole load of new age stuff to a bunch of crusties is going to make much difference. Its about motivating people en masse, so that real change can happen. The government has whole armies of civil servants behind them, and scientists, who tell them what's going on. They know what's wrong, they're simply not prepared to change it.'

Rory came across to the table with several bowls of food. 'That's crazy. Why not?'

Miki sank down in her chair, looking deflated. 'Loads of reasons,' she said in a tired voice, 'From fear of public backlash to plain, simple, greed.'

'But if people knew how bad things were...' said Jonas.

'Rather than being more concerned about what is

106

happening in the latest soap opera on TV?' said Miki. 'It's a challenge just to catch the public's interest and, besides, no one really trusts the news nowadays. It's all Fake News – and the more over-the-top it is, the better. And people keep doing bad stuff, breaking laws and the like and no one does anything. It's like all of them are waiting for an adult to turn up and sort it all out – but they're the adults!'

Rory sat down and passed out some serving spoons. 'God, are we doing the right thing, adding to this mess?'

'Of course,' said Miki, 'because we will reveal it's all fake at the end. We'll make people understand how they are fooled on a daily basis. It might be a first step towards opening their eyes about what really matters now. Far more use than selling someone a sweaty secondhand gym mat.'

Rory reached into a bowl and pulled out a wrap. 'This is my famous breakfast burrito,' he said. 'Let's eat them while they're hot, and before we start a revolution.'

Jonas waited until Miki had her mouth full of burrito and then he said, 'We're going to use Rory's as a base from tonight, since your parents are back. We meet there at 7.30 p.m. There'll be pizza.'

Miki grunted. Jonas took it for as good an acceptance as he was likely to get. He stood up. 'We need to leave. Can you email the details to Leo? His mum probably won't let him out, but we should try, seeing as he set it up.'

MIKI'S

After the boys had gone off to school, Miki washed up and tidied everything away. Red happily scoffed down the last of the scrambled egg. Miki brushed his coat. There was almost no sign of the ordeal he'd gone through. Hopefully her parents wouldn't notice any difference.

She opened up the website to check. Leo had put a hit counter in the corner. As she watched, it rolled over from 99,999 to 100,000. Miki stared at the screen. Then she logged out and in again. Leo must have made a mistake with the counter. She scrolled down and began to read some of the comments. A number of them were about people wearing white today, and a few from people who had painted their front doors white this morning. Was it really this easy to reach so many people? And was it this easy to convince them that lies were truth? Miki's heart lurched. How on earth could people be persuaded to save the earth – to do the real hard work of recycling, turning off power, voting for politicians who had plans to cope with climate change, reduce their consumerism? Real change would be hard and slow. These people pulling on their white jumpers for the day were looking for a quick fix, and if Miki had learned one thing from her parents' extended conversations over climate change, it was that there was no quick fix.

Outside a car pulled up. Miki slapped the machine shut and got up to meet her parents.

LEON

Leon sat at the back of Miss Wishart's class and wished he could take over from her. The poor lady was obviously struggling. She'd already corrected herself half a dozen times during this lesson and Leon could see a further three errors up on the board. 'And that,' said Miss Wishart writing a final line, 'is how you construct the counter. If you could all add that to your websites?'

Leon typed a few lines and a counter appeared at the

bottom of his website. It was a pretty, if dull, page that asked local people to log the number of seagulls they had seen in a day. Leon had originally wanted to make it about seagull attacks, but Miss Wishart had said no. Still, he knew the algorithm could be used for anything – including getting assets to log the number of times they saw a target in a local area. That was Miss Wishart's problem – apart from her lack of any real programming knowledge – she never saw the possibilities behind an algorithm. She never saw how the bare bones of them could be used for so many different purposes. He put up his hand. 'Done, miss.'

The rest of the class were struggling, because they were using Miss Wishart's faulty code. The harried teacher came over to look at Leon's website. 'Well done, Leon. And such a pretty site. I love the pictures of the birds and seaside you've included. Do you have knowledge of drop-down panels?'

Leon nodded.

'This isn't possible,' moaned a student.

'Can't be done, Miss,' said another.

'Won't work!'

'Obviously, it can be done,' snapped Miss Wishart. 'The youngest member of the class has already completed the task.'

Leon did his best to look saintly. 'Well done, Leon. You can do as you wish for the rest of the session. Perhaps you might like to add another bird to your website? Magpies perhaps. They're very distinctive.'

'Yes, Miss,' said Leon.

As soon as she walked away, Leon opened up a file and started to write down thoughts that had been brewing in his head that morning.

Aliens are amongst us

Project Blue Book, back in the 1950s, held files that proved aliens were already walking amongst us. Previously redacted, you too can find the data, if you're prepared to search through tens of thousands of pages. That's how the US keeps this intel secret. They release it, but bury it amongst tons of uninteresting, cripplingly boring, data, so that only your true and dedicated conspiracy theorist would mine deep enough for the truth. Of course, when these theorists post their conclusions, even demonstrate their finds, they are dismissed as cranks and obsessives. When you examine the US strategy for keeping information from the global public, it is a childishly simply system. Give the truth to the least trustworthy people and no one will believe it.

Recently they tried a new tactic. Footage of alien craft filmed by US fighter pilots was put out on the internet. The US admitted they were literally UFOs – Unknown Flying Objects – and a number of scientists testified that no vehicle they knew about could ignore the laws of physics and move in the manner of these UFOs.

And do you know what? Practically no one batted an eyelid. CGI in movies is so outstanding, that despite the US Government saying it was real, no one believed it. Tactic stage two – reveal the bald-faced, outrageous truth, and most people will think it is fiction, because the truth is too damn scary.

Let's step back a moment and think about any undeniable evidence that alien life forms exist. What could we count as proof? The ancient land markings, the Nazca Lines, that can only be viewed from space, drawn by a primitive people who had no knowledge of geometry? Or the fact that many respected scientists believe life here was generated by matter coming from outside our solar system, brought to the Earth by comets or asteroids. In particular, octopuses are often held up as a creature that is so anatomically different to us, yet demonstrably intelligent, that there had to be an outside – possibly alien – influence at play. More recently, Oumuamua, the strangely shaped, so-called extra-solar asteroid, was observed speeding up as it left our solar system, which shouldn't be possible. Few scientists doubt it was anything other than an alien probe.

Need more proof? Look no further than the heliopause that separates us from the rest of the galaxy. There have been countless films based on the premise that aliens have avoided us because we are so destructive – in some storylines they come to warn us before we destroy ourselves. But as every parent knows, what better containment is there for unruly children than a playpen? In our case the heliosphere. Yes, there are claims that this cloud originates from the sun, or from planets created at the same time as our sun, but really, do we believe that? A convenient marker between us and the rest of the galaxy. A boundary that slows down probes, as NASA has demonstrated, but through which Oumoamoa accelerated – against all known physical laws.

But you said aliens were among us, the more discerning reader may ask. I did. This is my conclusion: with so many signs of alien life, and yet, with our nations still inclined to war and destruction, don't you think that aliens would have left some kind of caretaker in this world? Not necessarily to protect us, but to warn them if it ever looks likely we will expand beyond this rock? Or, perhaps, I am wrong, and they are kindly beings who will, and may already have, stepped in to avoid global catastrophe. On more than one occasion during the Cold War, a signal was erroneously given to launch a nuclear strike, and, on each occasion, something occurred to stop the launch – either a person disbelieved the command, or a system failed. So, perhaps aliens do look out for us.

And who is to say they are even organic aliens? Perhaps they are nothing more than highly sophisticated artificial intelligences that advance as we advance, listening to us, monitoring us and sending information to its masters. Something to think about the next time you order your shopping from your smart voice assistant at home. Sure, you're only asking it to add extra tomatoes to the shopping list, but these machines are always listening, recording and monitoring us. Yes, that's right. You've already got an alien living in your house.

Leon sat back and reread his piece. It was artistic nonsense with just enough truth added to confuse, baffle and cause doubt. It was perfect. He uploaded it to the website and published it. Then he saw the email from Miki. He frowned. This called for an escape plan.

MIKI'S

'Darling! You're home! Does this mean you've given up

112

that ridiculous school?' Her mother posed dramatically in the doorway. Behind her, Miki heard a muffled 'Oompff!' as her father stopped short of knocking her mother over. Being taller than his wife, Miki could see her father's hat, eyes and nose above the boxes he was carrying. His eyebrows had disappeared into his hat in surprise.

Miki stood, awkward, with her hands clasped behind her back, one foot tucked behind the opposite ankle. 'Not quite. I've been excluded for two weeks.'

'Excluded!' exclaimed her mother, dropping the pose to step into the house. 'Whatever for?' Her father again mistook his wife's intent and stopped short with another 'Oompff!' The top suitcase, an old brown, battered one that had belonged to her grandfather, wobbled alarmingly.

'For fighting,' said Miki coming forwards. She dodged around her mother's outstretched arms and took the top case off the pile. 'You okay, Dad?' she asked.

Her father dropped the rest of the suitcases on the floor. They landed with a bang and a rumble that obscured most of her mother's scream. 'Don't worry, Meg. Miki's got the only one with anything breakable in it.' He came forward to kiss his daughter on the cheek. 'Thanks, darling. My arms were about to break. Who did you fight?

Miki carried the suitcase over to the table and put it down carefully. 'Just some girls,' she said. Her mother fussed around the fallen cases.

'At least you and they were breaking a stereotype, I suppose. Do tell me it wasn't all hair pulling and scratching,' said Meg.

'I don't remember what I did,' said Miki. 'I was very angry.'

Her father closed the door and threw himself – coat, hat

113

and all – down into an armchair. He sighed deeply. 'Seeing red, were you? What did they do?'

'They were making stupid comments about climate change not being real,' said Miki. She didn't want to tell them about the dog, and this was the most provocative thing she could think of. Hopefully, she wouldn't be punished by attacking climate deniers.

'Well, I have to say that is most ignorant of them,' said Meg. 'But one has to reason with people. Explain. Violence never changes anything.'

'It wins wars,' said Brian.

'And at what cost?' said Meg. 'Violence is never the answer.'

'You tell that to the service men who fought in WWII!'

'Was the fair good? Did you sell much?' asked Miki, attempting to stem the tide.

'It was fine until your mother took a workshop in psycho-pomp.'

'Psycho-drama,' corrected her mother.

'Whatever it was, you've been acting like a pompous drama queen ever since.'

Miki winced.

'I was not the one who chose to attend a composting workshop.'

'You know damn well that The Worm Turns workshop was not about gardening.'

Miki retreated backwards on tiptoes. With a practised stealth, she slipped upstairs to her bedroom. Red followed her, tail between his legs. Things were less than happy in the New Age downstairs.

Rory was meant to be in drama. He should be skipping across a makeshift stage of gym mats, proclaiming his lines and proving that he could do Peaseblossom far better than Susie Drummond, who whined and lisped her way through all the wonderful archaic words. Worse yet, he knew that off stage, Susie didn't have a lisp. 'It's my fairy voice,' she had told him. 'I'm applying to drama school. I'm going to be a real actress, not just someone out for a laugh like you. I have method. Besides, you're not even meant to be in here. Go away or I'll report you to the Head.'

At the time, Rory had felt a strong urge to slap her overly-made-up face, with its thinly plucked eyebrows and pouty outlined lips that looked like she'd got her mouth stuck in a drain. His desire to lash out shocked him so much, he retreated without answering. He walked away, head held high, but once out of the door he could feel the tears pricking at the back of his eyes. Behind him he heard the muffled laughter and chatter of the cast. Along with the glitz and glamour, such as it was at high school, with the costumes made of dresses from the 80s that various mothers had donated, and the plywood, Rory knew there existed a place where he might belong. Where wearing scarlet mascara or painting his nails were seen as foibles rather than sins. In that moment he hated Susie so much he wished she was dead. Then to his horror he burst into loud sobs.

Rory clamped his hands over his mouth, but the tears kept rolling. His chest heaved with the effort of gulping back his cries. The corridor was empty, but it wouldn't remain that way. Desperate not to be seen in this state he opened the nearest door and dashed inside.

He tripped over a mop and bucket and landed in a heap on the floor of the janitor's closet. He hooked the door closed with his foot. Darkness. He pulled his knees up to his chest and dropped his head, giving into the despair welling inside him. He cried and cried and cried.

A shaft of light struck through the darkness. Rory glanced and saw Mr Deacon standing there. A bubble of hysterical laughter broke from his throat. Deacon looked so utterly bemused, horrified even.

'May I ask what you are doing among the tools of Mr Willis' trade?'

'Sorry, sir,' said Rory, wiping his sleeve across his eyes. He put a hand against the wall and pushed himself up.

'Much as I appreciate the sentiment, sorry isn't an answer, Mr McColl. Has someone distressed you? Where are you meant to be?'

Rory shook his head. He gulped several times, pushing down sobs. Standing had banished the hysteria. He could feel his face turning red. He shook his head again. He couldn't find the words. All he could think was how desperately, earnestly, he wanted Deacon to leave. He couldn't remember wanting anything more in his entire life.

'Well, Mr McColl? What have you to say for yourself?'

Deacon started forward, reaching out an arm, as if he was going to pull Rory out of the cupboard. Rory flattened himself against the back wall. He wished he could catch the edges of the darkness and wrap it around himself. But Deacon had already drawn back. 'Now, I cannot come in and fetch you out,' said Deacon. 'I take it you want me to shut the door and walk away.'

Rory nodded.

'Well, I can't do that either. And you, Mr McColl, can certainly not stay in there all day.'

Rory stayed where he was.

Deacon sighed. 'We appear to have reached an impasse. Might I suggest a compromise. If you come out now, we can transfer to the physics base, which in reality is another cupboard, but with one tiny window. There is no one currently in the lab. You can then tell me what is bothering you. Otherwise I fear I will have to summon help and the situation will become more intense – and more public.'

It was the last part of his speech that convinced Rory. He stumbled out into the light of the corridor, blinking. Even so, he could see that Deacon looked at his face and recoiled. 'It's not blood. It's scarlet mascara,' said Rory. 'It's not very good.'

'Make-up is not encouraged at school,' said Deacon, 'but in this case it is infinitely better than you bleeding from your eyes like some stray Ebola victim. Follow me.' He led the way to the physics base, opened the door and ushered Rory in, before following him.

Rory climbed up onto one of the high stools that were used in the labs. Surrounding him were metal shelves on which oscilloscopes jostled for space with volt meters and circuit boards. Metres and metres of extension cable dripped off them like vines from a strange planet. Deacon went over to the small sink and collected a handful of paper towels. Then he dragged another stool forward and hoisted himself up with a modicum of difficulty. Rory saw himself being studied keenly to see if he smirked at Deacon's lack of physical stature. Rory had never felt less like smiling. Deacon held out the paper towels to Rory.

'It's fine, thank you, sir,' Rory heard himself say. 'I'm not going to cry again.'

Deacon offered them again. 'For your mascara, it's all over your face. If you let it dry like that it will take forever to get off.' The teacher flushed slightly. 'Or so my girlfriend tells me when she's been crying at the movies. I don't know why she picks films she knows will make her cry.' He finished, sounding slightly irritated. 'But then I doubt I will ever understand women.'

Rory took the towels and wiped at his face. He looked down at the smears on the paper. 'Thanks,' he said. 'Your girlfriend is right.'

'About the movies? Or the make-up?'

'I don't get why people want to see movies that make them cry either.'

'At least we agree on one thing,' said Deacon. 'That's a start.'

'I do appreciate this, sir, but I'd rather not...'

Deacon held up his hand. 'I realise my manner might not always seem the most sympathetic, but you must understand it takes a lot to control a class of adolescents. En masse, you are rather like a hunting pack. It's important not to show weakness before them.'

Rory smiled slightly. 'Especially Miki Barton,' he said.

Deacon shuddered. 'Wretched girl. Delights in being difficult. She's smart, though. Gets better grades than you.'

'I'm not the academic type, sir.'

Deacon considered him a moment. 'You might be if you applied yourself, but no, I don't think you're ever going to end up in an ivory tower. What do you want to do?'

'Be an actor,' said Rory. He shook his head. 'I've never told anyone that before.'

'I won't repeat it. But you will need dedication, a good memory and some talent. Do you have any?'

'I think so.'

'And enormous amounts of luck.'

'I know,' said Rory. 'It's not the easiest profession. Most of them,' he jerked his head towards the drama room, 'think it's only a bit of a laugh.'

'But you don't.'

Rory stayed silent. Mr Deacon waited. Finally, Rory sighed. 'I'm okay now, sir. I appreciate you taking the time…'

'But you're not going to tell me what's wrong,' finished Deacon. He sat back on the stool.

'Watch out!'

Deacon managed to grip the sides of the stool in time to stop himself falling backwards. 'Wretched things. No idea why these parrot perches are considered safer around bunsen burners than a decent chair…'

Rory gave a slight smile. 'I presume you'd prefer an armchair?'

'But not a chintz one,' said Deacon.

Rory shook his head. 'Oh, you're very much the buttoned leather wing-back type, sir.'

'I shall take that as a compliment,' said Deacon rising. 'Now, I really must…'

As the teacher turned away from him, Rory found himself speaking. 'I do appreciate this, sir. I know I'm a sort of odd fish as far as the others are concerned. Probably a neon blue one with sparkly edges.'

Deacon turned back, frowning, but he didn't look angry, Rory realised. He looked confused.

'I'm sorry I'm so loud in your class,' continued Rory. 'It's all…'

'Part of the act?' suggested Deacon.

'More of a cover story than an act,' said Rory, looking around and shrugging. 'I don't belong here.'

Deacon pushed the stool against a shelf and leaned on it. 'In this cupboard or on this planet, Mr McColl?'

'I know everyone says there is no such thing as normal…'

'Or they delight in not being thought normal,' said Deacon.

'That isn't it for me.' He took a deep breath. 'I have, or had, a diary at home. I wrote it up each day.'

'Very commendable,' said Deacon.

'As if I were a girl.'

He watched Deacon's face go blank, devoid of all expression.

'I call myself Katy in it,' he said.

'I don't know what to say,' said Deacon.

Rory felt tears prick at the back of his eyes again. He got quickly to his feet. 'I'm sorry, sir. Please forget I ever mentioned anything. I won't waste any more of your time.'

Deacon blocked his way to the door. 'I don't know what to say, Rory, because I think that is one of the bravest admissions I have ever heard.' He put out a hand and pushed Rory gently back to his seat. 'I have to confess I am not usually a teacher who has to deal with pastoral issues. I am very much afraid I might say or do the wrong thing. It is a most unusual feeling for me,' he gave a wry smile, 'and singularly uncomfortable. What would you most like me to ask you?'

'If I'm gay. I'm not. Or at least I don't know. It's not that I fall in love with boys. It's that I'm more comfortable wearing girls' clothes. I like make-up. I like not being…' he stopped, unable to find the words.

'Male?' said Deacon. 'You don't strike me as the kind of boy who wants to play football or do all those things that were thought of as boys' pursuits when I was young. For all your bluster, I've suspected you were empathic towards your fellow students. You often try to draw my ire if you think I'm being harsh on someone. Quite an unusual perspective in a teenage boy.'

'I want to be soft,' said Rory. 'I want to be bright and likeable and kind. I don't want to be part of a gang or a team – or in the boys changing rooms after PE.'

'Yes, I seem to remember as a teenager, I found other boys quite repellent.'

'But you said you have a girlfriend.'

'I do,' said Deacon. 'There are a great many ways to be a man – to be male – but I think you are happier thinking of yourself as a girl.'

'Is there someone wrong with me?' said Rory. 'I've read about theories…'

Deacon shook his head. 'There are great many ideas out there on the internet, and a great many psychologists formulating ideas, but to my mind all that is about labelling people. I wouldn't be too eager to label yourself, Rory. As I said, I'm not the best person to talk to, but it seems to me that you have a lot of thinking to do. You may not feel it, and I didn't at your age, but you have a positive wealth of time before you. Certainly, enough of it to afford you the luxury of taking your time deciding who you are and what you want to be.' He smiled. 'I can see why, even without talent, drama would appeal. It lets you try out so many skins.'

'Yes,' said Rory, 'I hadn't thought of it like that.'

Deacon stood up. 'I am going, with your permission, to

do two things. Firstly, I am going to suggest to the school counsellor that some sessions would be of benefit to you. However, I will not divulge any of this conversation to her. You can use the time as you will. Is that agreeable?'

Rory nodded.

'Secondly, I will see about removing the restriction on your taking part in the school play.'

'How?'

'I expect I may have to resort to blackmail.'

Rory gasped.

'I am only joking, Mr McColl. I am not yet quite sure what I will say, but I am certain enough of my intellect that I believe I will find a way.'

'Thank you,' said Rory.

'Now, I must get back to the cold tea waiting for me in the staffroom before my next class.'

'Thank you, sir,' said Rory.

'I haven't done anything yet,' said Deacon. 'But you can do something for me.'

'Anything, sir.'

Deacon paused with his hand on the door handle. 'Don't let it slip about my going to the movies to see romantic comedies. If you do, I fear I will not survive my next encounter with S4c.'

'They won't hear anything from me, sir,' said Rory.

Rory watched Mr Deacon strut off down the corridor. He felt a lot lighter. In fact, he wanted to skip, but that seemed a reckless action in a school that had such menaces as Mark Stuart. Instead, he went into the back of the library and surfed the internet for funny animal videos. He felt so much better that when he came up with a very silly idea, he had no hesitation in taking it forward.

MIKI

Upstairs Red didn't have his paws over his ears, but he had crawled halfway under her bed. Miki gave him a sympathetic look. 'I know,' she said. 'This is a bad one.' Below, in the living room, she heard her mother's voice rising in pitch. Red whined.

'She won't actually scream,' she told the dog. 'She regards that as too much of a feminine trope.' Red's tail, which was now all that wasn't under the bed, thumped weakly. Miki put down her sketch pad and went down on her knees. She reached under the bed and patted her dog. 'It'll be okay, Red. The trip must have over-excited them. Rather like toddlers after a party, they are tired and grumpy.' Red made another sad noise that was more a whine than a woof. 'Okay, you stay there, then,' said Miki kindly. 'I'm going to indulge in my human privilege of leaving the building alone.' Miki shoved a few essentials in a bag.

She crept down the stairs towards the kitchen and the back door. She had the feeling her mother had seen her, but she didn't stop, and no one called after her. Once out of sight in the hall, she took her coat off the peg and let herself out. Whatever was going on between her parents, she'd had enough. Besides, if her father was gunning for a regime change, she didn't want to get caught in the crossfire. Although she suspected by this evening, he would be cooking dinner and fawning over her mother in apology. She wasn't sure which was worse, the row or the aftermath. If only he'd stay strong for once, and not give in to her mother. Surely her father realised that in pushing against feminine tropes, her mother had pushed herself rather too close to being a bully in their marriage.

Outside, Miki tugged her coat around her. It felt colder than she had expected. Her green camo might look good, but she'd stripped all the lining out of it last summer and it did barely more than stop the wind. She had no desire to return to the house until the argument had blown over. Her parents rarely argued. They debated climate issues and called down ire on this or that public figure who was denying the truth. A real blow-on-blow personal insult match happened maybe once or twice a year. As she had marched into middle age, her mother had become more and more tyrannical it seemed to Miki. Her mother had become so decisive and determined, she often forgot to ask her family what their thoughts were on her latest project.

The arguments remained infrequent, but when one finally blew up it was all the more intense for the emotions her father had been suppressing for so long. They had yet to come to blows and she hoped never would. Her father was naturally a very gentle man, who liked an easy life, and had been perfectly happy as a director at the insurance company. He'd been equally happy to give it up, sell out his shares and follow his wife in her brave new life. It had been far easier than trying to persuade her to stay in the high end cosmetics laboratory where she had worked, and where one too many bunnies had finally ended their careers in the search for a perfect mascara. Whether it had been a particularly fluffy, lop-eared rabbit that had turned her mother's world upside down, or merely the onset of the menopause, Miki suspected she would never know. She'd been delighted when her mother quit her job, but had assumed she would look for one of equal (or more) seniority at an animal cruelty free company. What no one had suspected was that Meg had uncovered a desire for redemption, and was going full on eco-warrior to prove it.

It was all a bit thick, thought Miki. Teenagers were meant to be rebellious and regime-challenging, not the parents. She just wanted to go to school. Miki considered going there now, but decided against it. It would likely make things worse. Besides, was she really so sad she had nowhere to go but back to school? That wasn't cool.

She had her notepad and pencils in her bag, but no gloves. She'd freeze if she went down to the shoreline to sketch. She walked past a bus stop. Then she walked back. Someone had cracked the glass of the digital display. Rather than showing the next bus all it did was blink *8*888**. The bus route display board inside the shelter was also down. Only one hanging fixture showed where it had been. Miki swore quietly. Part of her understood the 'found art' aspect of the route map, but the more pragmatic part of her protested that now no one, herself included, would know where any bus was going. She checked the change in her pocket. She had enough for a return day fare. Right, she thought, I shall get on the next bus and see where it takes me. Her new friends might be happy playing online, but she wanted a real-life adventure.

RORY'S HOUSE

Rory and Jonas lay slumped on the floor. Leon sat at the computer, typing away. 'I think we need to ramp it up some more,' he said. 'We're getting excellent hits, but it doesn't feel like enough.'

Rory groaned dramatically. 'My belly. I'm so fat. Do you think I might be coeliac?'

'What are you thinking?' said Jonas.

125

'That I might be allergic to wheat,' said Rory.

'I think somehow we need to take it offline and into the real world,' said Leon.

'That's either a very good idea or a very bad one,' said Rory. 'I can't tell. Ouch. Oooh. It hurts. I'm either about to have a baby or an appendicitis…'

'Really?' said Leon, in a very disinterested voice. 'I was going to ask if there was any of the pepperoni left. I've been slogging away while you ate everything.'

Face averted, Rory passed him up a plate of cold pizza. 'You ate your body weight in carbs too,' he said.

'Hmm, maybe,' said Leon. 'But I'm far more active than either of you. If you don't start doing some exercise, you'll have a heart attack before you reach middle age. I could send you some information about it.'

'You're the one like a forty-year-old man,' said Rory. 'You're weird.'

'Thank you,' said Leon. 'I aim be forty for most of my life. I have even tried on a few cardigans, but I don't think I have sufficient height to carry it off yet.'

'Weird,' repeated Rory, 'and that's coming from me…'

'Why don't we look at what our readers most like – I mean what gets most comments or reposts?' said Jonas.

'An excellent place to start,' said Leon, taking a pretend pipe out of his mouth and waving it at him.

Rory rose to his feet. 'I need to go to the bathroom,' he said. 'I have a feeling I'm going to need more mascara for this.'

BREAKING NEWS

Police were called today to an altercation between two women in Joppa. The cause of the fight is unknown, but two washing lines, a fence and a policeman's nose were damaged.

OTHER BREAKING NEWS

A number of listeners have phoned in to comment on sightings of pumas in Scotland. One listener from Glasgow, Maggie McDermont, summed up their views with the comment, 'Any cat from Glasgow could take down a snobby moggy from Edinburgh. Our cats are way wilder.' Could the mysterious puma be nothing but a lost Glaswegian black cat?

FUTHER BREAKING NEWS

Are we due an alien invasion? Patrick Loss of PEAS, author of the *Emergency Guide: How to Befriend Alien Overlords*, told the press this morning, 'When we see an explosion of interest in aliens, as we have recently throughout the internet, and around the world, it is normally a herald of things to come. Remember, they are everywhere. Those who can read the signs know the time is near.' Have you seen any UFOs?

Breaking News is brought to you by Radio City Central: the local station you can trust.

SATURDAY 10th JUNE

BREAKING NEWS

Today Patrick Loss told a gathering of the press, 'They'll probably arrive in what looks like a meteor shower, and if people are happy to believe that, well, that's on them.' When further questioned, he would only say 'Wait and see. Wait and see.'

OTHER BREAKING NEWS

In more down-to-earth matters, local elections will be taking place shortly and voting cards will be dropping through your door any day. This reporter wonders what we'll see on the voting ballot this time. Any Scottish versions of Corporal Mop-head, or the Insane Partying Party, or simply the run-of-the-mill red, blue, yellow and green candidates? Or, dare I hope, that a meteor shower brings us a little green man to stand?

MIKI

Miki opened her eyes to bright light. 'Are you ill?' asked a stern female voice.

Miki sat up, 'No, Aunt Hildy,' she said.

'Well, the rooster is up, and so should we be. I'm away to church. I know better than to ask you to come with me. The least you can do is put the dinner on. I take it you can do that, and that my sister has not been totally lacking in your domestic education?'

'I often cook at home,' said Miki.

'None of your vegan muck,' said her aunt as she went out, closing the door behind her.

When the Glasgow bus had turned up, she'd hopped on with no real thought of staying away. But having arrived and found where the Glasgow School of Art was currently housed, she'd ended up in a nearby café chatting to current students about what it was like to attend one of the most famous art schools in the world. Then someone had invited her to a party, and somewhere around 2 a.m. she had realised that fascinating though her new friends were, there was no way she could get home. So at 3 a.m. she'd ended up on Aunt Hildy's doorstep. Aunt Hildy was her mother's sister, and while she had always disapproved of her sister, she let Miki know in no uncertain terms that she had now exceeded her mother in family disappointment.

'You reek of smoke and drink,' said her aunt.

'I was with some art students. They were smoking and drinking, not me.'

'Does your mother know where you are?'

During all this she kept Miki standing in the perfectly tiled hallway of her impeccable Glaswegian tenement building. Miki shivered with cold. She'd been unable to find a night bus, and against her better judgement, she had walked here. Her evident suffering did not appear to be softening her aunt's stance, who remained guarding the entrance to her flat like Cerberus in a floral nightdress.

'No,' said Miki. 'I think I've run away.'

'Well, if you have, it will be the first sensible thing you've done,' said Hildy and miraculously, she swung open the door to the warm flat. Miki hurried in before she could change her mind.

Now, five and a half hours later she forced her eyes open and stumbled into the kitchen. The makings of a roast dinner were laid out next to a neat list, including timings. Miki set to work.

LEON

'Will you stop? Mum make Leo stop. He's pinging soggy rice puffs at me,' said Alice.

Leon did his best to look angelic.

'Whatever,' said his mother, sighing. 'I need to get that lot to the jumble sale and sort it before the doors open. Why people think it is okay to donate the day before, I will never understand. More than likely half the stuff is rubbish.'

'I'd help, love,' said Leon's dad. 'But you know I have the five-a-side this morning. I can't let the lads down.'

'And what are you doing, Alice?' said her mother.

'You better not be off to see that Cliff,' said her father.

Alice threw a desperate look at her mother. 'I'm joining a revision group. We're going over the stuff for the biology prelim.'

Her father gave a low growl. 'I would have thought that was the last thing you need to revise,' he said from between gritted teeth.

'I didn't choose the group. The teacher divided us up. I've been looking at the notes till I'm blue in the face. I need someone to ask me questions. I need to do this.'

'I could help you sort stuff, Mum,' said Leon. 'I could even stay and help sell it. Tell people why we need to raise money to upgrade the school computers.'

'I don't know,' said his mother. 'It would do you good to go with your dad and get some exercise.'

'Lisa, we can't let him play!'

'He could stand in goal or something.'

'No,' said Leon and his dad in unison.

'It wouldn't be fair to the others,' said his dad. 'He's a very poor player.'

'That's no way to talk about your son.'

'No, Mum. I really am crap. Besides, I could answer questions about home computers – fifty pence a question.'

His mother eyed him suspiciously. 'You won't get any of the money, you know.'

'No, but we'll get better machines in school.'

'Oh, alright. C'mon.'

'But what about my revision group?' said Alice. 'Can I go?'

'Ask your father!' said Lisa, disappearing into the hall. Leon followed her but stopped to look at his dad. 'I wouldn't,' he said. 'You can't trust anyone.' He shut the door behind him just in time as Alice launched herself towards him.

JONAS

'Is your mother in?' said the woman on the front doorstep. In her late forties, she wore her long hair in a tight bun, over large blue-framed glasses perched on her nose and she had painted her lips with an excess of pink. When she spoke Jonas could see it had smudged onto her teeth. He wondered if he should tell her. A large satchel-like bag hung on her shoulder, and she wore a neat navy suit. Jonas thought she must be selling something; either double glazing or religion.

'Your mother?' persisted the woman.

'I'm afraid she is asleep,' said Jonas. 'My mother has a chronic condition and needs a lot of sleep. We're not in a position to buy new windows, nor can I wake her to discuss any–' he paused, 'spiritual matters.'

'Do I look like a religious zealot?' snapped the woman. She fumbled in her bag and produced her ID in a wallet.

Jonas peered at it, taking in little except for the dreaded letters DWP. 'As I said, my mother is asleep.'

'Your father then?'

'My father left us over two years ago,' said Jonas.

'Has he kept in touch?'

'I think that is a rather rude question to ask me on my doorstep, early on a Saturday morning,' said Jonas. 'I don't see how that is any of your business.'

'We need to know if he is sending you money.'

Jonas felt the blood rush into his face. 'No, he is not,' he answered as calmly as he could.

'Well, if you let me come inside, we need not discuss the details on the doorstep.'

Jonas grew angry. 'I have told you my mother is sleeping.'

'Not gardening this morning then? I can go round the back to check, you know.'

'No, she is not. And you're welcome to,' said Jonas, slamming the door in her face.

The doorbell rang. Jonas went back into the living room ignoring it. It rang again and again. He ran back to the front door and wrenched it open. 'What is the matter with you? My mother is chronically ill and needs her sleep.'

'So you say.'

'So says her GP, her hospital consultant and her CPN.'

'I wouldn't know anything about that.'

'You mean, you don't have any of the information we submitted about her MS at all?'

'Not to hand. It's not the way we do things. I need to investigate how mobile your mother is. She was reported to be gardening. Obviously, if she had MS, she would be in a wheelchair and unable to do so.'

Jonas' heart beat so loudly he was surprised she couldn't hear it. 'Do you,' he said in between taking deep breaths to calm himself, 'have any medical training?'

'I worked for ten years in a GP surgery.'

'As what? A cleaner?'

'As a medical receptionist. I find you a very rude little boy, what is your name?'

'Shouldn't that also be in your notes?'

'Well, as I have no idea who you are…'

'I have been talking about my mother. That should have given you a clue.'

'I need ID'

'And I need you to leave. If you don't, I shall phone the police and say you are harassing us. Which you are.'

'We have attempted to ring on several occasions and make an appointment with no success.'

'You must have been ringing the wrong number,' said Jonas. 'I suggest you try writing. Now, go away. If you ring that doorbell once more, I shall dial 999.' He closed the door. He walked back through to the living room and leant against the wall, waiting. He knew he had no reason to call the police, but hopefully the fuss it would cause would put the woman off trying the doorbell again. MS and wheelchairs. It was clear she had no idea how the disease worked. Letting her speak to his mother would only make things worse, but he couldn't keep on ignoring the phone calls and tearing up the letters. He didn't know what to do.

The only plan he had was to use the Fake News website somehow, but he still hadn't worked out how. He looked at his wristwatch. If he didn't move it, he would be late for Leo. He opened the door and peeked along the hall. There was no shadow on the other side of the glass front door. She'd gone. Jonas snatched up his jacket and bolted out of the house.

LEON

Leon couldn't have been more helpful as he took black plastic bags and boxes from the car into the gym hall. Not once did he complain of a trapped finger or a torn nail, or of simply being too tired to carry more, as he usually did when he helped his mother bring in the shopping. By the time all the donated jumble was piled up beneath the three trestle tables laid aside for the stall, his mother was regarding him with deep suspicion.

'Is there anything you want to tell me, Leon?' Lisa asked, opening the first box. 'Is it something that you've done?'

Leon shook his head. 'How do you want this stuff sorted? Clothes, toys and ornaments?' The last word was said with deep disdain as he picked out a flying china duck from a bag. Miraculously it was unchipped. 'I presume some people put these on their walls? In their houses?' His voice resonated so much with horror that his mother laughed.

'There was a time when such things were considered, if not necessary, extremely fashionable,' she said.

'Really?'asked Leon. 'Was this at a time of national instability?'

Lisa laughed again and came over to hug him. Leon suffered this, holding the duck stiffly at arm's length. 'One minute you're a little boy,' said his mother, 'the next minute you're a cantankerous middle-aged man.' She squeezed him tighter, 'my little conundrum.'

Leon broke away. 'Enough, Mother.' Then he giggled. 'How about clothes, toys and trash.'

Lisa nodded. 'As long as you don't label it that. Besides, someone's trash may be someone else's treasure.'

'You wish,' said Leon.

They both worked steadily for the next half hour. Lisa handed Leon some labels and a pen for pricing up. 'Use your best judgement,' she said. Leon labelled an orange t-shirt at 10p, as he felt sorry for anyone who had to wear the colour, but the flying duck he labelled, 'Rare Antique £50' as he felt anyone stupid enough to like it deserved to pay through the nose. Similarly, he labelled a skirt with mirrors at £40. Then he came across a sealed make-up set. He checked his mother wasn't looking then took off the plastic shrink wrap. 'Hey, Mum, it's not hygienic to sell partially used stuff, is it?' He held it up for her to see at a distance. 'Oh heavens,' said Lisa. 'Why don't people ever read the instructions about donations? Put it in a bin, Leon.'

'Actually, Mum, I was thinking I should go and speak to someone about setting up my question and answer stand.'

Lisa stopped sorting. 'You were serious about that?'

'C'mon, Mum. When was the last time anyone else other than me set up anything electrical in the house, let alone

135

fixed a problem with the computer?'

'Fair point. Go find Mr Deacon, he's in charge of the room plan.'

'Sure,' said Leon, despite the fact he'd never had a class with Deacon. 'Back shortly.'

His mother grunted something and turned her attention back to untangling a stringed dog puppet from a very moth-eaten, but well-loved blue bear.

Leon wandered casually across the room and then between the stalls. Once he was out of his mother's sight, he made a beeline for the door and headed out into the corridor. He checked his watch, gasped and began to run.

JONAS & RORY

'This does not look good,' said Jonas for the seventh time.

'It wasn't high on my priorities today to get stuck in the bushes with you,' said Rory. 'If I get my shirt caught on one of these wretched things you will never hear the last of it.' He poked feebly at the foliage.

'It's called nature,' said Jonas.

'It's prickly and smells bad.'

'That's the mud.'

Rory looked down. 'My Vans. I've only just got them clean,' he wailed.

'Ssh!' said Jonas. 'There's no point in hiding if you're going to make such a din.'

Rory pulled his lips in over his teeth and let them out with a low 'pumk' noise. 'Yeah, I suppose the worst possible outcome for you is being found in a bush with little old me.'

'Oh yes, worst possible scenario ever. Even worse than

136

having to fend the bloody DWP off your doorstep because they want to send your mum to jail.'

'What?' said Rory, horrified. 'They can't do that!'

'Want a bet?'

'I'm sorry. Anything I can do?'

'Yeah, shut up,' said Jonas 'Oh, don't look at me as if you're a puppy that's just been kicked. It's okay. I'm dealing.'

'But…' said Rory, then stopped under Jonas' hard stare. They sat together in silence for three more minutes that felt more like an hour to both of them.

'Besides,' said Jonas eventually. 'Everyone knows you're not my type.'

'Hah,' said Rory. 'You should be so lucky to be mine.'

Air cleared, they grinned at each other.

JONAS, RORY, LEON & MR DEACON

'Psst,' called Leon from the open door.

Jonas and Rory blundered out of the bushes leaving a trail of leaves behind them. 'You have a twig sticking out of your left ear,' said Leon in a pained voice. 'I take it you believe the term 'covert' is a new type of trainer. Let me explain to you. When hiding, the idea is that not only one should remain hidden, but that no one should ever know one has been hiding there.'

'Not now,' said Jonas, hurrying through the door.

'Who's Wan? Is he helping us?' said Rory.

Leon shut the door behind them. 'Look,' he said. 'I've put a paper wedge to keep the lock from engaging. I need to get back to the gym. I take it you know where you're going?'

Rory raised his eyebrows. Jonas sighed. 'Yeah, we do.'

'I've left a couple of cardboard boxes up there for you to carry things in. I don't imagine you'll want more than two.'

'Yeah,' said Rory. 'Not being octopuses.'

'Octopi,' said Leon. 'You'll have to get the stuff back in yourself tonight too.'

'What!' said Jonas. 'How can that possibly work?'

'I know it's not what we arranged,' said Leon. 'But the stupid teacher in charge has someone coming to pick up whatever is left over in a recycling lorry. A PR photo job. Usually the stuff gets cleared out the next day, which is how I would have let you back in.'

'But how can we possibly use it?' said Jonas. 'There's no point if we have to bring it back this afternoon.'

'For every problem there is a solution,' said Leon, taking a flat, black box out of his pocket. 'I think we can make this work. Rory's been training in these kinds of electrics…'

'Not by choice – and I've only had a couple of hours on it.'

'Let me let you in on a secret,' said Leon, thrusting the black box at him. 'There's this thing called the internet, and if you look not very hard at all, you can find almost anything. Besides, I don't see any other choice. Unless you want to call the whole thing off.'

'Maybe we should wait until Miki is back,' said Jonas.

'I didn't realise she was in charge,' said Leon. He tilted his head to one side 'Or is it that you miss your little girlfriend too, too much?'

Jonas blushed. Rory gave a crack of laugher, 'No offence,' he said, 'but the fabulous Miki would eat you alive. She's a firecracker.'

'She seems very sensible to me,' said Jonas gruffly.

'Yeah, you didn't have to try and pull her off Becket and Grime. All teeth and claws that girl. I think she works out.'

'Who or what are Becket and Grime?' said Leon.

'Friends Of Wan,' said Jonas, who was feeling slightly hysterical. 'Guys, this isn't possible. I say we call it off.'

'And it's my masculinity people doubt,' said Rory. 'Time to put on your big girl panties, Jonas. Think what would Miki do?'

Leon sniggered.

'I don't think Miki would do this,' said Jonas, slowing his pace.

'Too late. We're here,' said Rory, grabbing him by the wrist and tugging him forward.

'But what if someone sees us carrying stuff out?' said Jonas.

'Thought of that,' said Leon. 'Say you're taking stuff not wanted for the sale that the nursing home would like.'

'Which one?'

'Better not to give a real name,' said Leon, 'in case they ring up to check. Say something like Rose Home, or Duck Pond House.'

Jonas raised his hands in the air, curling his fingers, 'Leo,' he said in a strained voice. 'We are not spies on a secret mission to break into a covert facility.'

'How many times do I have to tell you it's Leon!'

Jonas spoke over him. 'We are three kids stealing equipment from the local high school and at least two of us are sufficiently well known personalities to be recognised.'

'I do hope one of the well known personalities is me,' said Rory, flicking at his hair and pouting.

'Your point?' said Leon. He tried to make his voice strong and confident, but his bottom lip trembled slightly.

'When whoever stops us finds out there is no Duck Bound Lodge or wherever, they will find us on Monday morning and ask us to explain. Bang goes – as you would say – the whole operation.'

'That is a good point,' said Leon in a small voice.

'Okay. Let's get out of here.'

'Hang on a minute, cowboy,' said Rory. 'Hold your bolting horses. Who says anyone is going to catch us? Besides, even if they do we can say we're taking the stuff round to the front entrance for the sale. As long as they don't catch us in the actual doorway, we can have been walking in from the outside world – you know that place where real life happens.'

'That works,' said Leon, grinning. 'That would do it. I should have kissed.'

Rory backed away in mock alarm. 'What do you say?' he said in a highly theatrical voice.

'KISS,' said Leon. 'Keep It Simple Stupid. Makes so much sense when you came up with that answer,'

'Agreed,' said Rory patting him on the shoulder.

'He means you're stupid,' said Jonas.

'He what?' said Rory. 'Oh, whatever. I'm going for it,' and he headed through the doors ahead.

'This is madness,' said Jonas.

'Yeah, he can't handle it on his own. He'll get caught. You going to let that happen?' said Leon.

'You little shit,' said Jonas to Leon. Then he ran off after Rory.

'And so my plan comes together,' muttered Leon to himself, grinning.

Clipped footsteps echoed from the next corridor. Leon moved towards them. 'Ah, Mr Deacon,' he said. 'I've been looking for you, sir. I have this idea. It's to do with helping people who are computer illiterate, much like yourself…'

MIKI

'I've tasted worse,' said Aunt Hildy. Miki glanced at the empty plate in front of her aunt, and the empty dishes on the table.

'I'm glad you were able to stomach it,' she said politely.

'You would have enjoyed today's sermon.'

'I doubt it,' said Miki under her breath.

'It was about pride, and so full of holes you could have put it on your table and called it a doily…'

'No problems on that front for me. My parents constantly let me know I'm disappointing them.'

'Have you called them yet?' said Aunt Hildy, dabbing her face daintily with a fine, starched linen napkin.

Slightly older than Miki's mother, Hildy acted like a woman from a different age. Her hair was styled, as she had often told her niece, after the style of the forties – an era that fascinated Hildy. Miki's father said he believed that, at least mentally, Hildy was from that time. He was constantly surprised she hadn't dug a bomb shelter in the back green. Sitting there in her neat cardigan and smart, old fashioned dress with just an edge of lace showing, Miki looked down at her Doc Martens and wondered how on earth they could be related.

'Is there something funny, miss? Your poor parents will be worrying their socks off.'

'I doubt it,' said Miki. 'They left me alone all of last week while they were off at their conference. For all they know I could have been staying out all night every night.

I've been suspended from school, you know.'

'Is that meant to impress me? Or are you wanting me to call social services for you? I mean, why else would you turn up at my house in the middle of the night.'

Miki blushed. 'I'm sorry about that. I couldn't think of where else to go. I mean, I didn't even know where I was going, but then the Glasgow bus came along and I thought...'

'You could do worse than visit your Aunt Hildy? Didn't your father warn you I don't have any dealings with frozen food? No ice cream here!' She paused, and said in a slightly gentler voice, 'What happened, Michelle, to make you run away?'

'I didn't...'

'I call a spade a spade,' said Hildy, sitting back in her chair and squaring her shoulders. 'You ran away. One of the few privileges of being a philosophy lecturer is that people expect you to be blunt.'

'I suppose I did,' said Miki slowly. 'They were having one of their rows. They only happen...'

'Oh, I remember. My sister has a fearful temper. Only loses it once or twice a year, but when she does.' Hildy stood and began to collect the dishes. 'Always thought you had more backbone to you than that, though. It's not the first time you've seen your mother lose her wig in a hailstorm.'

'Her what in a what?'

'Never mind,' said Hildy. 'Just tell me what is really bothering you.'

Aunt Hildy was known throughout the family for being as spiky as a cactus and as fierce as a bulldog. She was also known for being the very odd member of the family who was into something called War Reenactment. Most people didn't understand and even Glasgow taxi drivers were rumoured to be scared of her. She had a habit of jumping into their cabs on a Saturday with her gas mask under her arm, carrying her warden's hat and telling them. 'Shift yourselves! Don't you know there's a war on?'

Her unexpected kindness shook Miki. To her horror she felt tears flooding down her face. Her aunt put the dishes back down on the table and came round to pat her niece on the shoulder. 'Come on, lass, out with it. I'm betting it would take a muckle mess to turn you into a watering pot. You've more of me in you than you know.'

This was too much for Miki, who broke down, not so much into sobs, but into howls like a young wolf.

MARTY

His armpits sweating profusely, Marty slogged on up the hill to the school. He should have known this shirt, advertised as 99.9% pure cotton on the internet, would turn out to be mostly rayon. Rumours of some kind had reached his boss' ears and he'd run a fine toothcomb through Marty's expenses. The freelancing life might be the one for him, but until one of his stories took off he needed every penny from the sad little rag he worked for.

He hadn't dared take a bus up the hill, let alone a taxi. And all for one poxy photo that no one was ever going to use? A recycling lorry outside a school? Where was the news in that? He'd asked if anyone special was going to be there, but they hadn't even managed to get a reality TV celebrity – even an out of date one – to mark their precious eco moment. Not even a vlogger. How hard could that be?

The school was going for eco status, whatever the hell that was, and didn't want to detract from its message. That was the excuse Marty had been given when he had phoned. He hadn't listened to anything after that. He didn't like people sending 'messages'. It was like they were trying to do his job for him. It was up to him to create the story.

He'd never liked the colour green and he liked kids even less. He bet his boss wouldn't use the photo and claim it was badly framed or hadn't captured the essence of the moment, or some such other BS. His boss was only sending him because the school Head had kept phoning. They wouldn't use the bloody thing and they'd find a reason not to pay him. What a waste of a hot Saturday afternoon. He should be lying in the living room, curtains closed, watching football and drinking beer.

By the time he reached the top of the hill, his hair lay flat, plastered to his head with sweat and more pooled at the bottom of his spine in the small of his back. He stopped to sit on the edge of a wall and catch his breath. He had no illusions that anyone would offer him a cup of tea. If anyone recognised him they would only berate him for his article on that woman and her wretched boy...

Mere moments after he recalled Jonas, Marty saw the boy edging his way backwards out of a side door in the school. Without knowing precisely why, Marty dropped down behind the wall, out of sight. Jonas had a large cardboard box in his arms and was clearly struggling with the weight. After him came a skinny boy of around the same age. He wore red shoes, a turquoise sweater and jeans that had glitter down the sides. Dark red streaks ran through his hair. He was also carrying a box. The contrast to Jonas couldn't have been more startling. Marty's eyes swivelled back to Jonas: jeans, blue hoodie, neat brown hair probably cut by Mum. Altogether the boy next door. What was he and this strange bird of paradise looking so guilty about? What were they carrying? Whatever they were up to, it had to be more interesting than a garbage truck picking up a pile of landfill.

So as Jonas and Rory made their ponderous way down the hill, Marty followed. Darting between and behind parked cars like a bad extra in a police TV series, he stopped every now and then to snap a shot. The boys were still clearly struggling with the weight of the boxes. With luck, one or other of them would drop their box and he'd get to see what was inside. Even if they didn't they were going slowly enough he could keep up. Then, he muttered to himself, they would see what they would see. He knew something was up. Hadn't he always had a nose for these things? And that innocent-looking boy in the plain jeans, he was a troublemaker. The other poor sap was no doubt intended to be his patsy.

MIKI

'So this is where they moved the Art School,' said Aunt Hildy. 'It's such a shame you didn't see the old one. Lovely it was. Just like a tea room.' The edges of her lips curled very slightly. 'I'm more of a one for the discussion of atheistic myself than standing around in an art gallery. But then, if we didn't have artists we philosophers would have less to discuss. It can get pretty cut-throat, let me tell you, in the world of aesthetics and general philosophy. One of our Platonists had a major breakdown last year.

Miki found herself rubbing her eyes. This couldn't

145

actually be happening. 'This way,' said her aunt, leading her over to the reception desk by which stood a slightly nervous-looking young woman in a neat skirt suit. 'Sally is taking an elective philosophy class. Goodness knows why. She is terrible at it,' said Hildy. 'She's been a student here for two years. She can tell you what it's like to be a young person here.'

Miki found herself blushing. As they reached Sally, Hildy said, 'This is my niece, Michelle. I've got her to bring some of her sketches with her. I'd pay money. But don't let me influence your opinion. Her parents think she should be out saving the world rather than making art. But as Churchill said, what's the point of saving the world if we don't have art? Or words to that effect. It's almost as stupid as suggesting there is no place for philosophy in the modern world, when it's clear that the majority of the population have lost the ability to think. Anyway, as I said on the phone, we need your help.'

Sally swallowed. 'I'll do my best, Miss Barton.' Sally looked slightly confused, her gaze flicking between them.

'My mother's a bit of feminist,' said Miki. 'She made my father take her name rather than the other way round.'

'Oh, how splendid of her,' said Sally. 'And what a good idea.'

Hildy gave a loud sniff and said, 'I will leave you two young people alone. I'll be back in ninety minutes, at which time I look forward to hearing your opinions. You, Sally, as to whether my niece shows any promise…'

'Miss Barton, I really can't…'

'Rubbish, you're a student here, aren't you? We'd rather the truth, wouldn't we, Michelle? And you, Michelle, I want to know if you actually want to come here. Because

146

if you do, things will have to be arranged.' She walked off.

'I don't know what she meant by that,' said Sally, 'but if I were your parents I'd be scared.'

'Oh, it's a fairly level battlefield.' Miki held out her hand. 'Miki, please. I can't remember the last time someone, other than Hildy, called me Michelle.'

'Sal,' said Sally, shaking it. 'I would like to see your work, but you know, it's not my opinion that would count. I did think we might see if my tutor was in. He's really nice, but even he couldn't promise if you would get in.'

'Oh, I know,' said Miki. 'Besides, my parents would never let me. Hearing someone else likes my work and seeing this place is a dream come true in itself.'

Sal frowned. 'I probably shouldn't say this, but you know once you're sixteen in Scotland you can leave home whenever you like.'

'I never thought of that,' said Miki. 'I'd kinda of like to stay friends with my parents though.'

'Of course,' said Sal. 'But sometimes you have to remember it's your life. Let's bite the bullet and go and see if my tutor is in. He's pretty plainspeaking in a rip-a-bandage-off sort of way. If you haven't got a hope in hell, he'll tell you.'

'I don't suppose you know of any tea drinking parties I might attend this evening, do you?' said Miki. 'I'd really like to meet other students. No one I know back home is interested in art – or why it's so important.'

'Tea drinking?' said Sal.

'Definitely,' said Miki. 'I don't think Aunt Hildy would countenance anything else.'

Sal shook her head. 'She'd never believe it. Just say no one was doing drugs and she should be fine.'

'Okay,' said Miki, her eyes wide. 'They won't be, will they?'

LEON

Update on Fake News Team

I have renamed my subjects. It seems while the attachments of suspect girl's parents remain unknown and dubious, suspect girl has no political affiliations of any kind. Boys A and B likewise have proved to have no significant political attachment. It might be thought at this point I should withdraw my observation. However, all three have shown themselves to be potential civic agitators, with the two boys prepared to create major disruption.

At present the target of their machinations is the tendency of the articles, both in the press and on the internet, to exaggerate and even falsify news to increase their readership. Although this is an undeniable problem of our age, I am yet to be convinced that adding to this misinformation will in any way help the situation. I believe some grand reveal is planned, but I do not think my subjects have properly thought through what this will mean for them and their families. Or if they have, they have a somewhat idealistic and rose-tinted perspective.

For my part, I shall plead emotional ignorance, and act as if I was convinced by my much older peers into helping them with computer facilities, at which I am an undeniable child prodigy. Of course, if the secret services were to be involved in any way, I would immediately hand over this and my other reports. Otherwise I shall retain this material to be submitted as proof of my capabilities when I apply to my final choice of British Intelligence Division.

What concerns me most, and I think will be of interest to the secret services, is how boys A and B, although now not knowingly politicising their actions, could be made to do so. They strike me as exactly the idealistic individuals who could easily be recruited by people who claim to be motivated by good causes, but are in truth only out for money and power... They are both naïve about the world and far too trusting. In other words, boys A and B are ripe for the picking for some form of radicalization.

Leon sat back for a moment and looked at his screen. He needed to explain this part carefully. The word 'patsy' kept coming to mind. Patsy was not the right word. It was a ridiculous word. He must have heard it during one of their terrible family movies. He'd told his father a thousand times that modern fiction consumed through visual mediums was not worth his time...

'Leo, sweetheart, I can't get my smart meter to reset,' said Mrs Grimsby, grandmother to Ellen Hardy, who was in his class.

'It's Leon, not Leo,' said Leon automatically.

He looked up from the screen and clicked the shutdown button with his right little finger.

'Here's my 50p, love.' A remarkably crinkled hand slid the coin towards him across his makeshift booth/desk.

'Mrs Grimsby, you aren't meant to be able to reset your meter,' said Leon.

The old lady winked. 'I know, but Mrs Mason, who lives

three doors down from me, said her nephew did something wonderful to her meter and she hasn't had a bill for months. I reckoned if anyone would know what to do it would be a boy as bright as you.' She gave him a smile that revealed a perfect (too perfect) row of false teeth along her upper jaw and a twisted, crooked set below. With an effort Leon forced his eyes over the teeth to meet hers.

'That would be illegal, Mrs Grimsby,' said Leon. 'I can't do that.'

The wrinkled hand shot out across the desk, recapturing the 50p. 'I'll have my money back then! Don't waste your time,' she said to the man behind her. 'This boy doesn't know anything.'

The man behind stepped forward anyway. 'I'll give you a tenner, if you can tell me how to password protect my WiFi. Can't get my wife to stop playing some ridiculous building game. Supper is never ready when I get in – and it can't be good for her to be that obsessed, can it?'

Leon slowly and carefully told the man how to protect his WiFi. 'I can't guarantee your wife won't be very upset with you,' he said, thinking how he'd feel if he was banned from the internet at home.

'Oh, I'm sure she will be. Cruel to be kind, son. Only way to do it.' With that he pulled a tenner out of his pocket and handed it over. 'Worth double the price,' he said.

Leon thought for a single moment about pocketing the note, but he placed it in his collection jar.

'Leo, love, is it true that your voice assistant can spy on you?' said a very worried-looking mother.

'It's Leon, not Leo,' said Leon. He couldn't quite remember whose mother she was, but he was sure she'd been to his house to have coffee with his mother one weekend.

'Technically, yes,' said Leon.

'Can I stop someone listening?' The lady's face folded into further frowns.

'Do you think anyone is listening?' asked Leon.

'I don't see why they would be interested.'

'Then to be honest, there is probably no point worrying. The government can listen in to phone calls, even take pictures through your home computer, but that's only in the interest of preserving the peace. They're not interested in ordinary people – only criminals and terrorists. So you really have nothing to worry about. It's not like you have a secret superhero identity, is it?' He smiled and reached out a hand for the coin.

'So how do they know who to listen to or watch – watch!' The frowns remained, but the the lady went very white.

'I imagine they target suspicious people,' said Leon. 'Although they will also listen for key words.'

'Like what?'

'Er, murder, gun, poison, drugs – that kind of thing, you know?' said Leon.

'Oh dear God,' said the woman thrusting a two pound coin at him.

'Is there a problem?' said Leon carefully. He peered down anxiously over the desk to see if the woman had a suspicious packet with her.

'I belong to a book group that reads crime novels,' said the woman, one hand clutched to her throat. 'All of those kind of things come up in the stories.'

'There's a big difference between fiction and reality,' said Leon, breathing out. 'The authorities understand that.'

The woman leaned closer to the desk. 'But I write fan fiction! And sometimes I write in bed – and I don't wear a nightie!'

151

'Lady, I'm eleven years old.'

At this point the woman's face turned bright red. 'Here,' she said pulling another note from her purse. 'Pretend I never said anything.' She fled.

Leon put his new payment in the jar. He shook his head and muttered under his breath, 'TMI.'

Banishing the woman from his imagination, and seeing he had no more customers, he went back to his report.

I find it difficult to find the right words to explain. The boys both have the skills to be insurgents at 14 – at least I think they are 14. With training they could be devastatingly effective if picked up by the wrong people. The girl is not as far down the path, but she is interested in art. While I enjoy a good book as much as the next person, it is true that art can have major impact in the propaganda arena. I would suggest that it is worth watching that subject girl does not fall into bad company.

Also, I may have stumbled across a way to gather local intel. However, there is an issue that people may overshare in such an environment... again, I suppose this could be useful as long as operatives were supported to deal with any unsought mental images.

MARTY

Marty had stopped hiding between parked cars. Local people were beginning to give him odd looks. 'Hiding from the wife, mate?' one workman had called out. Fortunately neither of the boys had turned round. Whatever they were carrying was clearly heavy. He had managed to catch a couple of snaps when the street was empty. If the locals thought hiding between cars was odd, he dreaded to think how they would react to a man taking pictures of children surreptitiously. Not that they were really kids. More youths. Yeah, that would sound better in his article. Just the word, youths, suggested bad behaviour. But he needed them to turn round. Pictures of the backs of two teens carrying something did not make a good shot. Marty began to fear that he'd made a mistake blowing off the recycling photo op. He wiped his hand across his forehead. The afternoon sun beat down relentlessly. Sweat dripped into his eyes. He thought about how much he wanted a long cool drink. Maybe he should give up on journalism and become something easier – like a novelist. To make a living out of making up things all day. Those writers had it made!

The kids disappeared around a corner and Marty's heart quickened. This would be it. His nose for a story remained good. Like a bloodhound who had finally scented his prey, Marty bounded down the hill only to see the two boys disappear into a very ordinary-looking house.

Marty swore under his breath. Did he wait and see what happened or go back up the hill to the school? He had nothing but his instinct to show the kids were up to no good and if he didn't get an image as proof, he would not only not be paid for his afternoon but gain a big black mark against his name for missing the photo op.

Within moments of seeing the house he'd known there was no chance of creeping up to the windows to peek in. The gardens at the back had low fences and no bushes to hide in – not that he would be trying that again for a long time. He shuddered, thinking about what the internet, or the police, would make of him hiding in a garden to spy on the two boys.

153

What should he do? The bench under some lime trees decided for him. Marty collapsed onto it in a pile of camera gear and disappointment. 'Last chance saloon,' he muttered to himself. He could only hope that this unpromising lead somehow turned into the story of his life.

JONAS, RORY, LEON

Rory stood on the doorstep looking down at Leon, who had a small suitcase with him. 'I didn't think you were allowed out after dark.'

Leon brushed past him. 'Not dark yet and I've been storing up brownie points. Besides my mum likes you.' He hefted the suitcase. 'I told her it was a sleepover. You'd better tell your mum. I take it Jonas is staying too?'

'Really?' said the single-minded Rory, following him along the corridor. 'I didn't even know she knew me.'

'Apparently our mums are friends,' said Leon, entering Rory's room and throwing himself down on a beanbag. Rory noticed he put the suitcase down more gently beside him. 'Honestly, when you don't keep tabs on your parents they get up to all sorts.'

'Hello,' said Jonas. 'Anyone notice the missing equipment?'

'I thought you'd got it back in?'said Leon.

'We did,' said Rory, offering him a slice of cold pizza.

Leon sniffed at it. 'What are you, a dog?' said Rory. 'It was fresh this afternoon.'

Leon took it. 'Just checking.'

'Why does your mum like me?' asked Rory.

Leon shrugged. 'I dunno? Maybe she likes your eyeshadow?'

'Was she being sarcastic?' said Jonas. 'It seems to run in the family.'

Leon stuck his tongue out at him. 'No, when I said I wanted to go over to yours she said, "That's okay. He's a nice lad." So here I am, ready to be impressed by your hospitality and good manners...'

'Hey,' said Rory. 'We put in a lot of time and effort on it. Or I did.'

'An afternoon,' said Jonas.

'We did costumes,' said Rory.

'I'm in awe,' said Leon. 'Show me what you've got.'

'I'm not playing the sound now,' said Rory. 'The house was empty most of the day, but there's people back now. You'll have to take my word it's eerie.'

Leon pouted. 'Have you at least thought about how we're going to get in and out tonight?'

'Window behind you opens wide enough to let even Jonas out.'

'That's why you want me to stay,' said Jonas.

'Better if we keep us all together,' said Leon. 'Rory having us for a sleepover is the perfect cover and we can vouch for each other too. Call your mum. Say it was an idea that only just came up.'

'I know you don't think anyone is as bright as you,' said Jonas, 'but no one is that dumb.' He got up and went into the hall.

'I guess I should tell my mum too,' said Rory. 'Not sure how'll she take it.'

'Oh, please,' said Leon. 'She'll be delighted you have any friends at all.'

Rory winced. 'Yeah,' he said and went out of the room.

Left alone, Leon opened his suitcase and took out a shoe box. Time for stage one.

MARTY

'You have to believe me,' said Marty.

'I don't have to do anything,' said Sheila Stern (whose real name was Senga Harris), Sunday features editor of the *Edinburgh Tribune*. 'As far as this newspaper is concerned, I'm God and you are a worthless, slimy, garden slug.'

Sheila Stern sat behind a large desk, empty save for her computer, her notepad and a spiky cactus. A striking, rather than attractive, woman in her late thirties, she had heavy eyebrows, broad shoulders and long wavy hair, dyed and so overdone, it looked like a sheet of shiny corrugated iron painted black. No one seemed to have told her the eighties fashions were over, as she wore a bright purple trouser suit with chunky shoulder pads. She frightened Marty so much, he'd walked to and fro past the office entrance six times before he'd mustered the courage to go in. Sometimes, late at night, he thought about selling a story to a specialist UFO magazine editor he knew, on how Stern was actually an alien of the 'living amongst us' type. He'd write it under a pen name, so she probably wouldn't catch him. What stopped him from doing it was the nagging fear that it might be true. He knew this was illogical, but there was something just so damn odd about this woman. He half suspected she could read his mind.

Marty hung his head. With his muddy shoes and his jacket torn by bushes on the failed disability scandal piece, he knew he did not present the best version of himself. 'I've had a bit of a downward turn,' he said. 'Pretty sure things are on the up now.' He straightened his sleeves. 'I am not a slug,' he said in a voice that was weaker than he had intended. Should personnel talk to her about the way she treated staff? Or had she got them all webbed up in her alien hive?

Sheila Stern snorted and slipped an empty vaping pen between her lips. It appeared even God had to abide by someone else's rules. Marty failed to suppress a flicker of a smile. Maybe some of personnel had survived.

'What's so funny, worm?' she said. 'Because, personally, I'm not finding it funny that you missed a photo op with a recycling lorry.' Marty opened his mouth, but Sheila continued. 'And for what? So you could follow some young boys home? Did you lurk in the bushes this time too?'

'I hid between parked cars,' said Marty, who was thinking worm had to be a step up from slug.

'You do realise how this looks, don't you, McLaren?'

'I had genuine cause for all my actions.'

'You look like a perv!' said Sheila, loud enough that heads turned from all across the open plan office. 'A P-E-R-V, McLaren. And for all I know you are.'

Marty felt his face glow with embarrassment. 'I am not a paedophile nor a peeping Tom,' he said, loud enough for his voice to carry, but short of shouting. 'I have been maligned and misrepresented by agents who are attempting to undermine my investigations.'

'Yeah, right,' said Sheila. 'Tell that to the judge.'

'There is no judge!' This time Marty did shout. 'I have not been arrested nor even cautioned by the authorities about ANYTHING. I am INNOCENT, and you, Ms Stern, are wading into the waters of defamation. How many people heard you accuse me of being a person of perversions? Ten? Twenty? Under employment law alone, you are guilty of harassment. You appear to wish to add defamation to the charges I will bring against this paper.'

'You wouldn't dare,' snarled Sheila Stern. Her nose crinkled, her top lip folded up and she displayed uneven nicotine-stained teeth.

'WHAT HAVE I GOT TO LOSE, SHEILA? I'm broke. I owe the landlord and even my own mother won't return my calls.' Marty took several deep breaths. 'I've hit rock bottom. So as I said, the only way now is up.'

Sheila placed the vape pipe in her jacket pocket. 'Calm down, McLaren. Can't you take a joke? You know there's always a bit of banter in this office.'

'No, I don't. You've always made me work from home.'

'Yeah, well, you're a stringer. An independent guy, going where you want, investigating what you want. I bet you've half a dozen editors on a string, you dog, you.'

Marty reflected that Sheila Stern attempting to be friendly was not wholly unlike a great white shark asking you to check and see if it had got something caught between its teeth. He decided to try and tough it out. At least she hadn't morphed into anything. Maybe she was human, after all? 'So, Sheila, what you got for me?'

Behind him he heard the other twenty people in the room inhale in shock. Everything went quiet as everyone held their breath. No one other than the chairman of the media group called Sheila Stern, Sheila. The rumour was that even her husband, a thin, meek and worn down man only ever seen in the back of her car, called her Miss Stern.

Sheila Stern's hand flicked out towards her notepad. She uncurled the pen that had been hiding in her hand and scribbled something across the page. She tore it off and handed it to him. Marty took it with trembling fingers. She was giving him something from the notepad. Sheila only ever did that with things too secret to send by email.

He read it. 'You've got to be kidd…'

'But what if it is?' said Sheila Stern. 'It would be the story of a lifetime – of the century. Get me five hundred words by four o'clock, and I'll hold a space for you in tomorrow's edition in case it happens. Think big, Marty.'

JONAS, RORY & LEON

'Have you got any glue?'

Leon had leaves, twigs and what seemed to Rory to be general muck, spread all over his floor. 'Hey!'

'I've got newspaper underneath,' said Leon. 'How did you think we were going to get the show up there. I'm building a cammo box.'

'You're setting up an ammo box?' said Jonas, coming back into the room. 'I don't think that's a good idea. You don't have a gun do you?'

'Of course not,' said Leon. 'Dad said I had to be fourteen before I could join a shooting club. Do we need one?'

'No,' said Jonas and Rory at the same time.

'I said cammo, as in camouflage.' He sighed as theatrically as Rory could, 'Amateurs! I'm working with amateurs! Glue?'

Rory opened one of the drawers in his desk and pulled out white sticky glue, sticky tape and the glue so strong it can stick you to the table. 'Any good?'

'Excellent,' said Leon. He looked up at their frowning faces. 'Did you think we were going to wander around Arthur's Seat with the projector in our hands? It wouldn't be exactly discreet, would it? And you're meant to be almost grown-ups. Sheesh.'

'I did wonder,' said Jonas kneeling down beside him.

'You want me to leave my dad's camera in a box for anyone to pinch? He'd kill me.'

Leon sat back on his heels. 'Firstly, the idea is the box is well enough camouflaged that no one finds it, and second, I only need the SD card.' He held out his hand.

Rory took the camera out of another drawer and pulled out the SD Card. 'At least you had the sense to keep the camera out of sight,' said Leon, taking it. 'Projector?' He said, rather like a surgeon asking for a scalpel.

'So that's what that is,' said Jonas, passing over the black box from behind him on the floor. 'Rory said he didn't have time to explain.'

'I needed him to check that the slots were compatible,' said Leon. Rory inhaled and raised his eyebrows, but kept his mouth shut. Leon fitted the card in the projector. Then he put it in the box. 'I've got a portable USB charger in here, that should keep us going for a while, and a Bluetooth speaker along with the projector. I'm hoping you didn't try and sync the sound to anything too closely.'

Rory shook his head. 'That's quite clever,' he said.

'Right, now I need to sync one of your phones, so you can turn it on and off from a distance. It's a short throw projector – 500 to 550 lumins – which should do us. Who wants to be the operator?'

'Why not you?' said Jonas.

'I've got something else to do. Right, Rory it is. You look more like the type to spend time on your phone. Jonas can act as lookout. Check if anyone has enough presence of mind to realise you or someone is working the show.'

'I still don't understand,' said Jonas.

Rory handed his phone over. 'Neither do I, mate. We're in the presence of genius.'

'Exactly,' said Leon, his eye focussed on Rory's phone. 'I'm going off to plant the box. I'm smaller and in these dark clothes, less likely to be noticed. You might like to ditch the scarlet jeans, Rory, and not wear that sparkly scarf. It's getting a bit ragged anyway.'

'I still don't...' began Jonas.

'There is nothing wrong with my scarf!'

'Right, I'll make it easy for you. Short sentences. Simple words. Tonight is the first night of the big meteor shower. A lot of people who like watching stars will be out at Arthur's Seat to get a good view. Also the nut jobs from PEAS...'

'Protect the Earth from Aliens Society,' said Rory.

Leon nodded. 'Glad to see you read my piece.'

'It was rather persuasive in a pseudo-science sort of way.'

Leon grinned. 'Well, that's one part of the mission achieved. Anyway, the PEAS guys have got it into their heads that the meteor show is visiting aliens' ships and that NASA is lying to them.'

Jonas groaned. 'People always think NASA is lying to them. It must be such a pain making all those scientific breakthroughs for...'

'Yes, yes,' said Leon, 'poor NASA people. So when the shower starts, you, Rory, set off the box with your phone. How long does it run?'

'About three minutes.'

'Great. Long enough for people to be amazed and then run off to find their friends to tell them. Hopefully we'll get a fairly good crowd passing through. Should set up a bit of whisper tonight and then tomorrow night when we do it again...'

'Whoa!' said Rory. 'We're doing this twice?'

'Makes us more likely to get caught,' said Jonas.

'Not if you do as I say. You, Jonas, will film the show on your iPhone.'

'I don't need to go halfway up a dark hill to do that,' said Jonas. 'We've a copy right here.'

Leon pretended to beat his head off the carpet. 'We need a film like everyone else's. So it looks like someone from the website happened to be there when it happened. Then tomorrow we do a big feature and drive huge amounts of traffic.'

'And then we tell people it's all a hoax?' said Jonas.

'Not quite yet,' said Leon. 'We need a good ending to catch people's attention, not one that simply fizzles out. You know what I mean, don't you, Rory?'

'A finale,' said Rory, 'But what will you be doing?'

'Simple,' said Leon, displaying his biggest grin yet. 'I'll be running through the crowd jogging the arms of anyone sensible enough to catch this on their iPhone. We don't want anyone seeing it too clearly.'

'No, we don't,' said Jonas, paling.

Leon finished packing the box and punched a few holes in the top. 'For sound,' he said. 'Right, I'm going to put this at the end of the Crags, on the right-hand side of the gorge by the old ruin. Lots of long grass and gorse to hide it in, and a cliff face that, if I angle the box right, will bounce the sound off it as well as acting as a screen.'

'You've thought this through,' said Jonas.

Leon shrugged. 'No plan survives contact with the enemy, so be on your toes. Open the window and I'll go set it up. I'll wait up there. Better than going back and forward. We can all meet back here at midnight.' He checked his watch. 'Right, it won't be dark for three hours. Can one of

162

you put up something else on the website, so it doesn't look as if we had prior knowledge.'

Wordlessly, Rory opened the window. Leon hopped out. Crouching, he scuttled away from the house. Rory closed the window again. 'What do you think he'd do if we stayed home and played computer games?'

'We could,' said Jonas. 'I don't like any of this.'

'I was kidding. C'mon, Jonas, where's your sense of adventure?'

'Curled up at home watching TV,' said Jonas. 'Exactly where I want to be.'

But Rory was already sitting at the computer. 'What can I write? Everyone knows the old story about how bumblebees, according to the known laws of physics, shouldn't be able to fly.'

'Really?' said Jonas.

Rory flicked him a glance. 'Science caught up. Mind control stuff is old tin hat. We've done a whole thing about being paranoid that the government listens in to everything.'

'Does it?'

'Must be pretty boring if it does,' said Rory. 'There's GCHQ or something that's a listening outpost, but I can't see it listening to the likes of us. I've been holding back on octopuses are our alien masters, but I can't do that one tonight. C'mon, Jonas! Think of something.'

'Emus are the creation of a government genetic experiment that went wrong?'

'Not the best,' said Rory, 'But I think I can work with that.'

'What time do you call this, young lady?' demanded Hildy, opening the door to Miki.

'Eleven o'clock,' said Miki. 'You did say I could go to the party.'

'If you've come back pregnant, your…'

'Of course not!' said Miki blushing furiously.

'You'd better come in then.'

Miki followed her aunt through to the livingroom. 'I was later last night,' she said.

'Aye,' said her aunt, settling herself down into an armchair by the fire, which was on, despite the heat of the season. 'But that was a crisis. Now you're in my care. I phoned your parents. Fine conversation I had with them. Your father was sure you were round at a neighbours and your mother said you should be allowed to do what you liked.'

'Ha!' said Miki. 'Except go to art school.'

'I asked her about that. She said you'd never mentioned it before.'

'Well, I don't know if I had exactly – I showed them lots of my work – told them about my class…'

'Came at it sideways like a nervous horse, did you?'

Miki nodded. She perched on the edge of one of the sofa's arms, not feeling quite welcome enough to sit down properly. Her aunt picked up her book and settled back in her chair. 'The least you can do is make a body a cup of tea when you keep her up so late.'

'Of course,' said Miki, springing up. 'Did they say I could go to art school?'

Hildy shook her head. 'Dead set against it, the pair of them.'

Miki felt her eyes fill with tears. She sniffed and looked up, blinking. Someone had told her that you couldn't cry when you looked up. 'So that's that then.'

'I take it you enjoyed yourself?' said her aunt.

'I did.'

'Was it all you thought it would be?'

'More,' said Miki, sniffing again. 'Not that it matters. My life is over.'

'Stop being an overdramatic wee ninny,' said her aunt. 'Your life's barely started.'

'I suppose I could try and find something else to do.'

'Oh, for heaven's sake, where's your backbone, lass? If you want this thing then fight for it! We Bartons are descended from the Buchanans. We're a fighting clan. Is it fizzy pop that runs in your veins or a decent Highland malt?'

Miki shook her head violently. 'I did get offered alcohol, but I didn't take a sip, I promise.'

'Lord love you, hen,' said her aunt, sighing. 'You look like a spiky wee thing, but you've the backbone of a jellyfish. Go and get that tea and then we'll see what we can do to get you into art school.'

'You'll help me?' said Miki, surprised.

'Tea,' said Hildy. 'Not without that tea. Now be quick about it.'

BREAKING NEWS

We would like to apologise for personal opinions expressed by one of our reporters this morning. This station does not condone the rumour that an alien invasion is imminent or that there are aliens in government.

Breaking News is brought to you by Radio City Central: the local station you can trust.

SUNDAY 11th JUNE

STOP PRESS: THE EDINBURGH TRIBUNE BRINGS YOU THE STORY OF THE CENTURY. ALIENS SIGHTED. ET HAS COME HOME

MARTY MCLAREN

Very, very early Sunday morning: Edinburgh Tribune Emergency Editorial meeting.

Only one man in the world was prepared for what happened last night. As I stood next to Patrick Loss on that cold, dark hillside, I thought I was wasting my time. I thought Loss was simply another nutjob.

The meteor shower bloomed over our heads as bright and as busy as NASA had predicted. Nature giving us a celestial show. Beautiful, but nothing that hadn't been seen before. Then the noise began. As one, all heads on Arthur's Seat in Edinburgh, turned towards the high-pitched whine, that was followed by three short, sharp explosions.

Then we saw the craft, a strange, triangular space ship like nothing ever seen before. A hatch hissed open and out came a creature in a highly protective suit. It walked a short way from the craft before collapsing

167

to its knees. Then it turned – a mighty hush fell over the great hill – and the alien waved. It clearly and unequivocally signalled to us. It showed not only knowledge of our presence, but clear indication that it wished to communicate. Without thought I felt myself step forward, as if compelled by this alien presence. Ice water flowed through my veins, but I felt no fear, only a desperate desire to know, to meet, to take this alien invitation.

I was not the only one stirred by the sight. Around me voices rose in confusion, some expressing delight, some fear, but all desperate to know the truth.

But then the alien rose to its feet. It appeared suddenly taller, perhaps eight feet in height. It waved once more before making its way back to its space ship – and then in a blink of an eye, and with an ear splitting shriek, it was gone.

There is much we do not know, but one thing this reporter now knows for certain is that we are NOT alone in the universe.

Click here: to see the footage I shot

Click here: to read the interview with Patrick Loss, in which he predicts the aliens will return tonight.

'That,' said Richard Morley the Chief News-Writer, 'must be the worst piece of journalism I have ever read.'

Sheila Stern bit down harder on her vaping pipe. 'He has his own style. It's modern popularism. Modern. Something you wouldn't get, Morley.'

'But is it true?' asked the Editor-in-Chief.

'It's what McLaren thinks he saw,' said Sheila.

'It's a terribly startling headline,' said the new manager

from ads. She licked her scarlet lips. 'I mean that's a good thing.'

'It's poppycock,' said Morley.

'You going to stand by it, Shelia?' asked the Editor-in-Chief.

'Er,' said Sheila. 'I think we should give McLaren the credit. From our Special Correspondent?'

'Guest Correspondent,' corrected the Editor-in-Chief.

'Right,' said Sheila. 'That works.'

'You can't possibly publish this nonsense,' said Morley. 'You'll ruin the credibility of the paper forever. It was bad enough having an online version, but this is no better than…'

'Dickie,' said the Editor-in-Chief, 'We come from a different age. When we were cub reporters, getting so much as the name of someone's dog wrong was a firing offence. Now we have jokers in Number Ten who make up stuff on the spot. Alternative Truth they call it.'

'Fake News,' said the girl from ads.

'We all know it's bollocks,' said Sheila, 'But we print it anyway.'

'We'll sell out with this one,' said the girl from ads, pouting. 'If only I had had some warning I could have done some merchandising. I suppose we could take a frame from McLaren's film and sell that. Do you think we could get the alien to sign it?'

'There is no bloody alien,' said Morley.

'Everyone knows that,' said the Editor-in-Chief. 'But they want to read it anyway. Besides, we can always print a retraction blaming it on the Guest Correspondent. Does he have any known mental health issues, Sheila? We could always do a sympathy-cum-stab-in-the-back job. The public loves those.'

'I've got stuff on him,' said Sheila.

'Good girl,' said the Editor-in-Chief.

'Then we print it?' asked Sheila.

'There was never any bloody doubt we would, was there?' said Morley getting up from the table so quickly his chair crashed to the floor. 'Fake News, by God. Doesn't anyone in this place care about the truth?'

'Oh, I'm sure it's out there,' said the girl from ads.

JONAS, LEON & RORY

'Why don't you boys take your breakfast through to Rory's room,' said his mother loudly. Jonas had lost track of the number of people coming in and out of the kitchen. He recognised Rory's sister from school, but there were two younger kids sitting high on stools at the small breakfast bar. Two older boys also sat the main table, along with Rory's dad, a balding man whose face was covered in stress lines. Rory's mother stood at the cooker making pan after pan of pancakes, sausages and eggs. All of these were in separate pans that she juggled expertly, reaching over every now and then to catch the toast as it pinged out of the toaster. It made him wonder if anyone had ever thought of synchronized breakfast-making as a sport.

The three boys did as they were told. 'How many people live in this house?' asked Leon. 'It's almost as busy as mine.'

'I didn't know you had so many siblings,' said Jonas.

Rory shook his head. He said through a mouthful of sausage, 'I don't. My cousins are staying for a bit. Their dad works abroad a lot and their mum wanted to go too this time. It's only for a month or so.' He sighed. 'We're always having people to stay. Mum came from a really big family and she likes having people around.'

'Your dad looked a bit harassed,' said Leon.

'Yeah, he stresses. You wouldn't think to look at him, but Mum said she fell in love with him because of his long, thick hair.'

'What an odd reason to like someone,' said Leon. 'Must be to do with our simian ancestry. Basic sign of health or some such thing.'

Rory looked at him blankly, but Jonas almost choked and had to be hit hard on the back.

'Hey, boys,' said Rory's dad popping his head round the door. 'I've got to go into today, but I thought you might like to read this. Such rubbish, but it'll give you a laugh.' He threw a newspaper in to them. Jonas neatly fielded it before it hit Leon's plate.

He spread it out on the floor in front of them.

'ALIENS SIGHTED. ET HAS COME HOME' read Rory. 'Oh my God.'

The others joined him to peer at the front page. 'Marty McLaren,' said Jonas. 'He was the knob-end who tried to make a fuss about my mum. Ignorant...' he looked at Leon, 'man,' he finished lamely.

'I am familiar with all kinds of vernacular,' said Leon. Then he broke into a broad grin. 'They really went for it, didn't they? And that was only the dress rehearsal. Think how we can improve it for tonight!'

'Shut up,' hissed Rory. 'This is too big. Thank God there's nothing to tie us to it. Did anyone tell Miki?'

The boys all shook their heads. 'She'd not tell on us,' said Jonas. 'She's not that type.'

'Hmm,' said Rory. 'I think it would depend on how

171

serious it got. If they sent in the army and whoever inspects this kind of thing…'

'The men in black?' said Leon, trying to hide a smile.

'What has the movie got to do with it?' said Rory.

Leon opened his mouth to explain and then shut it again.

'Why didn't we tell Miki?' said Jonas. 'She would have stopped this before it started.'

'She didn't come over. Maybe we should go and see her,' said Rory. 'Get her perspective. I think you're probably right about her. Even thought she wants to study art, she's well – practical, sensible. Not at all like the wild image underneath. She might have ideas about how to dial it back.'

'Is it fair to involve her?' said Jonas.

'As yet no one has made any connection to us,' said Rory. 'They've no proof it was us.'

'Except the box under your bed,' said Leon.

Rory's jaw dropped. 'What?'

'You didn't think I'd leave it up there for the authorities to find, did you?'

'Authorities?' said Jonas faintly.

'Last night there were a few local police and a few reporters crawling over the site,' said Leon. 'But the *Edinburgh Tribune* is hardly a global newspaper. It's not even a national.'

'Yes, of course,' said Rory. 'It'll all be forgotten about by tomorrow.

'Hopefully, it'll get picked up on the internet. We should do a piece on it.'

'No,' said Jonas and Rory.

'Guys, it will look really suspicious if we don't.'said Leon. 'We'd be the only conspiracy website not talking about it.'

172

'It can't have got that popular already,' said Jonas.

'Depends on how convincing Marty's footage is. I think you guys did a grand job. It says there's a link for some video here. Turn on the computer, Rory, and we can take a look.'

The boys sat in silence, their breakfasts growing cold as they stared at the screen. It was extremely shaky and low quality.

'Not bad,' said Leon. 'It looks much like any other UFO film I've ever seen on the web.'

'Yeah, no one can make anything out,' said Rory.

'Exactly,' said Leon.

'You can see me wave,' said Jonas, his voice shaking slightly.

'You can see the alien wave,' said Leon. 'It's damn good work. Damn good. By the end this will be bigger than Roswell. What do you think we can improve on?'

'You're mad if you think I'm going through all that again,' said Rory.

'We'll get caught,' said Jonas. 'No point pushing our luck.'

'Why don't we take a stroll after breakfast,' said Leon. 'I can reassure my parents I'm alive and Jonas can check up on his mum. We can meet back here after lunch to discuss how things stand.'

'Might not be a bad idea to take a breather,' said Jonas. 'A few hours apart might put things into perspective.'

Rory shrugged. 'I'll walk you. This house is too busy anyway. You can take your shoebox with you.'

'I'll get my case,' said Leon meekly.

'You'll never guess who that was, Meg,' said Brian, coming back through to the table.

'Probably not,' said Miki's mother. 'We know a great number of people.'

Brian sat down and began to slowly slice up his cooling vegan sausage. 'No, I mean it was a real blast from the past. B.M.'

'BM?' asked Miki, looking up from her plate, and wishing she'd stayed to have breakfast with Hildy. Hildy had told her about a philosopher who would only eat white foods without a soul, and ended up practically living on beans. 'Very bright man,' she'd said. 'But you can take these things too far. We're apex predators, and I for one, am all for enjoying that – responsibly and ecologically of course.' Over her shoulder as she opened the fridge to put away the butter, Miki had seen packets of bacon and loops of sausages, in their half-open paper packages. 'Local farm,' said her aunt proudly. 'Isn't sustainable unless the population falls dramatically, but for now it's the best I can do.'

This sounded all too like the opening to one of her parent's diatribes on eco-friendly farming. Miki had distracted her aunt by pouring her a whisky, and once she was certain Miki didn't want one herself, they had settled down to discuss an individual's contract with society, and what an individual of conscience should feel able or not able to do once that contract was broken. It had been fascinating stuff, but although she had put up a good argument for collective anarchy, her aunt had invoked Seneca and won. Miki's forfeit was to travel home by the very early bus. Her

174

aunt always said no one put their backs into philosophy discussions now unless something was at risk. Miki had yet to ask what she did with her students.

'Before Michelle,' said her dad. 'From the era when we were young and mobile phones weren't even a twinkle in a robot's eye.'

'From the old days,' said Meg. 'I'm not sure I like the sound of that. Most of the people we've ever left behind we meant to leave behind.' She turned to smile at her daughter. 'Even we were young and foolish once.'

'Still are,' said Brian. 'At least at heart.'

'Don't drag this out, dear. Tell me who it was.' Brian flinched slightly at the endearment. He knew endearments usually preceded scolding. 'John Walters.'

Meg threw herself back in her chair with more than a hint of melodrama. 'John Walters! I haven't heard from him in decades. How did he even find us?'

'I've exchanged a couple of emails with him over the years,' said Brian. 'Nothing serious. He asked me to go to the football World Cup one year.' A wistful expression crossed his face, 'I said no of course. Very frivolous waste of time and money. The wages those footballers get. Disgusting.'

'To be fair,' said Meg, 'there have been studies that looked into the tribalism of football as something that could prevent actual war.'

'Now you tell me,' said Brian.

'Of course, the money footballers are paid undermines the idea that learning and scholarship is of value…'

'Who is John Walters and what did he want?'said Miki.

'We were at college with him,' said her father. 'He'll be in Edinburgh this afternoon. Asked if we could put him up for a few days. I said yes. I hope you don't mind, Meg?'

'Good heavens. It will be interesting to see him,' said Meg. 'I can't imagine what he might look like today.'

'Ugly, lanky chap, like a garden gnome that had been stretched on a rack.'

'He had that terrible beard he thought hid his acne,' said Meg.

'Only seemed to make it worse. Enormous adam's apple too. First time I saw him I thought he was choking on something – like a dead rat.'

'A rat?' asked Miki.

'Freshers Week. He was several years below us. He was getting what the Americans would call "hazed" something terrible. Always had that way about him, John. If anyone wanted to pick on someone they'd always choose John.'

'He did send out unfortunate signals,' said Meg. 'Ironic, considering what he studied.'

Brian barked with laughter. 'I never looked at it like that.'

'He sounds great,' said Miki. 'Why did you guys hang out with him?'

'It was your father's fault. When we came across some of the members of the rugby team setting about him, your father told them where to get off. Even punched one in the jaw, if I remember rightly.'

'Really?' said Miki, her eyes very wide.

'The blonde one ,' said Brian. 'The smallest one. What I remember after that is the three of us running for our lives. Fortunately the others were already half drunk.'

Meg smiled, tilting her head on one side. 'We did become rather good friends after that.'

'You wanted to look after him,' said Brian.

'He was like a lost puppy,' said Meg. 'No harm in him at all. We took him around with us, introduced him to some of our friends. Not that anyone else stuck like we did. He was very thoughtful. If we were taking a punt out he'd always bring a picnic. He got me tickets to my favourite band for my birthday. He remembered those kind of things.'

'Mu-um, were you sweet on him?' said Miki.

Meg laughed. 'Not at all. He was more like a little brother, and of course he idolised your father after he rescued him.

Brian shrugged.

'We stayed in touch for a while, but he stayed on to do a PhD. What was it in?' asked Meg.

'I don't know,' said Brian. He grinned. 'I remember he said once he thought he was being checked out by MI5, but I can't imagine he'd be any use as a spook.'

'He was – probably still is – an astrophysicist. His PhD was in an algorithm to find hidden planets or something?'

'Ah yes, capturing digital steganography,' said Brian wisely.

'You don't know what that means, do you?' said Meg.

Brian shook his head. 'Nope, but I'm pretty sure those words were in the title.'

'I remember,' said Meg excitedly, 'he was into UFOs, wasn't he?'

'He liked looking at the stars,' said Brian.

'He'll be here to see the meteor shower and see if that alien turns up again.' She laughed. 'Poor John, always so gullible.'

'What alien?' said Miki. The hair on her arms stood upright, her stomach heaved and after what had been an unusually pleasant breakfast with her parents (apart from the actual food), she had a feeling something terrible was about to happen.

177

'Oh, it's so funny,' said Meg. 'Do you still have a copy of the local rag? Your father saw it when he went out to get sausages this morning. He knew I'd want to read it. We'll recycle the paper, of course, but honestly, the power of mass hallucination among those corrupted by social media is not to be scoffed at. We should go up tonight. Take John on a little adventure…'

Her mother continued speaking, but Miki's attention was completely focussed on the newspaper piece and the low quality image that went with it.

LEON

Leon sat in front of his computer and smirked quietly to himself. His mother had been so delighted he had spent a night at a friends and that nothing untoward had happened, that she had agreed he could go out with his friends later to Arthur's Seat.

He logged on to the website and wrote a short piece.

Are they finally here? Have aliens finally contacted humanity? Out of all the world have they chosen a small Scottish city to be their first point of contact?

I agree it doesn't seem likely, but look here. Marty McMucky (Leon laughed so hard at this joke he had to stuff his fist in his mouth to stop his family hearing) has shot some distinctly grainy footage.

(Here he inserted a link to the *Edinburgh Tribune*'s website and also sneakily linked his website to theirs.)

So, folks, what do you think? Are we no longer alone? Is the truth no longer out there, but right here in a parochial Scottish field? Certainly, a load of folks are heading up to Arthur's Seat in Edinburgh tonight to see the second night of the meteor shower and whether or not our alien friends will return. So jump on a bus, catch a flight and head over to Bonnie Scotland. This really may be where it all starts. The end of an era and opening up the universe awaits. Or is this nothing more than a silly trick? You decide. Know that we will have eyes on the ground among the crowd, so if ET decides to do a meet and greet, we will be there.

He felt a little bad about mocking Scotland, but he hoped this way no one would even consider it was written by an actual Scot.

JONAS

Less than half way home, the first mobile satellite TV van passed Jonas. It quickly became clear he was going against the current. People were streaming in the direction of Arthur's Seat. It wasn't even lunch time, but many of them were carrying tents and placards. The placards ranged from 'Welcome Back ET' to 'Go Home Aliens' and a few giant 'PEAS' ones. The latter Jonas thought were particularly stupid. How on earth would aliens know what PEAS was? But then he saw two middle-aged men in suits carrying a sign between them that read, 'DO NOT BE FOOLED BY GOVT TRICKS'. Was that for the aliens or the people? he wondered. Jonas hadn't had to use his asthma inhaler for years, but he could feel himself becoming breathless. Could all this be down to him, Leo and Rory? Suddenly he felt very young. He felt an intense desire to confess. To hand over the whole problem to a responsible adult.

Unfortunately, he didn't know one. There was no way he was going to worry his mother about this. How the hell had Leo talked him into getting involved with all this? What on earth was the best way to shut all this down?

RORY

Rory walked halfway to Jonas' house before, overcome by the crowds, he had turned back for home. He'd registered how amazed and appalled Jonas was. Thoughts buzzed in his head. He needed to write them down. He remembered then for the first time in a week that he had yet to find his diary. He could vaguely remember how it had felt like the end of the world when he lost it. But no one had used it against him. No one had shared it on the internet. No one at school had eyed him askance, giggling. Overall, all the kids who had tormented him appeared to have moved on. Either that or he had stopped noticing them. In a moment of sudden clarity, he realised he didn't care if anyone posted his diary online. Yeah, it might be embarrassing, but he knew now what he would do if they did. He'd wear the very best dress he had into school the next day.

After his chat with Mr Deacon a weight had lifted off his chest. The world had become his very own glitter-filled oyster. He'd even found friends, real ones, not just people on the internet, who he would probably never meet – and then this. If he got caught and his diary came out there would be all too much media attention sent his way. He was aware how the press could twist things. His schoolmates knowing was one thing, a sleazy newspaper getting hold of it was another.

He turned up the path to the swing park on the edge of

the park. Delighted to find he had the place to himself, he swung idly on the swing set. It creaked and groaned. The paint was flaking off the supporting poles, but Rory saw none of this. He had played here when he was much younger, when he hadn't known how different he was from the other kids. Or at least they hadn't realised he was different. He knew deep down that he hadn't gone through any personal revelations. He had always been who he was.

What's the worst that can happen? he thought. Total exposure. He took a deep breath and considered what that would mean.

To his surprise, he realised that he felt more excited than afraid. He thought it through further. He didn't want them to get caught. There would be all kinds of trouble; especially for the others. But they hadn't done anything illegal that he could think of. No one had been hurt. That reporter might end up looking a fool, but he deserved that after the way he had treated Jonas' mother.

He swung back and forth. Eventually he came to a decision.

JONAS, RORY & LEON

'Deja vu,' said Rory, opening the door and looking down on Leon's suitcase. 'You're not thinking of staying over again, are you?'

Leon grinned and came in with a half skip/half hop. 'No, it's a school night. But I thought you might be okay with me leaving this here overnight. It'll be empty.'

Rory shrugged. 'Sure, you can leave it under my bed. You're looking very upbeat. How worrying. What have you done now?'

'Aha,' said Leon. 'You'll approve. Tonight's performance is going to be more razzle-dazzle.'

'I might, but Jonas won't. He's already here and he's talking of phoning the police.'

'To hand himself in?' said Leon. 'I thought you were the drama queen.'

Rory pretended to cuff him on the ear. 'Cheeky. I managed to talk him out of it, because as far as I'm aware we haven't committed any crime.'

'Hmm,' said Leon, cutting ahead of him. 'I guess it depends how you look at it.'

'What do you mean?' asked Rory. He closed the bedroom door behind him.

Leon put down his suitcase carefully. 'Well, there's been a number of police roaming around the park, so I suppose at a stretch they could accuse us of wasting police time.' He threw himself down on a beanbag. 'But then we didn't ask anyone to investigate. Your clever little movie didn't even suggest there was any kind of threat.'

'There are loads of police up there now,' said Jonas.

'But that's for crowd control,' said Leon. 'We didn't ask people to come and we could always argue they were only going to see the meteor shower.'

'Yes,' said Jonas. 'All those placards saying welcome ET... Oh, that's nothing to do with it.'

'Now, be fair,' said Rory. 'If that's anyone's fault it's Marty McLaren's.'

'What if we get caught?' said Jonas. 'What about what will happen to us?'

'What if we don't?' said Leon. 'Even if anyone figures out that it's a prank, it will go down as one of the best tricks in living history. And one done by a few kids. We'll be famous!'

182

'I don't want to be famous,' moaned Jonas.

'What's the razzle-dazzle?' said Rory.

'Ah, I was wondering when you'd ask,' said Leon and reached for his suitcase.

MIKI, BRIAN, MEG & JOHN

Miki wouldn't have been human if she hadn't felt her thunder had been stolen. After unexpectedly agreeing that she could go to Art School at breakfast, her mother had dropped the subject entirely, instead devoting herself to readying the house for the arrival of this John Walters. They'd barely had a mouthful of sandwich for lunch, her mother was too busy cooking. In itself this was a minor miracle for a woman who refused to do anything resembling housework on feminist grounds. But the smells coming from the kitchen were amazing. Her father had sped around the house tidying everything away and dusting with a ferocity that had the dog hiding and whining under the sofa.

All the time they had been exchanging reminiscences – 'Do you remember that time he fell out of the punt?' and 'do you think he will still have such bad skin?' and 'do you remember that time you got a tick in your leg and he got it out with a cigarette. That was clever' and 'did he ever finish his PhD?' And 'did he say what he's doing now?' And 'Remember how he always wanted a dog? He's not bringing one with him, is he? Red will have to go outside' and 'is he married?' And 'he didn't have a girlfriend at uni do you think he's…?' And 'I never did learn where he got his posters from.' And 'do you remember the time you and he humped stolen traffic lights over my college wall? We were mad. We could have all been sent down for that.' And so it went on. One or twice her mother turned to Miki to explain, but always ended up saying, 'You had to be there.' In the end Miki got out her sketch pad and curled up on the sofa.

'That's the doorbell,' called Meg from the kitchen. 'I hope he hasn't turned carnivore.'

'You've cooked vegan,' said Brian leaping up to answer it. 'No one will turn that down.'

'He could be fruitarian,' said Meg.

'No one's that daft,' said Brian opening the front door.

'Did you put the lavender in his room?' called Meg.

'Well, did you, Brian?' said a pleasant male voice.

'John, my man, good to see you! You look… you look… well. Come in. Come in.' Miki couldn't remember when she had last heard her father so flustered. She heard the door shut and the two men continued to talk as they came in.'

'I'm sorry to impose.'

'Really, it's nothing. Delighted to have you. Quite a blast from the past. We always meant to keep in better touch, but what with having a family and all that. Life sweeps by.' Brian laughed falsely. 'What about your family? Still at Oxford?'

'No, and consulting only now.'

'So, practically retired? At your age!' Brian laughed again. 'Meg? Meg? Where are you? Come out and meet John. You won't…' He stopped himself.

'Something smells lovely,' said John.

Miki finally saw what all the fuss was about. John Walters, tall, dressed in a dark, well cut suit, with neat dark hair and clean shaven, held out a hand to her over the sofa.

184

'I take it you're Miki? You look very like your mother did when she was seventeen.' He grinned showing excellent teeth. 'You're doubtless fed up of hearing that.'

Miki took his hand. 'No,' she said.

He raised an eyebrow and she felt a little heat come into her face. 'No, I'm not fed up because no one has ever said that.'

'Oh, your mother was quite the beauty when she was younger. Probably still is. That's not a bad sketch of Brian. You have talent. Going to art school?'

Miki nodded.

'Good choice. We need more artists in this weary world.'

'John!' Meg came into the lounge, a tea cloth over her arm and her hair slightly frizzy from the steam. Her astonishment was obvious in her wide eyes and slightly dropped jaw, and the way she stopped as if struck by lightning in the doorway. She recovered herself quickly. She came up to John and gave him a quick kiss on either cheek which he returned. 'You look very different,' she said.

'Sadly, we all grow older,' said John. 'Not so much like your little brother now, huh?'

'No,' said Meg. 'Most definitely not.'

Brian interceded. 'I'll show you your room. Meg needs to get back to the kitchen.'

'I never expected anyone to ever say that of you, Meg,' said John, smiling at her.

Miki's mother stood there staring. Then she shook her head. 'Oh, I hardly ever cook, but if someone wants something…'

'Done properly, one does it oneself,' finished John. 'I'm sure Brian is an excellent cook. But I must get to my room.

The suspense of whether or not Brian put lavender in there is becoming too much for me.'

'Of course. Of course. Come this way.'

'I take it he's improved with age,' Miki said to her mother, when the men had left. 'Doesn't look like he has acne now.'

'Oh, you know, as John said, we're all older.' Meg went out, tucking a stray curl back in place. Miki couldn't remember the last time her mother had bothered about her hair. She did it in the morning and then it lived on her head for the rest of the day, ending up however it wanted by the evening.

Miki followed her mother into the kitchen. 'Mother, did you like John when you were at Oxford?'

'Of course I liked him,' said her mother, bending over the stove and stirring something. 'Come and taste this and see if it needs more salt.'

Miki obediently tasted it. 'That's really good. No, I mean *like* like?'

'Are you sure it doesn't need a touch more or is it too much already?'

'It's fine. Mum, were you in love with John?'

Meg stopped and turned to face her daughter. 'No, I was not. We were close. We talked and argued about all sorts of things. I valued him deeply as a friend.'

'Over-explain much?'

'He was gawky and spotty.'

'Ah,' said Miki. 'You didn't fancy him. He looks a bit different now. Should I worry?'

'Now, don't you go getting a crush on him.'

'Hah!' said Miki. 'As if! He's an old man. Must be almost as old as you.' She wisely escaped to the lounge

186

before her mother could answer.

She found John sitting alone on the sofa, flipping through her sketch book, Red curled around his feet. 'I hope you don't mind. I couldn't resist.'

Miki minded rather a lot, but she shook her head politely.

'Come and tell me who these people are,' said John. 'I'd guess this one has a flair for the dramatic.'

Miki came over and sat down near enough to see, but not near enough to be actually next to him. 'That's Rory,' she said. 'He's desperate to play Peaseblossom in the school play.'

'Is he any good?'

'I don't know,' said Miki. 'I've never been into drama. I think he auditioned and he's involved. They tend to give the leads to the kids who are about to leave.'

'That seems fair,' said John. 'But if I remember my English Lit well enough, and there is no guarantee, I was a science major,' he smiled at her, 'Peasblossom is a small part.'

'Yeah, but it's the understudy for one of the female leads.'

John shook his head. 'And that matters? How ironic. Shakespeare wrote all his plays with the intention that men would play his female characters. Female players were forbidden by law at the time. Elizabeth I, wasn't it?'

'I wouldn't know,' said Miki. 'I'm not that kind of an arts person.'

'Oh, I wouldn't let your predilection for creating visual art prevent you from casting your net wider, as it were. Good art is a reflection of all aspects of life. You have to live life widely and fully if you ever want to be a great artist.'

'Great artist?' said Miki.

'I'm not a good enough judge to say more than you have talent, but I've always felt that the art I have truly enjoyed or has stuck with me during life, has been painted by people whose personality appears on the canvas. People who think loudly in paint, if you will.'

'I hadn't thought of it like that.'

'As your parents' daughter I have no doubt you will think loudly. It's whether or not your thoughts are worth hearing.'

'I'm not sure if you're complimenting me or insulting me,' said Miki.

'Neither. I have a bad habit of saying what I think. Some people find it refreshing.' He pulled a face. 'Others find it annoying. Who is this?'

The sketch was of Jonas. She'd caught him sitting at a window, staring out. 'He looks sad. Sad and thoughtful,' said John.

'Jonas. His mother is ill. He's her carer. He's a nice guy. Sensible, but okay.'

John laughed at that. 'And this is a young terror?'

'Leon.'

'What's he doing? You've made him look like a tiny mad scientist.'

'He's a bit of a computer whizz. He's younger than the rest of us. He got shunted up years 'cos he's smart. He's a funny kid. One minute it's like talking to a grown-up, the next you feel like you're babysitting and should be sending him to bed.'

'Child prodigies are always difficult – for others and themselves. So are you in class together?'

'I'm in some classes with Rory and Jonas, but not Leon

and not either of the others at the same time,' Miki said. 'Sorry, that's confusing. I mean we don't know each other from a class.'

'So how do you know each other?'

Miki told him about the morning someone had thrown paint over the dog. John reached down and fondled the dog's ears. 'Some people are not very nice. I've found that people who are unkind to animals are usually not worth knowing. The question has to be did they happen to have the paint to hand or was it planned? Do you know why it was done?'

Without meaning to, Miki started telling John about the fights at school, about Marty McLaren and the prejudice against Rory. John listened intently. Nodding and saying short encouraging phrases. Miki stopped herself short of telling him about the website and their fake news plan.

'It sounds like you have all been very supportive of each other,' said John. 'The boy whose nose you broke would seem to be a good candidate for throwing the paint on Red. Maybe you could check out if there are signs of redecoration at his house, if you have the time? Might help solve the mystery.' He paused and smiled, 'How did Leon join your little tribe?'

'He listened in at a window,' said Miki, laughing. 'Very Leon. One minute we were chatting away and the next, Jonas, I think it was, noticed the microphone on the window.'

'Don't tell me he blackmailed you with what he heard?' said John, laughing. 'He looks mischievous in your sketches, but not malign.'

'No, of course not. He came up with the whole idea…' Miki stopped and blushed scarlet. At that moment her father appeared from upstairs. 'I found it,' he said, brandishing an album, 'the story of our youth!'

'Is it safe to have that around your daughter?' asked John, looking away from Miki's embarrassment. 'We were a wild lot.'

Her father came into the room. 'He's kidding,' said Brian. 'The only time I was ever wild was when I punched that one guy out!'

'Not quite out,' said John. 'We had to run a good mile to lose him.' He reached out and touched her father on the arm. 'But I was very grateful.' He turned back to Miki, seeming not to notice her blush, 'Your parents guided my footsteps through my university years. I went up to Oxford young and I was not prepared for the world I entered. Your mother and father were my defenders.'

'It felt like we were your parents at times,' said Meg, coming back through.

'Dry run for this charming young lady, no doubt,' said John.

'Food is ready if you'd like to come through,' said Meg.

John made various protests about how they shouldn't have gone to any trouble, and greeted Brian's idea of looking through the album over dinner with enthusiasm. He praised Miki. He praised Red, who followed at his heels, gazing up with adoring brown eyes. Brian and Meg relaxed. Meg even suggested Brian opened a bottle of wine. Miki couldn't recall the last time she'd seen them so talkative without arguing. The three adults were clearly enjoying their reunion.

Miki played with the food on her plate and ate very little. She excused herself early, saying she was tired after her Glasgow trip. Her parents barely noticed her go, but John smiled and said, 'You'll come with us later, though?'

'Where?'

'Why, to go and see the alien, of course.'

Meg and Brian laughed.

'He means the meteors. We thought we'd all go up tonight and see what the fuss is about,' said Meg.

'If there's an alien there I'll eat my hat,' said her father.

'What do you think, Miki?' said John. 'Has ET come to visit?'

'I'm afraid I haven't seen that movie,' said Miki. 'I'm too young.'

'Oh you should. It's a classic,' said her father and with that he turned back to talk to John. Miki left the room, and for once Red didn't follow her. 'Traitor,' she whispered to the dog.

In her room, Miki texted Rory, Jonas and Leon.

MIKI> Guys, I no L told us not 2 text. Strange guy here, old friend of my parents. Asking questions. I think I just got played. We should meet. What's up with this alien?

LEON

MIKI> Outside yours in 10.

LEON & MIKI

Leon stood in the shadows beyond the street light. 'What's up?'

Miki started. 'I didn't see you there.'

'Over here,' said Leon. 'Out of the light. I don't want

anyone turning me in to my parents.' He gave an impish grin. 'I even have Xbox privileges restored during the week. I'm the man!'

'This is serious. There's an old friend of my parents here and I think he knows about our website.'

'Did you tell him?'

'No, of course not. My parents have finally agreed to let me go to art school. I don't want some kind of criminal charge on my head, preventing me from going. God, why did we ever listen to you?'

'More the other way round,' said Leon, still smiling. 'I only helped you formulate your ideas.'

'You're not taking this seriously, Leo. You're too young to understand. This could wreck my life.'

'Do you realise you are literally wringing your hands and pacing?' said Leon. 'I've never seen someone do that before. It's very attention-attracting. And how many times do I have to tell you? My name is Leon.'

'I'm upset, you silly child.'

'I'll own to the noun but not the adverb. We haven't done anything criminal. There's no defamation on our website. If anything, you could add it to your art school application as an art project to bolster it. As my father frequently points out, almost anything can be described as art today. I particularly like the idea of "found art". Saves me wasting time on pointless homework.'

Miki stopped pacing. She frowned heavily. 'I suppose that is just possible…'

'I wouldn't frown like that. You'll look like a origami paper fan before you're forty.'

'You cheeky…'

'Look at it from my perspective. I'm heavily involved

192

in this and I have a lot of ambition crammed into this tiny frame. Do you honestly think that I would do something to jeopardise my brilliant future?'

'I think you may be too young to understand what you've got yourself into,' said Miki.

'We haven't hurt anyone,' repeated Leon. 'Why on earth do you think your parents' friend has, as you rather dramatically phrased it, made you?'

'God, sometimes talking to you feels worse than being up in front of Mr Murray. How do you do that? You're only eleven!'

'So people tell me, but I do have a curfew, so if you could explain your panicked text?'

'I think he's a spy.'

'Really?' said Leon, his voice rising in pitch slightly. He consciously lowered it. 'Why do you think that?'

'It's something my parents said. But they also said he's an astrophysicist.' She shook her head. 'It seems ridiculous now I've said it out loud. This whole alien thing has spooked me.'

'No pun intended?' said Leon grinning.

Miki carried on as if he hadn't spoken. 'It's the kind of daft thing I can imagine you talking Rory into doing. Jonas is too sensible.'

Leon nodded. 'He's really sensible. Being his mum's carer makes him worry about things more than a normal kid. What he really needed was to blow off some steam.'

'Thank you Mr Pop Psychologist. But yeah, he'd never let himself get mixed up in this. It's a whole new level of pranking.'

'How do you mean?'

'I mean all the police resources and stuff they've had to bring in.'

'And your spook,' said Leon.

'Hopefully everyone will forget about our website.'

'I doubt it. There's been a ton of hits over aliens on it. It would make sense that GCHQ might send someone up to investigate. Have you told him our names?'

'He picked up my sketch book and asked who you all were and how we knew each other if we weren't in the same class. I ended up telling him all about us – not the website obviously, but before I'd realised…' she trailed off.

'Yeah, sounds like he got in your head. Clever guy. I bet you didn't even realise how much you'd told him until afterwards?'

'No, but Mum and Dad knew him at college and they're…'

'Oddballs,' said Leon. 'Not seditious oddballs, but oddballs.'

'Who mentioned anything about anyone being seditious – that means traitorous, doesn't it? Don't they lock you up in the tower for that?'

'And chop off your head? No, things are much more discreet nowadays.'

'What do you mean?' said Miki, her voice rising in panic.

'Keep it down,' said Leon. 'I said your parents aren't seditious. Now unless this guy claimed to work in Cheltenham I seriously doubt we have anything to worry about.'

'He did,' whispered Miki.

It was only with the greatest of self control that Leon stopped himself from punching the air and crying out in delight.

'Nah, Miki, I was only kidding. It's all fine. Nothing to worry about unless you believe the alien invasion is real.'

'Of course not,' said Miki with less than total conviction in her voice.

Leon laughed. 'I have to go. Please don't worry, Miki. We can meet up tomorrow, all of us, and have a catch up. The others will tell you there's nothing to be concerned about too. It's all chill.' He gave her a cheery little wave and ran off into the night.

MIKI, JOHN, BRIAN & MEG

Under a bright moon crowds filled Arthur's Seat. All that stopped them flooding the entire park were the bright yellow tape and patrolling policemen. An ambulance was parked up under the trees and several police vehicles lurked on the edge of the shadows behind it.

'Want a nip?' said Brian, offering his hip flask to John.

'Ignore him,' said Meg. 'He's regressed to being a student at a gig again.' She shivered. 'I didn't realise quite how cold it would be. Are you warm enough, Miki?'

Miki jumped at her name and backed into John. 'Woah,' said John. 'Guilty conscience, Miki?' He smiled to show he didn't mean anything unkind.

Or to make everyone else think he doesn't mean it, thought Miki.

'No, I'm not used to Mum worrying about my temperature. I'm normally left to be more independent,' said Miki. As the words left her mouth she realised how snappy she sounded. 'Not that that's a bad thing.'

'They've certainly gone to town,' said Brian, attempting to cut the tension. 'All we're missing is a fire engine.'

'There has to be an ambulance present when a crowd goes over a certain number. In fact, in the usual way of things you'd need a formal permit with a gathering of this size. Provision for sanitary facilities etc,' said Meg. 'I've been looking into it for when we run our festival.'

'Festival?' squeaked Miki.

'There's a chippy truck,' said Brian. 'Does that count? He must be doing a roaring trade.'

'In a Royal Park,' said John. 'I wouldn't want to be in his shoes if the police decide to crack down.'

'Why, is it treason?' said Meg with a smile.

'I believe you can only be hanged for arson in her Majesty's dockyards or for stealing sheep in Scotland,' said John.

'You seem to know a lot about it,' said Miki. John looked down at her and raised an eyebrow. 'Crowds and rules and stuff,' she added, her voice trailing away.

'Oh, that's from our student days,' said Meg. 'We used to organise gatherings and parades. John always helped out. Even when he didn't exactly agree with us. Perhaps you might be able to give me a hand with planning this new eco-festival.'

'I didn't necessarily disagree with your principles,' said John. 'More your methods. Besides, if I hadn't been there who would have kept you out of trouble? As for your festival, we'll have to see. I have a lot of telemetry waiting for me back at work right now.'

Brian stiffened and pointed at the trees. 'Hey, what's that?'

THE ALIEN INVASION

Miki looked under his arm and saw a light rising through the trees. The last leaves and bare branches fractured the light into long, thin shafts that fanned out across the night. 'Wow, it looks just like a movie,' said Miki.

'Doesn't it?' said John drily.

'Goodness, is this going to be a sound and light show?' said Meg. 'Has it all been a set up for a concert?'

'No one's selling tickets,' said Brian, shaking his head.

'Do you think it's actually an alien, Dad?' asked Miki.

'No, no,' said Brian, sounding more unconvinced at every word. 'But just in case we get split up we should arrange to meet back at the house.'

'Where else would we go?' said Meg. 'Anyway, it's clearly a prank. Don't you think, John?'

'Although it is often said that life imitates art,' said John softly. 'I have yet to experience reality so closely resembling a movie. What do you think, Miki?'

Around them murmurs and cries sounded. Phones flashed as people tried to take pictures of the light.

Then the light moved. It dashed along the treeline and swooped to the base of one tree. Then Miki saw a line of lights heading towards it. 'Police,' said John quietly. 'They need to catch whoever is doing this before the crowd gets difficult.'

'You think that could happen?' she asked.

John shrugged. 'Mob mentality is a misnomer. A mob has little sense. Last thing needed is for someone to panic.'

'But no one would believe this is an alien invasion, would they?'

'People believe what they read in the Daily Excrement,'

said Brian, breaking in. 'Most of that is clearly nonsense to an educated mind.'

'It's what I've always said,' said Meg. 'Education is the foundation of a decent civilisation and firm democracy.'

'But you don't like me going to school!' said Miki.

'I don't approve of the canon of knowledge currently proposed by the minister of education,' said Meg. 'If they taught what should be taught, it would be an entirely different matter.'

'Wow,' said Miki, 'Mind blown! Pow!' She made a gesture with her hands to show her head exploding. Everyone ignored her.

'You know,' said Brian, 'if this is an alien invasion, it would be ironic. Sardonic? If your last argument was about schooling. I mean here we are, all about to get blown apart by lasers streaming from metal tripods and...'

'War of the Worlds,' said John, looking down at Miki. 'Don't worry. If it was an alien invasion we'd know about it long before it appeared in a small Edinburgh park.'

'Not if they came through a portal, a rift in time or another dimension,' said Brian.

'I think you're frightening your daughter,' said John.

'I'm not scared,' said Miki.

'Sorry, Miki,' said Brian. 'Just getting a bit carried away. It's all a bit silly. We'll see whoever it is brought down here by the police in a minute, you'll see.'

'I'm not scared,' repeated Miki.

'You look worried to me,' said John.

'It must be the light,' said Miki. 'Doesn't it get harder to see in the dark as you get older?'

'Miki,' gasped her mother, 'Apologise at once.'

But John only chuckled. 'Look,' he said. 'Our light is running away.'

The orb of light that had been nestling at the bottom of the trees suddenly shot up, illuminating five silhouettes one of whom toppled backwards as the light bolted over their heads. Then the light simply vanished, but not before they heard the scream. The next moment two figures, one male, one female, and both pulling on clothing, appeared as silhouettes racing from the trees.

'Oh goodness,' said Meg, 'I hope whoever that is doesn't tumble down the hill. Now that light is gone I can't see a thing up there.'

'I think that was their idea,' said John. 'Obviously, they don't read the papers.'

But hardly had Meg spoken, when their eyes grew accustomed enough to the dark to see several torchlights bobbing around.

'We'll have to wait and see if they call the ambulance up,' said John.

'It'd never get up there,' said Brian.

'Either way, they'd take a stretcher up or the ambulance would move nearer up the road,' said John. 'We'll soon know if there is an injury.'

They waited. Miki felt herself trembling. 'Where do you think the alien went?' asked Brian. 'Gone to find a telephone box?'

Everyone ignored him.

Miki could no longer feel her toes. She rocked on her heels, trying to bring the circulation back into her feet. She felt on edge. John was right. It had looked too like an alien movie. She glanced over at the ambulance. There was no sign of movement. At least it seemed no one had been hurt.

Then like a wave, a sound rippled through the crowd as one by one they all turned to face the new spectacle.

Over by the rockface an alien ship had landed.

'Oh my God,' said Brian. 'It's real. It's bloody real! Meg, it's real. There are aliens.' He bounced with enthusiasm. Meg stood very still, but gestured to Miki to come closer. Only John appeared unruffled.

Brian saw the triangular shape of a giant spaceship. He blinked rapidly to get it to come into focus, but without success. He rubbed his eyes. 'Dammit,' he muttered. 'I must need glasses.' He screwed his eye up, and managed to make out a body emerging from the craft. A creature! He had never seen anything like it. It staggered forward. 'Lighter planet. Not used to our gravity,' he whispered to his family. 'Thank God it's bipedal,' he continued as the creature reared onto its hind legs. 'We're probably from the same seeds, sown billions of years ago across the galaxy. We'll be able to relate.'

'To think Central Casting were right,' said John softly. 'Aliens do look a lot like us.'

'I know,' said Brian turning to him. 'That series on TV when we were kids had me terrified that aliens would be giant insects, or man-eating crystal formations. This is such a relief.' John looked down at him, but his expression was unreadable in the dark.

All around them the crowd had fallen silent. Miki imagined them all holding their breath. 'Oh God,' she breathed. Brian put his hand on her shoulder. 'It'll be alright, honey,' he said. 'Intelligent life, no matter where it's from, always comes in peace.'

Brian watched as the alien lumbered across the side of the hill, paused to survey the waiting crowd and then, when it appeared to have seen enough, it meandered ponderously back to its craft, climbed, with some difficulty inside, and then simply vanished.

A roar went up as the crowd released its collective fears, excitement and relief.

However, Miki had seen something entirely different. She recognised the large patch of green glitter that Rory once told her he had spilt on his duvet cover when attempting an experiment to brighten up his school shirt. As she tried to get a sense of scale, she had realised that the figure couldn't be Rory. He was too tall to swamp himself entirely in the duvet. But it looked larger than Leon. That only left Jonas. She'd thought better of him. She had to admit that with whatever equipment they had used they'd done a good job. The image had been deliberately blurred enough that people would see what they wanted to see. The use of flying lights beforehand had been a touch of genius. That and articles in the news and on the bloody website had set up the situation beautifully. Honestly, when they got out of juvenile jail they could apply to one of those TV talent shows. Although it beat her how anyone hadn't seen the alien's pointy head for the pizza box it was. The logo was plastered all over the shop front in the High Street for heaven's sake. She ground her teeth.

'Anything wrong?' asked John.

'Anything wrong? Anything wrong?' said Brian. 'We've witnessed the event of a lifetime – of the millennium! Of, of, forever!'

'We'll see,' said John. 'I don't think Miki is as convinced as you.'

'Oh, she's always so cynical,' said Brian. 'The young! Let's go home and celebrate!'

Miki took a few paces back, while her father prattled away happily. Her fingers flew over her phone's keys as she sent a pithily-worded text.

BREAKING NEWS

Due to the laxity of our sub editors, it appears some listeners believed we believe there are aliens in government. While we agree the Westminster Government sometimes seems a long way from Scotland, and consists of a majority of people that do not seem to understand our grievances, we have neither proof nor suspicion that any Westminster MPs are aliens. It was merely a case of bad grammar.

BREAKING NEWS

It seems we have a most unusual candidate standing in the elections. Ms Felicity Bell has assured social media followers that all she will be doing is showing cat pictures and videos. Her press statement says, 'Everyone is so fed up with politics, but everyone likes cats. We need a more feline attitude to life. Time to lay back in the sun, rest and think, rather than giving a knee jerk response to every situation. Have you ever seen a stressed cat? I don't think so.' And it appears a great many people agree with her. Ms Bell's candidate deposit was crowdfunded within four hours.

MONDAY 12th JUNE

BREAKING NEWS

There has been an alien sighting in Edinburgh. A government spokesman said all steps to secure the area were being taken. He added, 'There is no reason for public panic.' Is this it, folks? Is ET finally here?

THE BARTON HOUSEHOLD

'Don't panic,' said Brian as the four of them sat around the breakfast table the next morning. 'How is telling people not to panic helpful? I've been awake all night. I'm going up to the site. We deserve to know.' He stuffed half a crumpet in his face and then pointed at it. 'Hrmpf merklay,' he said.

'I don't care what you say, you are no more going up there this morning than I would let you go again last night,' said Meg. 'If there is an alien on the loose, who knows what intergalactic diseases it might have brought with it. Which reminds me, Miki. Don't let the dog off the lead when you walk him today.'

'You think the aliens might be dognappers?' said Miki in disbelief. 'I must still be asleep. This is a nightmare.'

John calmly poured himself a cup of black coffee. Apart

from a slice of toast, this was all he had touched. He smiled at Meg. 'Not a big one for breakfast, I'm afraid.'

'Not worried this might be your last before the full alien invasion takes place?' said Miki. She immediately regretted the words, putting her hand over her mouth as if she could push them back in. 'I'm sorry, I didn't mean...' she murmured.

But John only raised his eyebrows and began to butter his toast.

'You do seem remarkably calm about all this,' said Meg. 'Aren't you a tiny bit worried.'

'Not especially,' said John. 'I have confidence in our long range telescopes. We might miss the odd asteroid, but we wouldn't miss an alien armada.'

'How comforting. No aliens, but possible surprise annihilation from sneaky space rock,' said Miki. She looked up from her phone which lay in her lap beneath the table, 'Sorry. I'm on edge this morning. I might be sarcastic from time to time, but I'm not normally rude.'

'I think I imagined goth sarcasm as being more downbeat,' said John, the corners of his mouth lifting slightly.

Miki gave a quick frown. 'You're thinking of emos.'

'What have emus got to do with anything?' said Brian. 'This is the most important day ever!'

'Don't you mean yesterday, dear?' said Meg.

Brian looked at her as if she had coshed him over the head. 'You're right. The most important day in my life is over. Nothing will ever top this.'

'Cheer up,' said John, rising. 'With a bit of luck an alien might capture you for interrogation. Thank you so much for breakfast, Meg. Could I ask one more favour? I have some business in town and I don't know my way around yet. Would you mind if I took Miki with me? I believe she's currently off school?'

'Suspended,' said Miki.

'I don't know,' said Meg. 'I mean is it safe out there? Besides your car has sat-nag.'

'It's out of date,' said John. 'Drives me mad, sending me up one way streets all the time or round in circles. Besides, you don't honestly think there was an alien on the hill last night, do you? You've never struck me as someone to get caught up in mass hysteria.'

Brian pointed his fork at John and cried, 'Disbeliever!'

Miki laughed nervously, not sure if her father was serious or not. Meg batted her husband's fork down with a casual hand. 'If it was an alien,' she said, 'I'm sure after a quick look at all our gawking faces, it turned tail and ran. Or at least it would if it had any sense.'

'Meg!' said Brian. 'That's so small-minded of you.'

'It's like John says,' replied his wife. 'In the bright light of day I can't believe what we saw was more than a hoax or some kind of promotional exercise. I'm half expecting the TV to start showing ads for Gins-that-are-Out-of-this-World.'

'I suppose you're right,' said Brian. His shoulders slumped. 'I'm going to try and hold on to some hope a little longer.'

John pushed in his chair. 'There's always tomorrow,' he said. 'Coming, Miki?'

'Sure,' said Miki. 'Why not?'

Once inside the car, John turned the air conditioning on and the radio off. Miki sat back in the leather seat. Long, black and sleek, she hadn't expected it to be so luxurious.

'Hire car?' she asked, as John reversed out of the drive.

'Mine.'

'Never been that interested in cars,' said Miki. 'But this doesn't seem like the kind of car a scientist might have.'

John drove off down the street. 'And what kind of car does an astrophysicist have? A blue one with stars?'

Miki gave a nervous smile. 'I don't know. I don't want to be rude…'

'Why break a habit?'

'But it seems awfully expensive for a government scientist,' said Miki, stung.

'But then you said you didn't know much about cars.'

Miki felt herself blushing. 'I know an expensive piece of machinery when I see it. Same as I know you didn't want me to come with you for directions. What do you want?'

John's response hit Miki like a bucket of cold water.

'I want you to help me put a lid on this thing you've started,' he said.

LEON, LISA, ALICE & MARTY

'There is no use crying,' said Leon's mother firmly. 'The whole town saw you running down the hill half-dressed, with that boy. I don't know what your father is going to do. I've never seen him so angry. I'm telling you your Cliff better not show up at our front door anytime soon.'

Alice hiccuped into her cereal. 'Bloody aliens. Why did they have to pick on me? It's not fair!'

'Language, young lady.'

Leon's phone pinged.

'Leon, what have I told you about having that thing at the table?'

'Sorry, Mum.' Leon put the phone back in his pocket.

Lisa nodded. The hall phone rang. 'Mum,' said Leon, 'your antiquated technical relic requires your assistance.'

Lisa scowled at him. 'Don't be smart, young man.'

As she left the room, Leon shrugged. 'Parents,' he said, 'tell you one thing one day, another the next.'

'You know what she meant,' said Alice. 'Little smarty-pants.'

'At least I keep my pants on.'

Alice had just got a decent headlock on Leon when they heard her father shout down from upstairs, 'Who is it Lisa?'

'It's some journalist,' Lisa called back. 'Says he wants to talk to our Alice.'

There was the sound of a large man thundering down the stairs. 'Why exactly do you want to talk to my daughter?' bellowed their father.

There was a short pause.

'No, she is not pregnant by a bloody alien! No, you can't run a story on her out-of-this-world lover!'

'You should get out of here,' said Leon from under Alice's arm. 'He's not happy.'

'No, I don't care if you give me a million pounds, you can't have an exclusive on her alien baby!'

'Why do I get the feeling this is somehow all your fault?' said Alice, squeezing a little tighter.

'Me?' gasped Leon. 'Earth to Alice. I'm not an alien.'

'It's all rubbish if you ask me.'

'That journalist wants to ask you. Maybe you could talk Dad round.' Her hold tightened again. 'Okay, maybe not that, but you find out who it is and ring them up yourself. They'd give you money for a good story.'

'How much?' asked Alice.

'Thousands. Ouch, Alice, not so tight. I'm not kidding.

It could be a front page story. It would sell loads of papers for them, you could ask for a lot of money.'

'Oh, yeah, what about?'

'Your alien lover – could be enough that you and Cliff could run away together,' he added, hope sounding in his voice.

'I suppose we could go on holiday together,' said Alice thoughtfully. 'I'd leave a note saying we'd be back. Then Dad would have to take Cliff seriously.'

'Good plan,' gasped Leon.

From the hall the their parents' voices grew in intensity. Then the doorbell rang. Leon and Alice froze as they heard the door being wrenched open. 'Hello, Mrs… Alice's mother. I'm Marty McLaren. I'm a freelance journalist. I thought I'd offer my services so your daughter could tell…'

The next sound they heard was a loud thud and their mother shrieking, 'Oh my God, what have you done?'

'Back door,' said Leon to Alice. She released him. They grabbed their school bags from under the table and fled.

MIKI & JOHN

Miki turned to stare at John. He continued to look straight ahead, his face expressionless. 'What thing?' said Miki. 'I was in Glasgow when the alien first appeared. You know that. I suppose when I stood next to my mum last night I was telepathically broadcasting the image.'

'Funny you assume I am talking about the alien hoax,' said John.

'What else would you be talking about?'

'And you use the word image – almost as if you knew it was being projected.'

208

'It was clearly a hoax,' said Miki, turning back and slumping down in her seat. 'Besides, you're driving towards the hill now. Why did you need me? You clearly know the way.'

'Don't be obtuse, Miki. You might not be directly responsible for all this, but you clearly know all about it. I imagine that's who you were texting last night.' He turned and looked at her briefly. 'In fact I know it was. The question is, will we be able to contain this situation?'

'You're not a physicist at all, are you?' said Miki.

'No, I'm an astrophysicist.'

'Yeah right,' said Miki, 'and I'm a little blue man from the moon.'

'It would make my life a damn sight easier if you were,' growled John.

Ahead of them the entrance to Arthur's Seat was blocked by two police cars. Several policemen were speaking to people, obviously turning them away. Behind them stood three further officers with semi-automatic guns clipped to the front of their harnesses. Miki began to feel afraid. It was rare to see armed police in Scotland.

A variety of satellite uplink vans lined the road. Yellow crime scene tape had been liberally draped over the trees lining this side of the park. Beyond and further up the hill, they could see more vehicles; some police cars and some bigger vans. Miki spotted a couple of dog handlers being led up the hill by their animals. John glanced over at Holyrood Palace. 'No flag. That's good. Tell me, Miki, that flag wasn't flying last week? If they had to evacuate a member of the royal family there won't be anything I can do to prevent the ton of shit that is about to come down on your head.'

Miki swallowed. 'I don't know what you're talking about,' she said, but even to her own ears her voice sounded unlike her usual self. She sounded – timid.

John rolled the car slowly forward. He wound down the window and a police officer peered in. 'I'm sorry, sir,' she said. 'We can't let anyone through. This is a restricted zone.'

John produced a small wallet from his pocket and passed it to her. The policewoman opened it and passed it back. 'I'll have to radio for instructions, sir,' she said. 'In the meantime if you could pull up over there.'

'Who's in charge here?' asked John.

'Chief Inspector Niall McKinley.'

'From Strathclyde?'

'No, sir, Edinburgh. But we've people from Strathclyde here.'

John smiled at her. 'You're probably not meant to tell me that,' he said. 'But it's good to hear Edinburgh is dealing with it herself. I'll pull up and we'll wait in the car. Thank you, officer.'

'Strathclyde?' asked Miki as John drove to where the woman had indicated they should park.

'Strathclyde is the anti-terrorism base for Scotland. There are attachments across the country, but that's where they keep the experts.'

'Terrorism?'

'Let's hope they are treating this as a training exercise rather than a deliberate attempt to excite civil disobedience and rioting.'

'What? That's ridiculous.' said Miki. 'How can you go from a prank to…?'

'To what?' said John, interrupting. 'To claiming we

are being invaded by aliens? Fortunately the Scots are, by nature, a level-headed lot. If this claim had been taken seriously elsewhere…'

'Like California?' said Miki.

'Your words, not mine. I was thinking somewhere people were more isolated or not as plugged into the global village.'

'I'm still not following. You're suggesting that people could have taken this seriously?'

'I take it you haven't been following what's happening in rural Italy recently? The rabbit?'

A figure with the sun shining behind them, so that they were no more than a looming shadow, knocked on the window. John pressed the button to lower it. 'Good morning. Chief Inspector McKinley?'

'Aye.' The voice sounded rough, with a distinct Glasgow twang. The inspector pushed his face over the edge of the window and glared at them. Miki drew back slightly. One word and she had almost gagged on his breath. His skin was pitted and pockmarked. A remarkable face for all the wrong reasons. His nose ended in a bulb laced with a spiderweb of tiny broken veins. 'They send you up from London? Cos you're not needed. We have the incident under control.'

'I'm sure you do,' said John. 'And no, I wasn't sent up. Rather, my daughter and I were on holiday when I heard about the incident. I came to see if I could offer any assistance. How serious is it?' He smiled. 'We've heard some ridiculous rumours.'

'Have yous indeed? And who's been spreading these so-called rumours?'

'We were in a café, weren't we, honey?' said John, turning to Miki. 'The Sea Hut or something? Lovely views of the sea.'

211

'Aye well, I'd take it kindly if you don't go repeating any such lies.'

A flash of annoyance crossed John's face. 'Rumour-mongering is hardly in my line.'

'The WPC told me where you're from.'

Miki watched as the two men sized each other up. The Chief Inspector placed one meaty hand on the edge of the window. 'So what exactly is it that you think you can do for me?'

John's smile grew thinner. 'Not knowing the situation makes it difficult for me to answer that.'

'I'm not going to be repeating things in front of yer lassie. We're a wee bit tighter on the need-to-know rule up here.'

'Of course not,' said John. 'My daughter will stay in the car. If you remove your hand from my door I will get out and we can talk out of her hearing.'

'How am I to know she'll stay in the car?'

John sighed and pulled out the key fob. 'You can take this and lock her in the car.'

'Wait a minute,' said Miki.

'Sorry, love,' said John, turning to give her an intense look 'They don't know you like I do. Try not to move. You'll only set the alarm off.' Without warning he pushed the button to raise the window and the policeman barely managed to get his fingers out of the way. Then he opened the door and got out. Miki watched as the inspector pointed the fob at the car. Around her echoed a series of clicks as the locks engaged.

Miki swore. She tried to give John a look to show what she thought of him, but he seemed to be deliberately standing with his back to her. She strained to see how

212

the inspector was reacting, only to realise that John had positioned himself so she couldn't see. She slumped down in her seat, scowling.

LEON & ALICE

'Hey, wait up! Not all of us do track,' said Leon. He bent over, puffing. 'Alice, come back. We're far away enough now.'

His sister slowed and turned.

'Where are we going anyway?' said Leon. 'One journalist is bad enough, but can you imagine the reception you're going to get at school?'

Leon watched, relieved, as Alice's face faded to a milk white under her make-up. He tilted his head, curious at the resultant colour. 'Weird,' he muttered.

'Where can I go?' said Alice.

Leon noticed her eyes were brimming with tears. He took a step back. 'It's not that bad. Something else will happen and the papers will lose interest,' he said and awkwardly put out a hand to pat her arm, rather in the manner of someone petting a grumpy Rottweiler.

'Like what? I'm not stupid. I know there are newspapers that would like nothing better than to run a sex-with-an-alien story.'

Leon winced. 'You don't have to give them one. Besides, only truly stupid people read newspapers nowadays. All the real news is online. As long as no one has an actual photo of you up there, it'll be fine. That guy, Marty Whatever. I've heard of him. He's a right chancer, but he's not going to risk getting sued.'

'I didn't even see any aliens,' said Alice, a tear rolling

213

down each cheek. 'Cliff and I had decided it was time to…'

Leon held his hand up quickly. 'TMI, sister,' he said. 'Look, why don't you take the bus into town and go and do whatever girls do in town?'

'Shopping?' said Alice. 'I couldn't. Besides, I don't have any money.'

Leon sighed. He pulled a wallet out of his pocket, took out four ten pound notes and passed them to her. 'This enough?'

'Where did you get that?' said Alice.

'I'm running some ad associate programmes on my websites. I have to split it with a guy who fronts it for me.'

'Huh?'

'You have to be over eighteen,' said Leon. 'Just take it. I didn't nick it.'

'I suppose,' said Alice, reaching out to take the money. 'Not sure…'

Leon gave a deeper sigh and handed over another twenty. 'Enough now?'

Alice, looking considerably more cheerful, nodded. She tucked the money into her bag. 'I expect you're right. It'll all have blown over by tomorrow.'

Leon nodded.

'Bye,' said Alice. 'Thanks.'

Leon watched her walk away. 'Sisters,' he said in a tone of utter disgust.

JOHN & MIKI

Miki woke from her doze to the sound of the door locks clicking open. John climbed into the driver's seat. He did not look happy. 'Seat belt on?' he said curtly.

'Never took it off,' said Miki.

John thrust the car into gear and reversed far too fast for Miki's stomach. She managed to swallow the bile that came up in her mouth. John stared straight ahead, not looking at her. 'I take it it didn't go well?' she said.

John didn't reply. He only drove faster.

'Em, it's a twenty mile an hour zone,' said Miki.

'If they can catch me they can give me a ticket,' said John.

Miki sat up further in her seat. She found herself scanning for hazards. She wanted to ask John where they were going, but he was driving so fast she was afraid of distracting him.

JONAS, RORY & LEON

Jonas and Rory had found a corner of the playground tucked behind the PE block. Without planning, both of them had arrived early. 'That was totally amaze-balls,' said Rory. 'Did you see the full size of the crowd we drew? Knocks the dream into a cocked basket.'

'Hat,' corrected Jonas automatically.

'Why the frown?' said Rory patting him on the back. 'Turn that frown upside down, man. You're a star.' He giggled at his own pun.

'As long as I am a star no one ever recognises,' said Jonas. 'I do hope Leon got that drone back okay.'

Rory shrugged, 'His drone. His loss. Hey, do you think he had a camera on it? Did he film it all? You can do that on some of those drones, can't you?'

Jonas turned his palms up. 'Couldn't tell you. Not my sort of thing. Oh, God, if he did film and it got found...'

'C'mon,' said Rory. 'If anyone had recognised you they would have been at your front door this morning, if not last night. Face it, we got away with it. Something to tell your grandkids.'

'Hmmpf,' said Jonas.

'Spill.'

'It's Leon. We keep forgetting he's a little kid. What if he boasts about it? Or just tells people because he thinks it's a good laugh.'

'Worse case scenario, we didn't hurt anyone. I still think we should do a piece on the website about the gullibility of the general public.'

'And stupidity,' said Jonas glumly. 'If it had been a real invasion who's to say the aliens would have been friendly.'

'True. Friendly is usually the last word you'd associate with a descriptor of an invasion.'

'I mean,' said Jonas, warming to his theme, 'no one can have truly believed they were waiting for an alien, can they? Wouldn't the wisest thing have been to leave town or at least hunker down and barricade your doors and windows?'

'You're thinking of zombies,' said Rory.

'It's not as if we made anyone go there…'

Rory nodded in agreement.

'Guys!' Leon hailed them. 'So this is where you're hiding. Heard about Marty McMudd's latest? He thinks my sister was having sex with an alien on the hill. He's offered to tell her side of the story. Can you believe it? Couldn't have stitched her up better if I'd tried.'

'Your sister?' said Jonas, paling.

'Yeah, she was up on the hill with Cliff. They got spooked by the drone's light.' He put his hands up. 'I had no idea they were up there, but this is even better than when

I fell through the roof onto them!' He bent over laughing and trailed off into giggles.

'So is she selling her story?' said Jonas.

'You've got to be kidding! My dad punched Marty on the nose. I was in the next room and I heard the crunch of breaking bone. You should be happy. That scum got what he was owed.'

Rory grinned. 'Another piece of good news. I take it she's not going to make something up?'

'Nah,' said Leon. 'Our dad would kill her. He's been angry enough about Cliff without her making a fool of herself in front of the whole city.'

'How did they find out it was her?' said Jonas.

'Silly mare ran down the hill with her top off and Cliff following, waving it at her. I bet the pictures'll be going round the school by now.'

'That's not cool,' said Rory. 'I get you like having spooked your sister and got her into trouble, but having that kind of photo out there on the internet, that's different. Horrible.'

'I don't know,' said Leon. 'It's not as if I'm going to look!'

'You should find a way of shutting it down,' said Rory. 'You're the computer genius. I wouldn't want that kind of picture going around, even if it was of my worse enemy.'

'But she was in public,' said Leon. 'Anyone can take a photo of anyone if they are in a public place. It's not like she got drunk at a party or something…'

'Not cool,' said Rory. 'Not cool.'

'He's right,' said Jonas. 'Has she seen the pictures yet?'

'I don't think so,' said Leon. 'She didn't mention it. Besides, I still don't think it's our problem.' He stuck out his bottom lip and crossed his arms.

'Man, you need to do something.'

'No, Rory, I don't.' Leon started walking away. 'We need to meet at Miki's after school,' he threw over his shoulder. 'She thinks there's a spy in town.'

Jonas had already begun speaking to Rory and Leon's last remark didn't register. 'He doesn't get it. He thinks its funny. He's too young,' he said to Rory.

'Yeah. I don't know Alice, but I'm guessing any girl would be mortified at pictures like that going around. There's certainly photos of me I wouldn't want to share.'

'TMI,' said Jonas. He thought for a moment. 'Look, I have an idea. Why don't we use the website for something good for once. I could write a piece on why such photos are not funny.'

'Don't you think you're more likely to make people go searching the internet than stop spreading it? People, especially kids, can be real shits.'

'Yeah, you have a point,' said Jonas.

They both leaned against the wall and sighed. 'You could,' said Rory, 'write something general about the evils of cyberbullying and how it wrecks lives? There's a whole load of people who aren't going to change their minds, but equally there might be some prepared to listen to reason. You could make it more general. About all kinds of cyberbullying?'

Jonas nodded.

'Only I don't think it's our regular readers you want to reach,' said Rory.

'No,' said Jonas. 'But I need to do something. I'll write something and then go looking for a site to post it on.' He stood up straight. 'Means bunking off school, but…'

'A man's gotta do what a man's gotta do,' said Rory with a grin. 'The fact you've got triple maths first has nothing to do with it, right?'

Jonas shrugged. 'I'll see you at Miki's after school?'

'Sure. Write well, young Hunter.'

'Hunter?'

'Famous journalist,' said Rory. 'Look him up.'

MIKI & JOHN

A bicycle wobbled out of a side lane. John swerved to avoid the cyclist and pulled the car back on track easily. Looking in the mirror Miki saw the cyclist and bike in a heap on the road. As she watched the woman stood up and waved her hand at the car in an explicit indication of what she thought of John's driving. He didn't even seem to notice. They were at the outer limit of the city now. John wasn't using the sat-nav, so she had no idea where he was going. They approached a roundabout and without slowing, John sped onto it and took the road for North Berwick.

'Are you taking me to England?' squeaked Miki.

John didn't answer.

'Please, would you stop? You're scaring me.'

John slowed the car and glanced at her. 'Why on earth would I scare you? I've known your parents since I wasn't much older than you.'

'Really? You don't think a strange man driving at breakneck speed out of the city, who won't speak to me, isn't scary?'

John slowed the car even further and pulled into a leafy layby. He pressed the unlock button. 'There, you can get out if you want, but I do need to talk to you.'

'Tell me where you were going.'

John sighed. 'I don't think so clearly in cities. Too many people to observe. I was heading out to – I don't know where, but I was going to stop soon, so we could talk. Maybe get a coffee.' He yawned. 'Tired and frustrated. Worse kind of me.'

'And you couldn't tell me that because…?'

John blinked at her. 'I didn't think about how you were feeling. It wasn't relevant at the time.'

'Wow, just wow.'

'Sorry. I'm not a people person.'

'You were very good at getting me to talk last night.'

'That's different.'

'A friend of mine said you were using a script.'

'More a technique,' said John. 'It's not my thing. I only have a rudimentary knowledge of…' he hesitated. 'Of that.'

'Basic training?'

John frowned. 'Yeah, right. Astrophysics 101.'

'I think we can drop that, can't we?' said Miki. She clenched her left hand down by the car door to stop herself from shaking. 'You're a spy, aren't you?'

'I really am an astrophysicist. Ask your parents. That's what I studied at uni.'

Miki sank back in her seat. 'Yeah, whatever. I don't think I have anything to say to you, can you please take me home?'

'I will,' said John, 'But I need to speak to a friend, before things get any worse for you and your friends. You may not believe this, but I am actually trying to help you – and in particular your parents.'

'My parents have nothing to do with any of this!'

'I know. But they have a habit of – er – attracting attention.'

220

'You mean from government agencies?'

John gave a thin smile. 'It's easier if you're frank. But yes, that's what I mean. There are only so many times a name can come up before action is taken. They do love their protests, don't they? I'm as keen as anyone on saving the planet, but these things have to be done in the right way. Your parents have been skating on thin ice for a while now. You do know your mother superglued herself to the roof of a tube carriage?'

'She did what?'

'I've done what I can…'

'So you *are* a…?'

John spoke over her. 'But there is only so much I can do. Inspector McKinsey is a difficult man, close to retirement and determined to go by the book. A proper Zeus. If I can't sort this then – well, it isn't going to be pretty.'

LEON

The number of juicy rumours going around the school about the aliens delighted Leon. He mentally stored up the best ones. His maths teacher turned out to be off sick, and it was easy to convince the substitute teacher he was meant to be in the computer lab.

He choose a computer at the back of room and logged into the website.

Dear Readers,

The world may still be turning this morning, but everything is different. Aliens have landed and they have been seen by thousands, possibly hundreds of thousands, of us. A local event with only a few people filming on their phones – and suddenly, the whole awesome spectacle has gone globally viral.

On our website we told of the impending event, we told you they would come again a second night, but only hundreds of you came to see the aliens. Did film crews turn up? I don't know. There has been nothing yet on the news. It's on the internet, even in the old fashioned newspapers, but the general news cycle, the trusty sources, guardians of the news releases to the worldwide population, they have stayed silent.

There can be only one of two reasons for this.

One: it is true. The aliens were here. Perhaps they still are.

Two: it is a magnificent hoax. But how could you tell?

This is the joy of the news cycle today – and not just that – the joy of all the information that floods into our homes on a daily basis – we have the choice of deciding what is true. A long time ago a philosopher, called Descartes, tried to discover what he could know about the world – and finally after many thoughts and written pages – mental gymnastics that still to this day bore students to an almost terminal torpor – he came to a conclusion. All he could know existed was himself – and even that he could only know because he thought.

And that's the thing. Do we still think? Or do we merely accept what we are fed? At school we were taught by rote. We trusted the authorities, even though we in all likelihood had no idea who they were, we trusted these invisible conveyers of the canon of knowledge to present facts and evidence to us through the school system of exams – or the university system

– we trusted them to teach us what we needed to know. To teach us what was true. We were not taught to question this sublime, invisible authority. Nor even to consider that different countries thought it important for children to learn different things.

But if we now consider that – who would we say is right? Do we hear our parents speak often of the useful things they learned in school? Things that have saved their lives, kept them earning a decent wage, and provided them with a moral compass to navigate life? Ask them and find out.

My point is, we have been taught to accept, not to question. My point is, now anyone can post on the internet, hijack social media, for their own ends, and the majority will accept whatever is offered to them. The more outrageous the offering or the more exciting, the less it is questioned.

In Descartes' terms we have ceased to exist.

Leon leaned back in his chair and pressed post. This evening he needed to make a decent report on the others, and then tomorrow he'd have his whole dossier ready to present when the IP address was traced. It would, sadly, bring the whole experiment crashing down like a house of cards, but you had to know when to call time on an operation. The possibility that the friend of Miki's family was a spy of some kind had accelerated his timetable. He stood up and stretched. If he was honest with himself he did feel a tiny bit of remorse about the collateral damage that would ensue. He quite liked Miki and the others, but if he was going to get recruited into one of Britain's Secret Services he had to be prepared to make sacrifices. Even if those sacrifices were other people he'd once thought of as friends.

MIKI & JOHN

'Zeus? Is that some kind of metaphor or are you really losing it?'

'Zero Effectiveness Under Stress.'

'That's quite clever.'

John pinched the bridge of his nose between the thumb and forefinger of his right hand. 'Could you possibly do me the favour of telling me the truth?'

'About?'

'Everything! The whole alien hoax. The conspiracy website. How deep in this are your parents? It *is* just some kids' pranks? Because I can tell you from where I'm sitting it's looking bad for the Bartons.'

'My parents have nothing to do with any of this!' said Miki.

'How do I know that's the truth?'

'I don't know,' Miki snapped back. 'Do you want me to pinkie swear?'

'How about, if I find out you have lied to me I will ensure there isn't an arts college in the whole of Britain that will admit you.'

'You can do that? You're only an astrophysicist, remember?'

'Try me,' said John.

'It's true my parents have nothing to do with the whole alien thing. I'm not involved either.'

John frowned at her. 'Be very careful what you tell me. I meant what I said.'

'It's true. I was in Glasgow at the time'

'But you knew it was being planned? That's why you gave yourself an alibi?'

'No!' said Miki, almost shrieking. 'I had nothing to do with this alien business at all.'

'If you're completely innocent I doubt I will be able to help your parents.'

'What?' said Miki. 'You want me to make a false confession?'

John shook his head. 'You watch too much TV. No, if I can't find who is behind this and broker a deal, I expect your parents will finally be taken in for questioning.'

'Finally?'

'They've been skating close to the wind for years.'

'What do you mean?'

'I mean, God damn it, I've been pulling your parents' names off various watchlists for years!'

Miki recoiled further back into her seat.

John took several deep breaths. 'Sorry. Sorry. I'm finding this all rather frustrating. I don't deal with people most of the time. I work with data. There're certain things I can manage, but generally my tolerance for most people expires within three or four hours.'

'I'm not sure I understand,' said Miki.

'I am brighter than most people, but I fail to understand social interactions on a general basis. Most conversations strike me as pointless and most people as stupid. It's the never-ending ability of people to talk rubbish in a desperate attempt to avoid obvious truths – like how stupid they are.'

'Do you think I'm stupid?' asked Miki

'I think that is a stupid question. Why should it matter to you what I think?'

Miki could see John was still breathing quickly, clearly struggling to contain his emotions. She made a decision. 'I will tell you the truth. I'll trust you, if you will trust me.' When he didn't reply she went on, 'I wasn't involved in the alien prank, but I recognised who was in the film. My friends, Rory and Jonas. I imagine the technical stuff was arranged by Leon. We had all been working on the fake news website. We wanted to show how people believed things they read too easily. I don't know why they did the UFO thing. It must have all been decided while I was away.'

'Why did you want to show people their foolishness? I presume you were going to confess about the website sometime? Anonymously or full confession?'

'I don't know. We hadn't got that far. To start with it was only the three of us. Someone threw red paint over our dog, and there was some stuff at school about me being feral – which I'm not. I didn't care about the last bit, but I was cross about Red – the dog. A journalist spied on Jonas and his mum, who has MS, and put out a story claiming she was a benefits fraud. He caught her on a good day. Rory – well, he has a secret, which he wrote in a diary and someone stole it.'

'You all had a vested interest.'

'Yes, Leon only joined us because he overheard us talking. He came up with the idea for the website. He's very clued up technically, for a small kid.'

'Why was he listening in?'

'Oh, he wants to be a spy.'

'Great,' said John in a tone that indicated the opposite.

'Thank you, for looking after my parents.'

'No problem,' said John. 'They looked after me when I needed it. Besides, I know they're harmless.'

'So what do we do?'

John turned the car back on. 'We go and see a friend of mine. Put your belt back on.' He pulled the car smoothly off from the roadside and to Miki's intense relief drove just the right side of the speed limit.

JONAS

Jonas turned the key slowly in the lock. He paused for a moment after he heard the bolt shoot back. Silence. Sometimes he thought his mother had the ears of a bat. He pushed the door open carefully, only taking the key out once he was inside and could steady the open door with his foot. He'd kept his hand around the bunch of keys, with only the front door one exposed. He muffled the sound of the keys as he slid them down onto the hall table. Even more slowly he closed the front door, lifting the snib before he did so and then lowering it only when the door was shut, so that it only made the smallest of clicks. He stopped and listened again. Nothing.

He put down his bag, shrugged out of his blazer and then, picking up both, he crept towards his room. It was one door down from his mother's. As he walked down the hall he could see her bedroom door was open. He sighed. He wasn't going to get away with this. He stopped in front of the doorway trying to think of a way of explaining why he was home. Inside the room the curtains were still closed. The lamp beside the bed on the nightstand was dimmed down to its lowest setting, throwing a faint circle of light on the edge of the bed and the floor. Jonas dropped his bag and blazer. His mother didn't move.

In the faint light he could barely make out an open

paperback novel on the floor. His mother's hand lay on the edge of the bed, palm upwards, fingers half curled – a hand waiting to be held. Jonas wanted to run into the room and at the same time he wanted to run away. His breathing quickened. He pushed all thoughts out of his mind.

She was asleep. She was just asleep.

He lurched forward into the darkened room. He had to fight with himself to take each step in the short walk to her bedside. As his eyes grew accustomed to the dark he could make out his mother's form, half slumped against the pillows. She didn't look comfortable.

'Mum?' he said. 'Mum?' Then more loudly, 'Mum, wake up! Wake up, Mum.'

His mother didn't move.

Thoroughly frightened, Jonas snatched at the lamp, turning it up full. His mother, Trisha, lay there unmoving. The corners of her mouth were turned down and her mouth was open. Her face looked so wrong, drawn and white, with her eyes half closed. Jonas threw himself onto the bed, clutching at his mother. 'Mum!' he screamed. Still, she didn't move, but he felt the warm skin of her shoulder against his face.

'Oh God, Mum? What's wrong?' He scrabbled in his pocket for his phone and dialled 999. 'Ambulance please,' he said in a shaky voice. 'It's okay,' he told his mother, 'I'll get help. You'll be alright, Mum. You'll be alright.'

The operator came on the line. 'It's my mum. I've come in and she's collapsed or something. She's in bed, but she won't wake up and her mouth is all odd. She's all white, but I touched her skin. She's warm, so she'll be okay, won't she? She has MS.' He knew he was gabbling, but he couldn't stop himself.

228

The operator interrupted him gently, asking his name. He told her. Then she asked if he could see his mother breathing.

Jonas' legs gave under him. He sat down heavily on the floor. 'No, I can't,' he said. 'She's dead.' He burst into tears.

RORY

Rory crouched, panting, behind an piece of scenery. It was green, a tree or a bush. Part of the ever growing set for *A Midsummer Night's Dream*. He'd thought he'd be safe here. Mark Stuart and his gang never came up to the drama department. He clenched his jaw to stop his teeth chattering. He waited. Would they bother to scramble up on the stage to look for him? He closed his eyes and crossed his fingers, hoping they had got bored with chasing him and moved on to easier, more findable prey.

He heard the heavy door open. The hinge spring still hadn't been oiled and screeched a protest as the door was flung open. 'C'mon boys,' said Mark Stuart loudly, 'let's find our fairy. Where else would a fairy hide but in a fairy forest?' He laughed unpleasantly. 'Do we think he's in the basket?'

Rory heard the sound of the props being chucked out of the prop basket. Something broke with a clatter. The boys search ceased. Rory quivered. Surely now they'd clear out rather than get into trouble over breaking stuff? That was different to breaking people. Broken stuff was found and questions were asked. Broken people went off clutching their bruises and black eyes, swearing they'd walked into a door or something. No questions were asked. No questions answered. Anything but get another beating from Stuart and his cronies. One boy, in year two, the boy who had a squint. When he'd told, Stuart had found him outside school and broken his leg. No witnesses ever came forward, so the police could do nothing. In the end his parents had moved him to another school and Stuart's reign had become supreme.

Rory could hear them muttering again. Moving away. There were only three of them, including Stuart left, the others must have got bored.

Rory's phone rang. In a blind panic he pulled his phone out of his trouser pocket to turn it off, but he fumbled it, and instead of turning the thing off, the phone shot out of his hand to land on the stage. He saw the name on the display as he grabbed it.

'Jonas, mate. Now is not the time…' He broke off. Edging further back onto the stage, he said very quietly. 'You crying?'

'It's Mum,' said Jonas. 'I thought she was dead. I'm in an ambulance. She's really sick. Really sick. I don't know what to do. There isn't anyone else…'

'Calm down,' said Rory. 'Where you going? The Royal?'

'The Royal? The guy's nodding,' said Jonas between sobs.

'Right, I'll get Mum to bring me up,' said Rory. 'She's a midwife. She knows how to talk to doctors. I'll be there before you know it. It'll be fine. I have to go now.' Rory turned off his phone. Shit, he thought, shit. Poor Jonas. His mum was like, all he had left in the world after his dad had cleared off. Imagine having no-one – having no-one to the extent he had to call him, Rory. Poor fu—

'Come on out, little fairy. We want to see you dance on your twinkly little toes. No one's going to hurt you.' The

230

three boys burst into laughter. 'Not too much.'

One of Stuart's minions spoke, 'What colour do you think fairies bleed, boys? Glitter pink?'

'Glitter pink? What the f—? You one too? You little f—' said Stuart. 'Want us to start with you?'

'No, Mark,' said the minion. 'Only trying to be funny. Honest.'

'Well don't. You aren't.'

Rory heard more footsteps behind him. The others hadn't got bored. They'd circled round to trap him. How would he get to Jonas now? He thought of his friend – Jonas was sensible, liked to do the logical thing. He didn't have Rory's desire for fun, or his energy, but then he didn't care that Rory wore cheap bright mascara that made his eyelids swell. The only comment he'd ever made was to pass Rory some cotton wool from his mum's bathroom and suggest he might want to put cold pads on the swelling. Rory knew he pushed Jonas' buttons, infuriated him at times, but he'd never mocked Rory. Never been mean or even particularly interested in what Rory wanted to wear or be. He hadn't drawn away from him in case people thought he was gay like Rory. Not that Rory was even sure he was gay. But all his other so-called friends, apart from Miki and even Leon, that little brat, those three were the only ones who had accepted him for who he was – someone just like them. Someone trying to work out who they were.

And now, because of these lame-brained cretins, who couldn't tell Royal Navy from Royal Blue, who wouldn't know hot pink from pale rose, he wasn't going to be able to be there for his friend. His friend, who thought his mother was so sick she might die. Then Jonas would be alone. Rory came from a big family, but all the same he knew all too well what it was like to be alone.

Inside him, something snapped.

He stood up before he realised it. He walked out into the middle of the stage.

'Here I am,' he said.

Mark Stuart gave a cry of triumph as he and his boys raced towards the stage. One of them must have flicked some switches because one of the stage lights came on. Without thinking, Rory moved into it. As he stood in this spotlight he felt his anxiety slip away. This was where he belonged. This was where he was going. Mark Stuart and his little friends were only blips on the way.

Stuart clambered up on the stage. 'You going to dance for us now then?'

'Fuck you,' said Rory. His voice didn't come out as strongly as he wanted. Project, he told himself, project.

Stuart staggered backwards, pretending to be shocked. 'Ooh, look boys. This one might have balls after all.' He made a swipe for Rory's trousers. He obviously expected him to move backwards, because his hand brushed across Rory's fly. The onlookers made a noise. Rory recognised it as what his drama teacher would call a 'crowd jeer'. He took his cue.

'If you wanted a feel, you only had to ask,' he said.

Stuart blustered and swore.

'Not that I would have let you,' continued Rory. His voice sounded clearer, stronger now. 'You're so not my type.'

'You little fu—' said Stuart. He crossed the distance between them in one stride, swinging his arm wide to punch Rory in the face. It was a poor move. Rory turned sideways and caught the other boy's fist with his hand. He held on tight. 'Got under your skin, have I, big man? You know what they say about homo-haters? They're still in the closet.' By now the others were on stage and had closed to form a ring. Whether they would stay back or join in, Rory didn't know.

Stuart gave a roar. He didn't manage to free his wrist, but he kicked out hard at Rory's knee. Rory's leg crumpled and he collapsed. He held on to Stuart's wrist for dear life. 'What? Right here, right now? On the stage? You are a one,' he said. He kept his tone light, but his leg hurt like hell. He let go and rolled away from Stuart, then he stood up, looked him square in the eye.

'See how your mates aren't helping you?' he said before Stuart could move. 'That's because they believe me. You train your dogs to believe anything they're told and that's what they'll do. Believe anything about anyone – even you. Not very nice, is it?'

Stuart charged him. Rory caught one of the stage ropes and pulled himself up. He swayed backwards and forwards. The audience laughed and clapped.

'Come down,' shouted Stuart. 'Or I'll f—ing pull this rope down. Then you'll be in trouble.'

'Come down and you'll what? Beat me up? Cause me lots of pain? What's the point of that?'

'I'm going to hurt you,' said Stuart, grabbing the rope and pulling. The pulley at the top creaked.

'Yeah, probably, but you're never going to hurt me enough, are you? Unless you kill me nothing will change. You're a fly in my life, Stuart. A bump in the road I have to endure for a while. Then you'll go off and work in a burger joint while I get a life. You're nothing. You're going to be nothing.'

Stuart's minions stood watching. He glanced around at them. 'What's the matter with you lot?'

No one answered him. Stuart grabbed hold of the rope and pulled with all his strength.

The rope, Rory, the pulley and part of the stage rigging crashed to the ground. One large stage light wobbled on the end of its mounting. Rory landed on his back under a section of rigging. The fall hurt, but he did his best to use his drama skills, slapping his arm against the stage floor as he came down to negate some of the impact.

Stuart's minions started at the noise and, with a pack mentality, fled. Stuart himself stood frozen as bits of rigging fell around him.

Rory staggered to his feet. He glanced up. The stage light drooped alarmingly. Instinctively he reached out and pulled Stuart over towards and on top of him, less than a second before the light crashed down where the bully had been.

Rory kicked his way out from under the startled boy. One of those kicks might just have connected with something soft. Could be his head, thought Rory. 'You're welcome,' he said, standing up. Then he bent over the fallen boy. 'And just so you know. I wear dresses and I look damn hot in them.'

MIKI, JOHN & THE HACKER

John drove down a small lane that seemed to have been designed more for cattle than cars. Miki braced herself against the dashboard and the door. 'You're sure he lives down here?' she said.

'It's a she,' said John as he weaved his car in and out of

potholes, 'and no, I'm not sure. It's the last place I heard she was. We've only ever talked online. I'm pretty sure our turning up at her door is going to freak her out. Let's hope she doesn't have a gun.'

'What?' said Miki, paling.

'These eccentric types that try to – well not go off the grid – obviously – but be anonymous or missing from the system – they can be a bit odd.'

'Odd, as in she might shoot us?'

'As I said, I generally deal with this type online.'

'Online in a squat?'

'There'll be a neighbour somewhere round here she's piggybacking on.' He glanced at Miki. 'Piggybacking on their WiFi,' he said.

'Oh, right. But can she get on to the dark web like that?'

'What's left of it, yes,' said John. 'Besides, that's not why I need her.'

'We could have asked Leon. He's pretty good for his age. Better than any of the adults at school. He runs rings round the computer department.'

'Hmm,' said John.

'What do you mean, hmm?'

'I'm sure he's good. But K4 here is in a different league.'

'Don't tell me that's her hacker name.'

'As far as I know, it's also her legal name. She's divorced, or is it emancipated, herself from everyone else in her life.'

'Why? Did something bad happen to her?'

John looked at her full on and the car jolted across a large pothole. His attention whipped back to the road. 'Jesus,' he said. 'That's my bloody undercarriage gone.'

Miki felt laughter bubbling up inside her. She suspected it was hysteria. She was in a car with a possible spy, who

235

was more concerned about the underside of his car than that some lunatic known only as K4 might shoot them.

RORY & HELEN

'I'm telling you now, young man, this had better not be a wind up. I'm on shift in two hours.'

'I keep telling you. It's for real.'

'What ward has she gone into?'

'I said I don't know. He called me from the ambulance. He was a mess.'

His mother sighed and pulled into the staff parking lot. She wound down her window and waved her card at the machine.

'They make you pay?' said Rory, distracted.

'Uh huh, and looking at the time, you'll be getting the bus home.'

'Dressed like this?' said Rory. 'These are my best jeans. And this jacket is vintage. The bus is filthy.'

His mother's face was turned away from him as she expertly reverse-parked her car, but he heard her sigh again. She turned off the car and confronted him. 'Look, Rory, you said you thought your mate's mum was dying and he was all on his own. This best mate of yours that you've known for what – a week?'

'He's always been in my year.'

'You know what I mean.'

'Okay, we've been pals for two weeks. But he's a really good guy. He's different from the others.'

His mother raised an eyebrow. 'Different like you?'

Rory snorted. 'No. If there was a class in conforming, he'd ace it. He's the poster teen for nice boys.'

236

'I don't get what you two have in common,' said his mother, getting out of the car. She waited till Rory closed his door and locked the car. She looked at him over the top of the car. 'I don't get this.'

'That I might have a friend?'

'Yes, frankly, yes. You've always been the butt of everyone's jokes.'

'Thanks, Mum. Thanks for that,' said Rory. He set off towards the hospital without waiting for her.

At reception they were diverted to a general ward. As they stood by the lift, Helen said, 'At least she's not in surgical. That's good.'

'Taking the surprise well, Mum. Confess, you didn't believe she'd be here at all.'

'Well, I suppose I should apologise for that. But you have to admit it's all a bit odd.'

Rory was spared a reply as the lift door opened. Once inside he stared fixedly at the numbers above the door, willing the lift to go faster.

MIKI, JOHN & K4.

'I guess we are going to have to walk from here. Even if I didn't care about my car, which I do, we'd only get stuck.'

'Isn't this the part where you tell me to stay in the car for my own safety?' said Miki.

'What am I, the FBI?' said John, getting out of the car. 'I wouldn't even be here if it wasn't for you and your friends. You're coming with me.'

Miki squinted ahead. Among the undergrowth, she could just about make out a roof and one wall. It seemed more likely to be a dilapidated shed than anything. What made her nervous was that the rest of the structure lurked between trees, and shadows obscured it almost completely. Anything or anyone could be there. John slammed the car door and a flock of birds scattered from the branches. Miki shivered. She got out. 'Aren't you meant to protect me?'

John looked over at her, bemused.

'I mean, don't you take an oath to that effect or something?'

'You either watch far too much TV or you have me confused with someone else. Probably both.'

'Do you at least have a gun?' said Miki, as John started off towards the trees.

'Of course not,' said John. 'We don't generally shoot each other in this country.'

'I hope K4 agrees,' said Miki to herself.

'Almost certainly not,' said John. 'She's an internet terrorist. She'll need to keep up her street cred, or should that be super highway cred?'

Miki fell silent. With luck it would be an empty shed and they would leave. She'd insist he took her straight home.

Her heart sank as the building revealed itself as they approached. At one time it must have been a shepherd's hut with only two rooms, but sometime in the past some severely misguided soul had extended it. A corrugated attempt at a plastic conservatory had been added to the back and a box-like structure bulged awkwardly out of the roof. Someone had covered the lower windows with brown paper. Paint peeled from the windowsills and front door. The colour had been lost to time, moss and erosion. Moving through the treeline Miki smelled the damp, earthiness of the trees. It reminded her strongly of decay. What was the movie where people ended up being buried in shallow graves in the woods? When their bodies had been found, they were crawling with bugs. Everyone in the cinema had screamed. 'I think this was a bad idea,' said Miki. 'Let's go. There's no one here.'

'Nothing human anyway,' she added under her breath.

The light was fading and the scenery around them was growing more and more like a horror set.

'Hey, K4! You in here?'

Silence.

'We should go,' said Miki. 'I want you to take me home.'

'Come on. I've wrecked the underside of my Lexus on your drive. The least you can do is offer me a drink.'

Still nothing.

Miki moved closer to John. 'Please. Let's go. I'll tell you everything.'

John ignored her. 'K4!' He shouted. 'It's SpyGlass'

'Spyglass?' repeated Miki.

'Did I say that already?' said John

'No,' said Miki, her eyes wide. 'No, you didn't say that.'

Miki heard the door creak before she registered it had opened.

'Ah there you are,' said John, as calmly as if he was welcoming someone into a teashop. 'Miki didn't think you were in, but I've always imagined this was the kind of place where you'd stay.'

Miki barely took in what the woman looked like. Her eyes were focussed on the shotgun pointed straight at them. The ends of the barrels seemed huge, wide and very, very dark. Packed with death, whispered a voice in Miki's mind. She froze. However, John didn't seem to have noticed the gun and walked forward, his hands out to the side, palms towards her.

'This isn't happening,' thought Miki. 'This is the kind of thing that only happens on TV. It isn't real. It can't be real.' She finally registered the woman's face. She had a ring through the left side of her top lip. Both sides of her head were shaved, but a streak of long, jet black hair grew along the centre of her scalp. Miki couldn't see how long it was, but she could see a silver peace earring and an angel stud on K4's left ear. On her right there seemed to be four holes with silver horns poking out of them. A final ring pierced the side of her ear. She had the pale face of someone who prefers being indoors. Her clothes were a mishmash of multi-coloured layers with green, possibly ex-military, trousers. She couldn't be much taller than Miki and she was extremely thin. Miki wondered if she did pull the trigger whether she would end up flat on her back with the gun pointing at the sky like a skinny dark chimney.

Meanwhile K4 and SpyGlass continued to talk.

'Where'd you hear that name?' demanded the woman.

'SpyGlass? That's my online name. You're K4 aren't you? I mean I'm almost sure this is where I tracked you to before I left Gloucestershire.'

The woman tucked the gun more neatly into her shoulder and looked down the barrel.

'Why were you tracking me?'

'I've been spoofing you for ages. That's the basis of our deal.'

'So it was you who sent the tactical team to that Shrewsbury coffee shop?'

John shrugged. 'I didn't send them anywhere. It was all their own idea. By the way, when it comes to hacking into a certain minister's account and then sending embarrassing emails from said account, you need to cover your tracks more carefully.'

'Shit! They backtracked that?'

'Yep, we're pretty on the ball, you know. You got lucky I noticed.'

K4 lowered her gun. 'If all this is true, I owe you a solid. But what the heck are we doing talking in rl? Not like you at all, SpyGlass. That your girlfriend?'

'No, daughter of an old friend of mine.'

'You have friends?'

John let the comment go. Miki realised she had been holding her breath when K4 lowered the gun again and her body greedily sucked in air. She choked. John thumped on the back.

'Don't think she's ever had a gun pointed at her before,' he said.

'And you have?' said K4

'Oh, there's so much you don't know about me it could fill a book,' said John.

'You're certainly better looking than I expected,' said K4.

John flushed slightly. 'Thank you, I think. Can we come in now? There's something small with far too many legs trying to crawl inside my shoe. It's probably venomous.' He shook his shoe. 'Do you have a first aid kit?'

K4 let the gun dangle by her side. 'Yeah, it's you. Come on in.'

RORY, JONAS, TRISHA & HELEN

Trisha had a single room to herself. She lay in bed with an oxygen mask over her mouth and nose. Her eyes were closed and around her was a barrage of beeping, flashing machinery with tubing connecting her to it. Jonas sat in a high backed chair holding his mother's unresponsive hand. He seemed calm, but his eyes were red from crying.

Rory moved into the room. 'Jesus,' he said. 'God, Jonas, I'm sorry. Is she going to be alright?'

Jonas swallowed hard and shook his head. 'Don't know,' he managed to say, before he bit his lip and looked away.

Helen pushed past her son and crouched down beside Jonas. 'Hi, Jonas, I have the misfortune to be Rory's mother. I'm a nurse. I'm going to talk to the doctors and find out what's happening. They may come and ask if they can have your permission to tell me. Would you like them to?'

'Yes, please. They didn't tell me much, but I couldn't take in what they said. I kept thinking…' He broke off, gulping for air as he tried not to cry.

'Is there anyone I can call, honey? Anyone else? Your dad?'

'He walked out on us when Mum got diagnosed with MS.'

'Do you think your mum would like us to call him?'

Jonas shook his head. 'No, she wouldn't, but I wouldn't know how to reach him anyway. He's gone. It's just me and Mum.' Jonas dropped his head and began to weep quietly.

Helen rubbed his back gently. 'I'll be back in a few minutes. Rory will get you a cup of tea and a biscuit. You might not realise it, but you need that.'

Helen opened her purse and handed a note to Rory. 'And be quick about it!' She gave him a stern look. Rory did as he was told.

When he came back his mum hadn't returned. He offered the tea to Jonas. 'You'd better drink it. I know Mum when she gets like that, all medic-like. I got you a Twix as well. Didn't know if you were allergic to peanuts. So many people are nowadays.'

Jonas took both. 'Thanks,' he said. 'Sorry about earlier. Crying, I mean.'

Rory pulled up a plastic chair. 'Shit, man, if it was my mum in hospital, I'd be crying too. I mean she's not nice like your mum is, but she does care. A bit like a friendly barracuda. Except with her patients. She's like a fluffy lamb with them.'

As if alerted by his comments, Helen appeared in the doorway. She gave her son a hard stare. Then she jerked her thumb at Rory to get out of the seat and sat down next to Jonas. 'Right, love, they are going to keep your mum in for a couple of days. There's some tests to do, just to check things out properly. The doctor won't exactly say what he thinks is wrong yet, but I got him to say it was likely she was going to be okay. I had to force him pretty hard to say that, but he's being careful.'

'So what is it?'

'There are two main possibilities. One worse than the other. You sure you want to know?'

Jonas nodded. Rory looked out the window. He watched the reflection of the conversation. It felt private and painful, but he thought if he left it would be worse.

'The worst it is likely to be is a form of epilepsy. A few people do develop it later in life. If it is that, then your mum will live, but she'll have to take medication regularly and her life would change a bit.'

'How?' said Jonas.

'Let's cross that road when we come to it. There are different sorts of epilepsy and we don't even know if it is that.'

'Okay,' said Jonas. Rory heard his friend's voice waver. 'What's the other thing?'

243

'It might be simply stress. Has your mum been under a lot of pressure lately?'

Rory spun round. 'That bloody journalist. He deserves to go to jail.'

Helen waited for Jonas to answer. 'He took a picture on a good morning, of Mum working in the garden. She was kneeling down and digging in the flowerbed. She says making things grow makes her feel good. She had to spend the rest of the day in bed, she was so tired.' Jonas squeezed his mum's hand more tightly. 'He didn't understand. He called us benefit cheats. He sold the story to a newspaper and put it up on the web.' Jonas swallowed. 'It's not true. Since Dad left we don't have hardly any money. Mum manages to make things stretch so we pay our bills, but that's it. He made it sound as if we were living in luxury like some kind of celebs.'

Helen said a word Rory had never heard her say before. 'Don't look so shocked, son,' said his mother. 'Just because I don't like you swearing doesn't mean I don't know the words. I was young once myself. I think there might be a lot to sort out when your mum comes round. I hate to pry, love, but is your dad still paying the mortgage?'

'I don't think so. Mum says she hasn't heard anything from him since he went.' He swallowed. 'He said he couldn't cope with Mum being so ill. It upset him too much.'

'I know he's your father, love, but I tell you, if I see him, I'll give him something to be upset about!' Helen's lips closed into a thin line. She was not a slight woman and as she crossed her arms, the muscle in them was obvious.

Jonas smiled for the first time since he'd found Trisha unconscious. It was a small smile, but it was a smile. 'I'd like to see that,' he said.

'I also think, love, that it makes it more likely that this is all down to stress. That's quite a burden your mother's been carrying.'

'I do my best,' said Jonas. 'I don't want her going into a home.'

'I'm sure you do, love, and no one's talking about sending her to a home. You both need a bit of help, that's all, and I'm sure we can sort that out. Right, now I'm going to give you and Rory money for a taxi to your house, so you can pack some things and come back to ours for the next couple of days.' Jonas began to protest. 'Your mum needs rest and she'll be happier knowing you're somewhere safe rather than sitting worrying beside her. She might not be conscious enough to talk, but I'd bet any money she can hear. You can stay with us as long as you need. Family's always coming and going, so we have plenty of room. Rory, you get that big mac and cheese out of the freezer for the pair of you tonight for tea. Your dad'll be home by seven. Oh, and I left your diary on your desk. Found it when I was hoovering behind the back of the sofa. I was keeping it to teach you a lesson. You should be more careful. Not all people respect privacy like I do.' She looked across at the bed. 'But after today, it seems a bit petty. Not that you've even asked me about it. I guess it's not that important to either of us.' She gave him a quick one-armed hug.

Rory stood there, beginning to reassess everything. There had never been any danger of anyone knowing his secret. He hadn't needed to tell Mark Stuart anything.

'C'mon Rory, look lively. Jonas must be starving,' said his mum, giving him a friendly shove towards the door.

Inside, the hut smelled damp. Miki hesitated, waiting for her eyes to adjust to the dimness. She realised that newspaper had been plastered over the window. Why? To keep the room warm? She couldn't see any source of heating, or was it that K4 was on the run? The woman moved around and Miki heard a tap turn on and then something being filled. Gradually she began to pick out the scene.

The door opened straight into a room that appeared to be a kitchen. A white old fashioned china sink, a battered, ancient electric cooker and fridge stood against one wall. A large, well scrubbed pine table, surrounded by four mismatched, peeling painted chairs, took up most of the rest of the space. Miki sat down on one. It creaked alarmingly, so she sat as still as she could. While Miki took in her new surroundings, John hopped on one foot as he shook out his shoe. A rolled up leaf fell to the ground. He sat down hard on a chair and regarded the sole of his foot. Then, very gingerly, with his thumb and forefinger, he pulled off a piece of flattened worm. Holding it up for a moment and peering at it, he exclaimed, 'Ugh!' and dropped it distastefully on the floor. 'This place is disgusting.'

'Did you just drop a worm on my clean floor?' said K4.

'You're the one who chose to live in the middle of this mudfest,' snapped John.

Miki picked out the gun resting against the far wall. Currently out of K4's reach, she wondered if she should go for it. She had little idea how to handle such a weapon, but she could always pass it to John. At this moment, the man in question was sitting down and smoothing out his sock before putting his shoe back on. He didn't look like the kind of man she'd seen in the movies that could handle a gun. Maybe it was best if she watched and put herself between the gun and K4 if the woman decided to go for it. Hopefully, John would then step in and do something useful. Miki sighed. He definitely didn't conform to her idea of a spy. Less 007 and more man-in-a-supermarket.

'This is nature, SpyGlass! These trees are what let the earth breath. Let us breath. Not even you can exist wholly online.'

'So now you're an eco-terrorist? You change your central tenets as frequently as I change socks!'

'What is that now? Three times a day?' said K4.

'So my feet get hot. It's a recognised medical condition.'

'Have you two ever been married?' said Miki.

'To each other?' the two adults said at once and both pulled faces. 'No.'

'Why are we here?' said Miki to John. 'I mean, really great hair, K4, and you're without a doubt the most interesting person I've ever met.'

She broke off as K4 rummaged in a drawer. She held up a pair of clippers, smiling what appeared to be a genuine smile. 'Want me to do yours?'

'ADHD,' whispered John in her ear.

'No thanks,' said Miki. 'Maybe when I go to Art School.' She looked hard at John. The spy pulled himself together.

'I'd like your help, K4. These kids were running a website full of fake news.'

'What, you?' said K4. 'Why?'

'For me, it was about all the rumours people spread about my parents – them being anti-vaxxers, eco-guerrillas, that kind of thing. Which they're not. They an eco-friendly business. That's it. You want a recycled yoga mat, they're your people. The idea was we were going to get people to believe a load of rubbish and then show them how they couldn't and shouldn't trust everything they believe online.'

K4 bit her bottom lip. Miki realised that she could only be a handful of years older than she was. 'Yeah, I can see that,' said K4. 'I would have done something more direct–'

'Like subscribed various bishops to porn sites?' said John.

'I told you that was a mistake,' said K4. 'I was too young, wasn't thinking. Not cool to use exploitation material to hit at the Man. Makes me as guilty. I appreciate you taking it down.'

'It's how we met,' explained John. 'Online.'

'Yeah, and you thought, this is someone I can work with... I'm kind of a spy-spy,' said K4.

'She means an asset,' said John. 'We help each other out from time to time.'

'Are you the Barton's kid?'

'Yes,' said Miki.

'Yeah, your parents really get around. I've lost count of the number of watchlists I've pulled them off.'

Miki slumped in her seat. 'Shit, so that bit's true.'

'Hey, I think they sound cool – if a bit naïve. Your mum's always posting all this stuff about fighting to save the planet. She sounds like a right eco-guerrilla. Doesn't mean actual fight, though, does she? Means more, put your recycling out. Her language is too emotive. Can give people the wrong idea,' said K4. 'Still, better than my parents. Mum was always high and dad thought I'd make a good second wife, so I left.'

'Your father?' Bile rose in Miki's mouth. She'd heard about that kind of thing, but... 'God, I'm sorry.'

K4 waved sympathy away. 'What doesn't kill you leaves you with serious mental scarring, but I got away. I do SpyGlass favours and he helps me out when I sail a bit close to the wind.'

'Now we're all on friendlier terms, let's get down to business. I want you to make it look as if this website was run by someone else. Shouldn't be too hard. There must be a number of people you'd like to drop in it? Subject to my approval, of course.'

'Let me get my laptop,' said K4. She went through to the other room.

'You knew her story?' said Miki quietly.

'I found it out,' said John.

'Is that why you help her?'

'I wouldn't give much for her sanity, surviving prison,' said John, 'and she makes a good asset.'

'But her parents – her father – should be in jail!'

'He's on a watchlist,' said John, 'But without her accusation nothing is going to happen. And she doesn't want to look back.'

'But,' said Miki. 'That's wrong. He should be punished.'

'I'd personally be happy to see him in front of a firing squad,' said John. 'But it's not my business. My testimony would only be hearsay.'

'But can't you arrange for something to happen to him?'

'Miki, I'm an astrophysicist who works on government algorithms, I'm not an assassin.'

'What?'

'An algorithm I developed to detect invisible astral bodies also kind of works for language. It's complicated. And not that interesting to someone who wants to study art.'

'So Leon was right when he said you couldn't be a field agent?'

'It wouldn't be my choice,' said John. 'But I seem to be in the middle of a bloody field right now.'

'So you help my parents and you helped K4 – and abused your position to do so?'

'I've already said, K4 is an asset...'

Miki continued. 'You're actually quite a nice person, aren't you?'

John frowned and pinched the bridge of his nose with the thumb and forefinger of his right hand. 'Please don't go around saying that, I'll lose my job.'

At that moment K4 came back in, an open laptop in her hands. 'Not going to be as easy as I hoped. Someone used a school computer to post. Rookie error. It's going to take a while to remove that. Want to crash here while I do this?'

John and Miki looked at each other. 'Leon,' said Miki. 'Little shit wants us to get caught. He's selling us out.' She glowered accusingly at John. 'He wants to impress you.'

BREAKING NEWS

Government sources both here and in Westminster continue to refuse to issue a full statement to the press about the alien appearance in Edinburgh.

BREAKING NEWS

Are these aliens immigrants? Do we need a quarantine area? Are they eligible for council housing ahead of earth-born people? Are they political refugees? Will it be dangerous for earth to give them sanctuary. These

250

and other questions discussed by our official panel of alien experts at 9pm tonight.

BREAKING NEWS

Italian Cyclists claim to have ridden five days without sleep.

Breaking News is brought to you by Radio City Central: the local station you can trust.

TUESDAY 13th JUNE

BREAKING NEWS

Be Prepared
Tune in at 1pm to listen to our prime special alien advisor describe how to set up a grab bag for when the Alien Invasion begins

BREAKING NEWS

A farmer in South Wales claims all of his lambs have disappeared overnight. Did the aliens drop by for a midnight snack? If they are carnivores what else might they eat?

BREAKING NEWS

Special alien pull-out in our sister magazine tonight. Our advisors suggested we should get all relevant information in print for when the aliens turn off our electricity. Magazine is normal price plus £20 for the alien pull-out.

Italian cyclists say they are doing it all in the memory of the talking rabbit. They want to raise money to save animals from being eaten.

JONAS & RORY

Jonas lay on his back on the camp bed in Rory's room and stared up into the darkness. The contraption, something that Rory's father had somehow brought back from his army days, felt like sleeping on canvas and wire. Jonas suspected that under the sheets and pillow that might be exactly what it was. Rory's sister Susan had made it up for him, while Rory had attempted to make him eat half-defrosted macaroni cheese until Jonas had roused himself enough to reheat it properly. How could someone be incapable of using a microwave? thought Jonas. Rory had seemed totally lost in the kitchen which was weird. Maybe the stress of everything was getting to him too.

Beyond the discomfort and his general sense of uprootedness, Jonas thought about his mother. He thought about the stress she'd been under. Rory had explained part of it to his father when he got home. Apparently his wife had rung him, but he'd asked Jonas a couple of questions. One of them, that was still bothering him, had been, 'Was his father at least still paying the mortgage?'

Jonas had to admit he didn't know. He'd never thought about how the house was paid for. It was simply his home. The thought that his mother might have been running up enormous debt and didn't feel as if she could tell him made him feel sick. He liked the house, but he loved his mother. If they had to lose the house to lessen her stress and make her healthy then he was ready to start packing now. He'd thought they shared everything, but while he was away pranking the internet his mother had, literally, been worrying herself to death. He had to remember to tell her when he next saw her that he was old enough to know everything now, and if it came to choosing between losing the house and having her still around, he never wanted to see the place again.

In his bed, Rory tossed and turned. He could hear the camp bed creaking alarmingly. Eventually he said, 'Is that thing as uncomfortable as it sounds?'

'Worse,' said Jonas. 'Not that I'm not grateful to your family…'

'Susan said she set it up because she didn't think it was a good idea to leave you alone in the spare room.'

'What did she think I'd do?' said Jonas. 'Steal a pillow? Eat one?'

Rory gave a humourless chuckle. 'No, you idiot. She thought you might be sad or lonely if you couldn't sleep. She likes me and thought I'd cheer you up – do my comedy routine.' He paused. 'Sorry, not been up to much. I got a bit of a shock today.'

'You and me both,' said Jonas.

'God, no, I didn't mean like that. You win on the trauma stakes hands down, mate.'

'Thanks.'

'No, it's just that,' Rory paused and stared up at his ceiling. He could still make out the outline of the fluorescent stars he'd had up as a child. What had happened to them? He wanted them back. 'My mum handed me back my diary.'

Jonas sat up in bed. 'The one you lost that …'

'Yeah, that talks about me as Katy. That one.'

'Where did she find it?'

'Down the back of the sofa – she didn't say which. In here or in the living room. She said she'd been holding on to it as a lesson to take care of my stuff, but it seemed rather petty now.'

'A lot of things do.' Jonas sighed. 'Did she read it?'

'She said not.'

'Does she know about you?'

'Hell, I don't even know about me,'said Rory.

'You know what I think? I think, despite the hours your folks work you all seem close. You keep in touch. I think, even if they don't say they know, they won't be surprised. I bet Susan knows what you do with the dresses and make-up she gives you and she doesn't care.'

'She wouldn't,' said Rory. 'She'd use it as an excuse to get new stuff. But yeah, if they haven't guessed… maybe I should start wearing dresses openly at home. When I saw your mum lying in the hospital bed, it made me think no one is here forever. Not that I think your mum is dying,' he said quickly.

'Yeah, I know,' said Jonas. 'Like a whole lot of stuff isn't important any more. The website – the pranks…'

'No,' said Rory, sitting up and turning to face Jonas in the dark. 'The opposite. If we're only here for a short while then we shouldn't need to pretend to be who we aren't. We need to find the courage to be us – I need to find the courage to be me. That's what I've been thinking about. If I hadn't thought the diary had been lost I'd never have gone along with Leon's plan and that would have changed everything in my life for the worse. I told Mark Stuart who and what I was. He was scared, not me…. Because

I reckon, deep down inside, he's scared of everything and I'm not anymore. I'm going to be me from now on for as long as I live.'

Jonas didn't answer.

'You still awake?' said Rory softly. 'Because I think I just made an important decision and I'd hate to have to go over it all over again at breakfast. It's more dramatic in the moment.'

Jonas gave a small snort of laughter.

'Ah, my audience is awake. What a relief,' said Rory.

'But you can't say the UFO thing was worth doing. It was childish and we're probably going to be in trouble for that. I really don't want to put any more weight on my mum.'

'I don't think we broke any laws,' said Rory. 'Not even in the rubbish we put up online. That's kind of the point, isn't it? Some people will believe anything – and that's wrong. That's what leads to people getting hurt. Like your mum and Miki's dog. So the UFO might have been a bit over the top, but it proves the point. People need to think more.'

'But what about the police, the ambulance people – all those officials that got brought out? Someone has to foot the bill for that.'

'Yeah, well, they can bill us if they want. Wait till I'm a famous film star and I'll pay off our debts.'

'Seriously?'

'Seriously. I intend to be famous,' said Rory. 'And seriously, there would be no point giving us a bill we cannot pay. Besides, not being eighteen, we're still technically kids. The worst we might get is a bit of a telling off from a policeman. I know! We can even claim it was community theatre. That gives you a free pass with most things as long as there aren't any injuries. We can put it on again for the Fringe next year and charge for tickets.'

'Not in the Royal Park,' said Jonas.

'So, we'll find somewhere else.'

'You're mad, you know that?' said Jonas.

'Your mum's going to be fine. It's all going to be fine, you know that?'

But Jonas didn't reply. He'd finally put his head back down on the pillow and was fast asleep.

MIKI, JOHN & K4

The grey early morning light shone through the holes in the curtain. Miki yawned and stretched. Her mouth felt dry and tasted like the mud pie that child with the weird pimples, who always smelled of wee, had force-fed her in nursery school. What a weird memory to pop up. She hadn't thought about Rachel in ages. Rubbing her neck, which ached horribly, she sat up, blinking, and looked around. Confusion flooded her. Then she smelled something weird, like dog poop.

'Shit!'

John lay slumped in a chair, his jacket across him for warmth. Miki looked down, identified where the smell came from. In one swift movement she threw off the mouldy blanket someone had thrown over her. Then she turned and whipped a curtain back. It dissolved into a dusty mush between her fingers. 'Shit!' She used the remnants to smear a slightly more opaque section of the grimy glass. It was definitely bright daylight outside. As if to confirm this her stomach gurgled with hunger. 'Shit!'

'Do all teenagers swear with as little imagination as you?' asked John. Miki turned to face him. John yawned, shivered slightly and pulled his jacket on. 'How on earth does she live without heating?'

'K4?' he called. 'It's bollock Baltic out here. Mind if I make the girl and I a cup of tea?' He turned back to Miki. 'Always better to ask the person with a gun before you nick their tea, don't you think?'

'What's the time?' said Miki in a rasping voice.

John got up. 'God, you sound as if you need tea more than me. And that's a lot.' He wandered over to the back of the room and poked his head through the next door. 'Nope, she's not here. Let's hope she's done what we asked. I suggest we wait a couple of hours before I use one of those computers to check. Stealing tea is nothing next to using her rig.'

'What's the time?' repeated Miki.

John glanced at his watch. '10 a.m. Heavens, I haven't slept as long as that in ages. Pity it wasn't in a comfy bed. What do you take in your tea? I advise against milk.' He picked up a pot and looked in it. 'Probably best to avoid the sugar too. Ants.'

'John,' said Miki, feeling like she was going burst any minute, 'I've been out all night with you. My parents are going to go mental. They've either organised a national search by now or they'll be planning our wedding.'

John dropped the pot. It smashed, sending white sugar across the floor. Several startled ants scurried away.

'You mean you never stay out overnight? You're sixteen, aren't you? A bit of a wild child if your friends are to be believed.'

'I'm fifteen,' said Miki, 'and I only – I only say wild things – and hit people sometimes.'

John pinched the bridge of his nose again in a gesture now so familiarly annoying that Miki had to restrain herself from hitting out at him. 'Your parents know me. They know you'd be safe with me.'

'Really?' said Miki. 'They know you're a field agent who can look after himself?'

'There's no need to shout,' said John. 'No, of course they don't know any such thing. Firstly because I'm not and secondly because they don't know where I work. But I think you will find they trust me as an old, honourable friend, who would do his very best to look after their daughter.'

'So global search it is. Dad probably thinks we've been taken by aliens.'

The front door creaked and buckled as something was hurled against it. John grabbed Miki by the wrist and pushed her behind him. The door gave and K4, holding a bag brimming with mushrooms in one hand and a box of eggs in the other, grinned at them. She held both up. 'Breakfast?'

'No mushrooms for us,' said John quickly. 'How far are you along?'

'Oh, your bit of work? All done.'

'Then I think we should get back to my parents,' said Miki.

'I need to know what you've done,' said John.

So K4 told him.

JONAS & RORY

Rory slipped the shimmering fabric over his head. It settled in waves of silky blues, greens and whites around

259

him. He held up one arm so that the long, full sleeve fell dramatically. 'What do you think?'

'Do you have to do this now?' said Jonas. 'I don't want to stop you, but haven't we got enough going on right now? Couldn't it wait one more day?'

'Mate, if I wait another day, I don't know if I'll have the balls to do it. How do I look?'

Jonas shook his head. 'Like a little boy playing dress-up in his mother's clothes. It's far too big for you.'

'Rory! Jonas! Breakfast!'

'Too late,' said Rory. 'Time to go.'

Jonas followed him down the floral-papered hall to the kitchen. His stomach felt all light and floaty, and there were spots in front of his eyes. 'Rory,' he hissed, 'please!', but Rory strode ahead.

They walked into the kitchen. Rory paused dramatically in front of the table at which sat his mother, his father and his sister. Jonas found he had no chance of nudging past. All three stared up at Rory. Jonas took in their various expressions of horror and closed his eyes. He willed it all to be a dream, but he could still hear them.

'Good heavens, Rory,' said Helen. 'You cannot possibly wear that.'

'How the hell did you get that?' said Susan. 'That's Lori's. I said I'd fix her hem.'

Another voice spoke, Rory's father, but it didn't make any sense. There were no words. More a low moan. Like a cow calving, thought Jonas. He squinted, one eye slightly open.

Rory had pulled himself into an acting pose, spine straight, chin slightly lifted, 'Mother,' he declared dramatically, 'You may not realise…'

'That,' said Helen, 'is an evening dress and completely unsuitable for breakfast.'

'W-what?'said Rory.

'And it belongs to Lori. You must have picked it up by mistake when I gave you those clothes for the "drama department",' said Susan. She did air quotes around the last two words. 'You better not have got anything stinky on it. Lori loves that dress.'

'I can see why,' said their mother to Susan. 'The colours do shimmer in the light.'

Rory's father continued to make the low moaning noise. His wife tapped him sharply on the back of his hand with her fork. 'Shut up, dear. It's only a dress, not a syringe full of drugs,' she said kindly. 'We'll talk about this later.' She looked back at her startled son. 'Now, Rory, sweetie, go and put on something more appropriate for breakfast and I'll tell you how today is going to work.'

Rory slowly retreated from the room. Jonas hesitated in the background. 'Sit down, dear,' said Helen. 'Did you know about the dresses?'

Jonas took a seat. He nodded.

Helen reached out and patted his hand. 'I'm glad he could tell someone. Do you…?'

'No,' said Jonas quickly and loudly. 'I don't.' He took a breath. 'Not that there's anything wrong with wearing dresses. I just don't want to.'

'That's just as well,' said Helen. 'Rory can get very competitive.'

'I suppose I'll have to help him buy make-up now,' said Susan. 'With all the other things I have to do…'

'I wouldn't let you if you paid me,' said Rory, coming back in a polka-dot mini dress. 'I'm allergic to the cheap stuff you buy.'

'Now, that's more practical,' said Helen, 'but you will have to practice sitting with your legs together. You can't do that man-thing in a dress.'

Rory pulled his knees together.

'Good,' said Helen. 'No matter what you're wearing, no one wants to see your danglies on public display.'

Rory blushed crimson. 'M-m-mum!'

LEON

Leon sat looking at the printed version of the dossier he had compiled on his friends. He'd backed it up to the cloud and he had it stored on both of his computers. There was no way this was going to vanish. He was wearing his clothes for school as if he expected it to be an ordinary day. He checked his watch. He'd thought they'd have been here by now. Surely they'd be able to get the information from the school records to see who had posted the article? Maybe it was different with schools because they were kids. Maybe spies weren't allowed to hack into school computers. He frowned. That didn't seem right. The whole point of being a spy was you were allowed to operate outside the lines. Surely such mundane rules wouldn't apply to them?

'Breakfast!' called his mum.

Leon put the printed pages neatly on the centre of his desk. Then he changed his mind and put them in a drawer in case someone else came into the bedroom first. Then he thought that a decent wannabe spy would put them somewhere secure. He slipped them inside his pillow case. That wasn't the best place…

'Leon! Now!'

Quickly Leon pulled them out and stuck them under his

mattress. Hopefully the secret service people, when they came, would appreciate that as a child in his parent's house, special safes and combustible trapdoors were beyond his means.

Leon's breakfast passed without incident. He walked to school as slowly as he dared, keeping his ears open for the sounds of sirens, and looking for black vehicles with tinted windows about to swoop down on him. All he saw were some third years tossing a second year's lunch around. The kid in question ran backwards and forwards, an awkward piggy-in-the-middle, wailing in despair. Inevitably the lunch box split open. Egg mayonnaise sandwiches rained down and splattered on the pavement. A single pepperoni sausage rolled down a drain and a cat ran off with some kind of iced biscuit. The second year sat down and cried. One of the third years retrieved a can of coke that had fallen into a shrub and handed it to him. The others jeered at him for being soft. He threw a punch that both the others dodged, and then they ran off together, leaving their victim holding the sole remaining portion of his lunch.

As for how walks to school usually went, this was quite an event. But today it seemed a positive letdown. He stopped to help the second year gather up the bits of sandwich that had landed on the grass, partly because he felt he should have helped and felt sorry for the guy. But mostly because he wanted the extra time to allow the secret service to catch up with him.

They didn't appear. But Petey, the second year, who appeared to have a very bad cold and no handkerchief, was very grateful and followed him to school telling him how he would have dealt with the bullies if only he hadn't been ill, in more and more hyperbolic language.

Leon managed to shake him off by dropping behind a hedge when Petey was midway through describing how he thought he could manage a flying kick when his temperature came down. Peering through the leaves, Leon had to stuff his fist in his mouth to stop himself giggling, as Petey stopped and looked around in confusion. He waited until the boy was far enough ahead and then he stood up. He sauntered along slowly. Eventually he reached the school gates. He stood staring up at the school sign.

'What's the matter, nerd? Forgotten how to read?' One of the senior boys rode by on his bicycle. Without thinking, Leon dodged the swinging school bag aimed at his head. 'Weird,' he muttered to himself and headed into school.

By the time registration had finished and the first lesson had begun, Leon was beginning to think there must be something wrong with the school computer – or at the very least its links to the outside world. Or hadn't what he'd done been obvious enough? As his teacher droned on about poetry written about life in WW1 trenches, Leon wracked his brains for something more outrageous, but even more clever, to do.

The low, atonal murmur of Mrs Monroe stopped as a knock sounded on the door. A small girl, with bushy hair and badly washed-off make-up, handed Mrs Monroe a note. The teacher cleared her throat.

'Now listen up, class. This is serious. Has anyone seen Miki Barton?'

Leon sat bolt upright. 'What's happened, Miss?'

Mrs Monroe scanned the note again. 'It appears she's gone missing. Do you know something?'

'No, Miss,' said Leon, slumping back down in his seat. Inside he was fuming. They'd only gone and picked up the wrong pupil. Obviously, because Miki was older, they'd assumed she'd been the ringleader. He bit into his pencil. This required some serious thought. Was Miki the kind of girl to take the credit? Probably not. She had far too many opinions about justice. But what if she thought she was protecting him? Leon let out a groan.

'Are you alright, Leon?'

'No, Miss. My stomach really hurts. Can I go see the nurse?'

'Very well.'

'Got your period, have you?' called Hamish Steel, a football fanatic who Leon disliked intently. As Mrs Monroe scolded the boy. Leon walked past and discreetly spat on his head, a nice big white gob of saliva. He managed to get it right at the crown where it nestled nicely into the scalp. Being vertically challenged, Leon reckoned Hamish should get plenty of comments at break.

MIKI, JOHN, BRIAN & MEG

As John drove up to the Barton's house a police car passed them. Miki's head swivelled.

'I doubt the police would be interested in a teenage girl who's been missing for one night,' said John.

Miki sighed. 'Maybe in your day, John. But this is a different world. Kids aren't even allowed to play outside anymore.'

'I do have something of a handle on the modern world.'

Miki shook her head. 'On the modern world of the internet, maybe. Are we really going to go with the breakdown story and the long walk to find a garage?'

John nodded. 'Then you fainted, so I got you to a doctor. He said it was lack of food.'

'I never faint. Why didn't you think to phone my parents?'

'It was so hectic,' said John. 'And then we got the last two rooms at the B&B in the middle of nowhere – and by the time I got to bed my phone was out of charge.'

'And the next morning?'

'I wanted to get you home as soon as possible.'

'I cannot believe you think this is going to work. Have you ever had to make up a cover story for anything?'

John muttered something.

'What?'

'I said we have people who specialise in that kind of thing.'

'Good grief,' said Miki. 'This is so going to be fun. Not.'

Meg opened the front door before John had even turned the engine off. Miki leapt out of the car and ran to meet her. Meg embraced her.

'Ouch,' said Miki. 'Not so tight. I've only been away a few hours.'

Meg said nothing, but continued hugging her and rocking slightly from side to side. Brian followed her out, his hair standing wild in all directions. Miki, with some difficulty, extracted herself from her mother's embrace. 'At least you weren't worried,' she said. 'Looks like you just woke up.'

Brian shook his head. 'I've not been to bed,' he said in a low, intense voice, his attention focussed past Miki. She turned to follow his gaze and saw that it centred on John, who stood by the car. 'We need to talk,' said Brian in the same strange voice. 'Let's take this inside.'

Meg and Brian sat in two armchairs opposite a small sofa, so Miki and John were forced to sit together. The sofa was old and sagged. Miki held on to one armrest to stop herself sinking into it and over towards John.

'Mum,' said Miki. 'It's fine. I'm alright. Nothing bad has happened.' Miki thought her mother's face relaxed slightly. The tightness around her jaw relaxed, suggesting she was no longer gritting her teeth.

'What do you mean by bad?' snapped Brian.

'We're both fine,' said Miki.

'It's the craziest story,' said John. 'We…'

'I bet,' interrupted Brian in a voice that was becoming more and more like a growl.

Then, to Miki's horror, John told them the story he'd rehearsed in the car. To be fair, she thought, he told it well. He added enough detail to make places seem real and included amusing anecdotes of the crazy locals who had helped them. Neither of her parents responded and when John finished with a deprecating laugh at his own foolishness, his laugh fell into a cold, bottomless pool of silence.

Meg and Brian said nothing. Brian's expression was wooden. Meg kept her head up, but she couldn't meet Miki's gaze.

'I'm sorry I worried you,' said Miki. 'But we're back now. Isn't that what matters?'

'Yes,' said her mother turning to Brian. 'They're back. Let's leave it at that. If Miki says she fine then I believe her. It's all I need to know.'

'Fine,' said her husband. 'I'll let it go if Miki answers me one question. Why didn't she call us on *her* phone?'

'Guilty conscience, Leo?' said Mr Deacon.

Leon jumped in his seat. 'No, sir. Nothing at all, sir. I was listening, sir.'

The nurse had checked Leon over. Declared there was nothing wrong with him that a good lesson with the nice Mr Deacon wouldn't fix. She was of the opinion Leon 'had too much on his mind, being so young and advanced so much above his age.' She even, to Leon's absolute horror, suggested he got his mother to give him a nice glass of hot milk before bed to ease his tummy and give him nice dreams. Would he like to see if she could get something now for his tummy? Leon left as soon as possible, afraid that any minute she'd offer him a lollipop. Now, back in class, a nice glass of hot milk and a lollipop in the first aid room seemed like an excellent idea.

Deacon prowled around Leon's chair. Leon had seen him do this before. It was as if the teacher imagined himself as a tiger getting ready to pounce, when the reality was he had to squeeze between the narrowly packed rows of desk and always managed to knock pupils' books and pencils to the ground. Although Leon noticed Deacon never deigned to apologise or pick anything up. This was his first experience of being the teacher's prey.

'Only I couldn't help noticing,' said the teacher on his second lap of Leon's desk, 'that you've been very tense all morning. Much as I would like to attribute that to my superior teaching, even I don't find nineteenth century textiles and the cotton mills that interesting.' Sutri Rajh's pencil case hit the floor, scattering glittery pencils everywhere. Sutri gave a small anguished gasp as she

268

scurried to retrieve the pencils before Deacon came round again and stood on them.

'In fact,' said Deacon, 'if I was of a mind to be poetic, and I am, I might say every nerve of yours was aquiver. Are you waiting for something to happen, Leo? Is there something you know that we don't? Please share such a riveting piece of information with the class. We are all ears, aren't we, everybody?'

No one responded. Instead Leon registered a collective intake of breath. Everyone was waiting for him to do something clever – something Leon-like. But it was clear to Leon it didn't matter what he said. Until today he hadn't set a foot wrong in Deacon's class, and had evaded being pierced by what the teacher liked to think of as his rapier wit. Deacon was enjoying himself immensely. So Leon decided to tell the truth. 'I'm waiting for someone from the secret service to recruit me, sir,' he said.

Deacon, who had been expecting pretty much any excuse but this, was somewhat nonplussed. However, he'd been a teacher for almost two decades. He knew not to show weakness. 'Ah, of course. I should have guessed,' he said.

For a single second Leon wondered if Deacon was a liaison with the school for MI5. Then he dismissed the idea as profoundly ridiculous. 'Yes, sir. I sent them a message telling them where I am last night. Not a direct message, obviously. One in code.'

'Naturally,' said Deacon. He raised his eyebrows and looked around at his class. At the back of the class a couple of the boys tittered.

'Gather your things, Leo. You need to be ready for the call, don't you? Come on, now.'

Bemused, Leon packed his bag. The class watched with

growing amusement. This was much better than learning about looms and industrialisation.

'All done?' said Deacon, finally pausing in his prowling, 'Then I believe you should wait outside the headteacher's door. If he manages to see you before I get there, feel free to tell him your little story.'

Blushing crimson, Leon made his way through the maze of desks. Of course, the headteacher was far too busy to see him and Deacon seemed to have forgotten all about him. Leon had had enough. Instead of going into lunch he went home.

JONAS & RORY

Rory compromised. He wore the mini dress, but teamed it with a pair of long shorts. 'You'll start a new fashion,' said his sister.

Rory ignored her.

At the hospital they found Trish looking much better than yesterday. Helen came in briefly before she started her shift. 'Good to see you with colour in your cheeks,' she said. 'I hope you don't mind, I kept the boys off school. It's not like they're doing much except revision now. They can catch up at the weekend. I thought it would do you and Jonas good to see each other – and well, Rory, any excuse to stay off school.'

Trish looked curiously at Rory.

'Oh don't mind the dress,' said Helen, blushing. 'Rory's taken a fancy to – er, wearing them. As they say, anything's better than drugs.'

'You don't need to fight my battle, Mum,' said Rory. 'I'm sure Jonas' mother has more on her mind than my sartorial arrangements.'

'I was wondering if that's a vintage dress, Rory. I think my mother had one like it. It might be a Zandra Rhodes. You should be careful of it.'

'I suppose it could be,' said Helen, considering it. 'No drinking soup while wearing it! I must be off. I'm on ward 6 today. They're so overstretched, but I mentioned you to the hospital counsellor and she's going to drop by later with some practical suggestions.'

'Oh, I don't know,' began Trish.

'Her name's Sophie and she's dead nice.' Helen bustled off.

'Boys,' said Trish. 'Don't you dare leave me.'

The counsellor didn't turn up before lunch. Jonas found himself sidelined while his mother and Rory talked vintage fashion. He only woke up when Rory got out a notebook and started showing his mother some sketches he'd made of outfits. 'I didn't know you did that,' said Jonas.

'Yeah, like I was going to show this around the school.'

'You've got a talent, dear,' said Trish. 'You certainly know how to put colours together.'

LEON

Leon's parents were still at work, but he'd left his window slightly ajar, as usual. It was the work of moments for him to slip inside. He made himself a sandwich and got a can of Pepsi from the fridge. He'd never skipped school before, but since they only took the full register that went to the office in the morning, he doubted anyone would miss him. If they did they'd probably think someone had sent him home as it would be on record he'd visited the nurse.

He sat down at his computer. If he'd known skiving

was this easy he might have tried it before. He logged on and started trawling through news sites. He was halfway through his sandwich when he read something so startling that a big chunk fell out of his mouth and landed on the keyboard.

Marty Mclaren, Freelance Journalist Behind Alien Hoax & Joke Website

Little known journalist, McLaren, who was having no success in breaking into the major news channels, is now known to have been behind the alien hoax recently perpetrated in Edinburgh. It seems McLaren decided that if he couldn't get a reporting job he might as well make up the news. The hoax has been an enormous success for him. Convincing hoards of people and costing the taxpayers thousands, possibly even tens of thousands, for crowd control, policing and forensic examination.

It appears the UFO hoax was the final stage in a long campaign. McLaren has been, for many weeks, running a fake news website that has gathered over one hundred thousand followers and widely disseminated a host of fake news items....

The article continued to list all the items Leon and his team had created, plus a few extra ones. Despite his rising anger, Leon felt the one about the Cult of Squirrel worship was inspired. The piece ended with...

Mclaren is now in police custody. Whether he will be charged, or ordered to pay back the costs of his antics, is

272

yet to be learned. One neighbour reports that as he was being taken away McLaren was shouting about 'two teenage boys' and 'a recycling lorry'. Mrs Williams, who saw him removed by the police, commented, 'He kept shouting about it all being linked to the school – and how some kids were getting revenge on him. Complete nonsense. He always was a bit odd. Coming and going at all times of day and night. He's obviously gone off his head. I wouldn't be surprised if they locked him up.

Leon picked up the bit of sandwich from the keyboard and ate it. He barely noticed what he was doing. All he could think was how very much he wanted to find McLaren and wring his neck.

MEG, BRIAN, JOHN & MIKI

'I forgot I had it with me,' said Miki.

'You expect us to believe that?' said Brian.

'There was a lot going on,' said John, gamely. But Miki could hear the concern in his voice. The truth was she'd got so used to following Leon's instructions not to use their phones that she had, honestly, not thought of it. It wasn't that she'd forgotten she had it, precisely. Rather that it hadn't occurred to her to call or text. Besides, what could she have possibly said? That she was in a shack with a notorious hacker in the middle of nowhere? It occurred to her, rather too late, lame as it was, John's story had been much more believable than the truth.

'Look, Mum,' she said. 'Let's tackle the elephant in the room. I haven't slept with John. He didn't ask me to – and

I'm not interested in him in that way. Neither does he think of me as much more than an annoying schoolgirl.'

'Well, I didn't actually say… think…'

'But that's what you're wondering, isn't it? Look, cards on the table, as Dad says. I got involved in something I can't talk about and John got me out of it. If anything I – we – owe him a favour for well, clearing the thing up.'

'Is this something to do with your work?' said Meg to John.

'In a way,' said John. 'I can't talk about it.'

'Oh my God,' said Brian, 'the aliens were real. You met a real life alien, didn't you, Miki?'

Miki and John stuck to their statements that they couldn't discuss the matter that was now sorted. Later, after an awkward lunch, John said he had to return to work. The whole family, including Red, followed him out to say goodbye, then departed: Brian to walk Red, and her mother to get back to her tie-dying. Miki lingered behind. 'That was ridiculous,' she said. 'Aliens.'

'I don't think your mother believes that,' said John. 'But she believes I got you out of something. I'd avoid being alone with her for a bit until you do something else outrageous and all this is forgotten.'

Miki smiled. 'All my outrageousness is now being reserved for art college.'

'Good,' said John. 'Don't call me when it happens. I don't want to know.'

LEON

After much raging and shouting, Leon sat down at his computer. He wanted to immediately write a rebuttal of

274

everything he'd read. However, another three groups had already claimed his fake news website had been theirs. No, if he was ever going to prove he had done this, he was going to need the others.

It would have to be tonight.

LEON, MIKI, JONAS & RORY

Miki arrived at Rory's house shortly after four p.m. 'Is Jonas here?' she asked when Rory answered the door. He was wearing a pink kaftan and a purple turban.

'Lovely to see you too,' said Rory. 'Yes, he is.'

'I heard about his mum. How horrible for him.'

Rory ushered her into the house. 'She's on the mend. It might turn out to be a good thing, because now my mum's involved. She's very into social advocacy.'

'Hmm,' said Miki. 'I need to talk to you all. I've texted Leo to come over.' She paused before Rory's bedroom door. 'Are they doing the *Arabian Nights* at school?'

'My house, my rules.'

'There is no rule that could make pink and purple look good,' said Miki. 'You look as if you belong in one of those fake plastic pink castles little girls get at Christmas. The ones that come with the unicorns and bubble fountains.'

Rory shoved her in the small of her back, so she more or less fell into his room. The doorbell rang again and Rory went to answer it. Miki found Jonas sitting on the camp bed. He smiled when he saw her. 'So sorry,' began Miki. Jonas stopped her by holding up his hand. 'It's okay. It's a relief to have someone else involved to help,' he said. 'Rory's mum has been fantastic. I only hope my mum continues to let her help.'

Leon burst through the door, followed closely by Rory. 'Have you seen who's taking the credit for our website?' he cried, throwing a printout into the centre of the room. 'Only Marty McLaren. There's no mention of us at all – and he's not denying it.'

Miki picked up one of the papers and read it. 'I need to tell you guys something.'

'All our hard work. Everything we were trying to achieve and this scum takes the credit,' raged Leon.

Jonas, who had also been reading a paper, said, 'Why wouldn't he deny it? It looks like he might be going to jail for this. We can't let that happen to him.'

'That's about the only good thing about it,' said Leon. 'He's a lowlife scum. Worse than my sister's boyfriend and he has acne. I think he pops it in our bathroom when he visits. I've found pus on the mirror after he's been in. He's gross.'

'Probably thinks he can get a book deal. McLaren, not your sister's disgusting boyfriend,' said Rory. 'Looking at how much trouble he's in. I think we might all have had a narrow escape.'

Miki breathed a sigh of relief. 'I'm glad you think that because it's kind of my fault Marty's getting the blame.' Three pairs of eyes turned towards her. Miki took a deep breath and tried to stay calm.

'It turns out that the guy visiting my parents may or may not work for one of the intelligence services.'

'I knew it!' said Leon, jumping to his feet and pumping the air with his fist. 'So when's he coming round?'

'It seems,' said Miki, raising her voice and giving Leon a serious stare. Leon sat down and Miki continued, 'it seems that my parents often end up on watchlists because of their

– er – eclectic interests and apparently, my mother's blog. Which I'd never read before today.'

'Is she Battling Barton?' said Leon, temporarily distracted. 'It comes across as a radical's call-to-arms. Do you have guns in your house?'

'No, of course not. But Mum seems to get a bit carried away sometimes.'

'Yeah, right,' said Leon. 'Some of the things she says, she's lucky she hasn't been carried away by the police. What was in the last one? Something about if the streets must run red to save the green blood of our planet…'

Miki raised her voice and spoke over him, 'John was at university with them – an undergrad when they were doing their PhDs.'

'Your parents have PhDs?' said Rory. 'Doesn't that mean they're really smart?'

'You'd think so, wouldn't you? But not so much when it comes to the real world. It turns out John's been taking them discreetly off these watchlists for quite a while. Battling Barton causes a lot of trouble. Anyway, when our website caught his employer's attention…'

'I knew it!' said Leon, jumping to his feet once more and pumping the air.

'And there was the alien invasion as well – we so have to talk about that one. What on earth did you think you were doing? So many people believed it.'

'Great, wasn't it?' said Leon. 'Better than any of us had hoped.'

'Well, you'd disappeared,' said Rory, 'and the website wasn't drawing the local people in. Only the crazies.'

'We did get a bit carried away,' said Jonas.

'You think?' said Miki. 'They had police up there.

277

Ambulances. Helicopters. It must have cost the government a fortune. Do you want to pay that bill?'

'We didn't ask for any of that,' said Rory. He looked at Leon for support.

'We're minors,' said Leon. 'What are they going to do?'

'Get our parents to pay? Send us to a special school for disturbed kids?' said Miki. She watched as the other three grew a bit paler.

'No,' said Leon. 'We would have been headhunted. At least, I would have been.'

'Except it's not happening, is it? John knows exactly who we are. He took me to see one of his hacker contacts, and she shifted the blame – the digital trail – to McLaren and a few other people.'

'Who?' asked Leon.

Miki shrugged. 'The woman has a habit of wandering around with a loaded shotgun. I didn't feel like asking too many questions.'

'But this John knew about us?' persisted Leon.

Miki nodded.

'So he'll do a report on us?'

'No,' said Miki, shaking her head. 'I made a deal with him. We don't do anything like this again and we get away with it. A one-time-only chance to start over and never do anything this stupid again.'

'And he didn't say anything about me?' said Leon. 'I mean, me in particular? Did you tell him it was my idea. That I set up the website?'

'I didn't want to cause any of us more trouble,' said Miki. 'I told him as little as possible. He already knew a fair bit.'

'That's not fair,' said Leon. 'You've ruined everything.' He bit his lip. It didn't help. He broke into loud, noisy sobs.

Miki looked at him, bemused. 'You don't understand, Leo. We're safe. It's over.' Leon gave a wordless cry and bolted out of the door.

MIKI, JONAS & RORY

'He won't come out of the bathroom,' said Rory. 'He's stopped howling at least. But someone is going to want to go in there soon.'

'So we think he set us up to – what? Try and attract attention from the secret service? To show how good his hacking skills are?' said Jonas.

Miki shook her. 'I met a real hacker. Leo might be good for his age, but I doubt he'll ever be in her league. It's hard to explain but there was something about her…'

'Leo's a clever kid,' said Jonas. 'But being bumped up years at school doesn't make you a genius. Who knows? Maybe he'll be good enough some day to work in white hat hacking, but he's dreaming if he thinks anyone is going to pick him up as a child spy. That's the kind of thing that happens in the movies. What an idiot.'

'He's much younger than us,' said Miki. 'He still believes that sort of adventure could happen to him.'

'I feel used,' said Rory. 'I mean, I'm trying to feel sorry for the kid. He's really upset, but I'm beginning to get the feeling he didn't care about what we wanted – about what we wanted to show people.'

'I suppose that's sort of happening with McLaren,' said Miki. 'I don't think he'll be charged.'

'Probably he'll make up a book about it,' said Jonas. 'Say it was all him.'

'It kind of does what we set out to do, doesn't it?' said Miki.

'What, give McLaren his day in the sun?' said Rory.

Jonas shrugged. 'We should be grateful we got out of this. Miki's right. But it doesn't feel good, does it? I'm going to check on Leo.'

Miki sat down. 'It does feel unsatisfactory,' she said.

'Did we ever know what we wanted out of it?' said Rory. 'I mean, you were afraid for your parents. I was afraid for myself. Jonas wanted to get McLaren for landing his mum in trouble – and it seems little Leon wanted to be spotted as a spy.'

'I wanted people to stop believing everything and anything they read on the internet, but in a sort of revengeful manner,' said Miki. 'I wanted people to be caught out. To realise they'd been tricked by some schoolkids. Being tricked by a slimy journalist isn't quite the same thing, is it?'

'Do you feel bad about McLaren?'

'Not really. K– The hacker told me some of the other scummy stories he'd written. He really did prey on the weak.'

'And now he'll make a million or so off a book deal.'

'You think?' said Miki. 'Ouch, that hurts.'

Jonas came back in. 'Leo said he had to get something to show us. I let him go. He's still in a bit of a state.'

'Do you think McLaren will make a lot of money off a book deal?' said Miki.

'Maybe,' said Jonas. 'It seems to me there's very little justice in the world.' He turned to Rory. 'Your mum is brilliant. She's really going to war on my mum's account. There's no way my mum or I would have had the strength to do it. Getting through every day was about the most we could do. It's good to know there are some good people in

280

this world.' He hunkered down on a beanbag and looked miserable.

The doorbell went again. Rory went and quickly returned with Leon. Leon passed around the file he'd been hoping MI5 would find.

'Jeez,' said Rory when it was his turn to flick through the pages. 'Screenshots and all. You little git.'

Jonas gave a couple of sharp laughs when he read it. 'You were definitely selling us out.'

'Didn't you care what might happen to us?' said Miki. 'You are one self-centred little…'

Jonas cut in. 'Don't. You'll set him off again. At least he's owned up.'

'Still not feeling the love,' said Rory.

Miki paused in her reading. 'Did you see this appendix?' she said. 'He's got down, spot on, why we were up for doing it all.' She read, 'Above all, having suffered from the mendacious attention of social media and its incurable desire for stories, regardless of their basis in truth, the group wanted to teach others not to accept what they saw online, but to question everything. Despite everything they did, this noble cause – this desperate need to counteract a society driven by the notion of five minutes of fame – can, I believe, forgive them any misdirection or confusion they may have caused. After all, their final intention was to come clean and demonstrate to all the truth of their beliefs. They were prepared, in the end, to be sacrifices in the name of truth and transparency. The group was prepared to stand up in the name of what they believed in and weather the storm. How many of us can say the same?'

'That is kind of nice,' said Jonas.

'A bit overblown if you ask me,' said Rory.

'Pretentious, certainly,' said Miki. 'But it reads like he was trying to keep us out of trouble.'

'Yeah,' said Rory. 'The great kid spy…'

Jonas cut him off. 'You know, I really, really hate that McLaren is getting the credit for our website.'

'He's going to jail,' said Miki.

'He's going to get a book deal,' said Rory. 'I don't like it much either.

'If we hadn't done the alien thing…' said Jonas.

'Too far,' said Rory nodding.

'It was clever,' said Miki. 'Stupid, but clever.'

'You haven't said a word in ages, Leo,' said Jonas. 'Are you recording us or something?'

'No,' said Leon, his voice a little squeaky. 'I wanted you to have all the facts.'

'Why?' said Rory suspiciously.

'So you could decide whether or not to do the final interview. To claim responsibility for what we did.'

'Are you mad?' said Miki.

'So you don't mind that an adult came along and ruined all our plans because he thought he knew better?' said Leon.

'You mean John? He rescued us,' said Miki.

'I didn't think you were the kind of female who wanted rescuing,' retorted Leon.

Miki winced. 'Well, not normally…'

'And you, Rory, all your worries about social media are over, are they? Your diary is safe and that's all that matters. You're safe.'

Rory didn't reply. Leon turned to Jonas. 'You needn't say it,' said Jonas, 'next time it'll be someone else's mum. I see that. We have no idea what McLaren will put in any book of his, but we can bet it won't be anything like how Leon summed us up.'

'What are you suggesting?' said Rory.

'You've got to be kidding me,' said Miki.

'If we don't, we'll regret for the rest of our lives that we didn't,' said Jonas. 'Isn't that what they say? You regret most the things you didn't do?'

'Not if they're stupid dumbass things, you don't!' said Miki.

'You still want to make the confession video?' said Rory.

'We have Leon's document, complete with screenshots to prove it was our idea,' said Jonas. 'That's why he showed it to us.' He smiled at Leon. 'You might be a little git, but you're a clever one.'

Leon watched them all with big, wide eyes.

'Oh hell,' said Rory. 'I'll do it.'

'Me too,' said Jonas.

'Okay,' said Miki. 'But if...' She got no further. Leon had sprung to his feet, his small fist pumping the air, 'I knew you guys would come through!' he shouted.

BREAKING NEWS

Tonight on Channel 4, see what everyone is talking about. Four kids go to war on social media. Meanwhile investigative journalist, Marty McLaren, is released in disgrace from jail after false confession.

EPILOGUE

Jonas' mother received help from several charities during her successful benefit fight. As a result of the confession broadcast, a lawyer came forward and offered to help her with her divorce and gain child maintenance from her absent husband. Jonas and his mum moved to a smaller house in the same area. All the others visit frequently. Eventually Jonas' mother agreed to take half the money that K4's FundMe page had raised. She gave the other half to various charities. She used the rest to launch her own internet channel where she discussed what it was like to have MS, made Jonas discuss what it was like to be her carer, got other MS patients to come and discuss their journey, and made sure she pointed her viewers to as many sources of help as possible, included setting up an ASK A MUM column. Which made Jonas both very proud and very embarrassed.

For the rest of her school career Miki was no longer teased. Despite turning over a new leaf and concentrating on her grades rather than being rebellious (at least most of the time) Miki continued to be treated with enormous respect by all her teachers. Her place at the Glasgow School of Art was confirmed.

Meg, after several loud discussions with Brian and Miki, agreed to tone down the language in her Battling Barton Blog. Although she refused point-blank to stop writing it.

Rory now has his own YouTube channel. He is currently in talks to become an ambassador for a new brand of allergy-free unisex make-up.

Occasionally, the others call Leon Leon to make him happy, but most of the time they still call him Leo. Leon has learnt what it is like to have proper friends, and only complains about them getting his name wrong once a day. He also has a new computer. His father has a bigger overdraft. On it, Leon receives the occasional untraceable message that suggests various courses of study and books he should read. Many of the books have to be specially ordered from the library. Leon is so busy learning from these extracurricular sources that he has not caused any more trouble on the internet – so far.

Praise for Fake News

'A gleeful comic romp packed with invention...'
— Philip Caveney, author of *The Sins of Allie Lawrence*, *The Calling, The Crow Boy* trilogy and many more.

'Hugely enjoyable!'
— Paul Hudson, Librarian, Portobello Library.

'Fresh & pithy, this makes for a very original & funny read. I thoroughly enjoyed it.'
— Alex Nye, author of *Chill, Shiver, Darker Ends* and *When we get to the Island*.

ACKNOWLEDGEMENTS

With huge thanks to Clare Cain for her time, care, attention and belief in *Fake News*. Grateful appreciation also to Graeme Clarke for a wonderful cover design.